Death at the Double Inkwell

Shonell Bacon

CLG Entertainment
Writing that Stands Out in a Crowd

http://www.clg-entertainment.com

Manufactured in the United States of America
Second Edition

Dedication

To my human trinity - their love and support (on earth and above) keep me grounded and forever moving forward: my mom, Brenda Henson, and my maternal grandparents, Audrey "G" Bacon (1931-1998) and Charles "Pop Pop" Bacon (1929-1998)

Acknowledgements

First, I have to thank my Lord and Savior. It sounds trite, but it's not. Because he gave me the love and gift of word play, I picked up my diary at the age of ten and began writing screenplays and articles in it.

My mother and my siblings have always been there for me and supported every literary goal and dream I've ever had. I write because I love it, but on those days when fear and doubt infiltrate me, my family is always there to make sure I don't give up. Thank you, Mom, for telling me I'm great and reading my stories—more than once. Thank you, JoPo, for reading all of my synopses, LOL. Thank you, Mikey and Tone, for being proud of me and tooting your sister's horn from time to time.

There isn't enough space to say thank you to all that have been there for me, so know that you are all in my heart and I am blessed to have had you on the journey.

I do, however, have to thank one other person. God definitely blessed me when he placed Samara King in my life. She is my *sister from another mister*, and through tears and laughter, shouts and much prayer, she has constantly pushed me over the years to put my work out, to show that I am indeed a talent. Because of her faith and push, I took the leap. Thank you, Sister.

It might seem weird to acknowledge a book, but *Death at the Double Inkwell* would not have been written had it not been for Mary Higgins Clark's *All around the Town*. It's because of this book and a novel writing class that the words of DDIW filled pages.

SHONELL BACON

A Rude Awakening

Like most Monday nights, Sarah Brockman found herself in bed alone. She stretched, twisted, and turned, trying to find the right spot to sleep in since she didn't have her husband as her buffer.

After ten minutes of wriggling, Sarah sat up.

Her husband was off, as usual, in Cleveland or Chicago, New York or L.A. Some place other than home. *Attending to business,* he always said.

Probably to get back at me, she thought. Since her own *stepping out,* Sarah had long wondered if Mark's business came in the short/petite or Amazonian/statuesque variety.

She hated him for leaving her in this big house alone though her pushing him away didn't help matters. She hated the weird creaks and moans of the settling house. At least once a night, she reached over to her nightstand for the mace or the steak knife she kept there. Her husband called her paranoid. She preferred the term *cautious.*

Sarah ran her fingers through her pale, golden hair before finally falling back onto the mattress and closing her eyes.

"Just fall asleep," she whispered. She grabbed her husband's pillows from his side of the bed and pressed them close to her, digging her slender fingers into the pillowcase.

The shattering of glass startled her. She leapt from the bed and grabbed her knife, the mace, and the phone on the nightstand. She raced into the walk-in closet and sat on the floor. Her fingers shook, but she managed to hit TALK on the phone. No dial tone. Tears streamed down her sun-kissed cheeks. Clothes, swaying on their hangers, brushed her shoulders. Through the thin slats on the bottom half of the door, Sarah saw the grayness of the room.

"God, please, help me," she whispered up through her clothes, hoping her message reached heaven.

DEATH AT THE DOUBLE INKWELL

Even from the closet, Sarah heard the soft whoosh of the bedroom door opening. She rubbed her stomach and swallowed down a lump of vomit and a scream.

She breathed into the phone, wishing there was someone on the other end to help her.

Through the slats, Sarah saw the shades of darkness change in the bedroom from a dark gray to black. The intruder stood just inches from her. Her fingers itched to hold onto her rosary and pray. She needed something or some higher being to tell her that she would be okay because she didn't believe it. Amidst the silence and the fear, Sarah couldn't help but wonder why the alarm didn't go off.

The door opened.

Sarah screamed as she stared into the barrel of a gun.

The mace, the knife, and the phone slid from her hand, thudding onto the carpeted floor.

Seconds ticked by as they stared each other down. Sarah saw nothing but black—the intruder's black clothing, gloves, mask, scully cap, gun.

But it was the eyes, all big and brown and full of menace. She could have sworn she had seen them before, but she'd never known anyone in her life so full of hate.

"Please," she said. "You can have anything you want, just please don't hurt me. "I'm—"

The intruder grunted. "This ain't even about you, bitch," he interrupted. He then laughed—the sound so chilling Sarah closed her eyes tight to keep from seeing one who could be so evil.

"My sweet Sarah," the intruder said.

Her face slackened. She recognized the voice.

She never opened her eyes again.

Chapter 1

*J*ovan Parham Anderson gripped the wrinkled silk sheets and gritted her teeth as her husband thrust himself into her.

"Relax, Jo," Cordell whispered. "Stop being so uptight." Jovan closed her eyes as they began to well up with tears. *Relax?* she thought. *You bastard.*

She sucked in a deep breath as Cordell's hands took hold of her breasts and tweaked her nipples—a move that would have normally excited her now made her stomach lurch.

Jovan moved her arms around to Cordell's back and dug her nails deep into his flesh.

"That's it," he grunted in her ear. "Hurt me, Baby."

Cordell grabbed Jovan's full hips and rammed into her, causing her to cry out. "Yes." He groaned.

"You're hurting me, Cordell," Jovan said, panting. "Slow down."

Jovan pressed her hands against his chest, but he hunkered down and pumped ferociously inside her.

"Stop," she yelled.

A deep rumbling sound erupted from his mouth, and Jovan knew he was about to orgasm. He lowered his head and took one of her nipples into his mouth. He nipped it. Jovan yelped and began hitting him in the face. "Stop, Cordell," she said. "Please, you're hurting me."

In a flash, Cordell had her hands above her head; he never lost his deep, quick rhythm inside her.

"Don't ever hit me again," he said in a low voice. Jovan's eyes widened and tears leaked from them, sliding down into her ears. She watched as Cordell's eyes rolled up into his head. He bit his lower lip. "Unhhh," he moaned. "I'm there." He pushed himself as far into Jovan as he could as his moans overshadowed her screams.

He fell upon Jovan and for several moments, the only thing that could be heard was Cordell's heavy breathing and Jovan's whimpers.

"For God's sakes," he said, "stop your crying." He rolled over, sat up, and placed his feet on the floor. "If you did your womanly duties, I wouldn't have to stay all pent up and act like this."

"I asked you to stop, Cordell," Jovan said. She opened her eyes and stared at his smooth, brown back. "You come in here past one in the morning, frustrated over work, and think you can just take me when you want."

The sirens from police cars silenced their argument, temporarily. Cordell jumped from the bed and spun around. "Jo, stop being a bitch and get over it. You're my wife, right?" She stared for a while before nodding. "Get over it," he repeated. He snatched his black slacks off the back of the chair in the corner of the bedroom.

"What are you doing?" Jovan asked.

"Going out," Cordell replied.

Jovan looked at the clock. "It's barely six in the morning."

"I need air."

"You haven't been here but a few hours."

"What did I just say?"

Jovan stared at Cordell, the man she had vowed to love. The man who had just taken her though she cried for him to stop. *Air*, she thought. In the past, she had doubts about Cordell. Did he lie? Did he cheat? Did he still love her?

But now, in the bedroom with sex lingering in the room, she *knew* he was going for more than air.

"Hmm," Jovan whispered.

"Got a problem with that?" Cordell asked. When Jovan didn't respond, he slid his shirt on and stepped into a pair of Nike Air. As he swiped his wallet off his nightstand, he turned

4

to Jovan and added, "Clean up the bed."

She watched him leave then looked down. Spots of blood dotted the otherwise snow-white sheet.

"That son of a bitch," Jovan said as she carried the sheets to the laundry room to wash. Her normally spry, hip-twisting walk became an open-legged shuffle as she trudged downstairs.

In the kitchen, she initiated a pot of coffee and poured herself a cup when it was done. She made it into the living room and peeked out the curtains of the bay window. Police cars, black Cadillacs, and the coroner's van took up the entire block. She watched as detectives walked into the house two doors down from hers: The Brockmans.

Jovan immediately placed her coffee on the window seat and walked as fast as she could out the door. All her neighbors were out in their yards, dressed in nightclothes.

She crossed the lawn to her next-door neighbor, a short, portly judge who was known in the neighborhood as the enforcer. The neighborhood was far too upscale for such a person, but it always brought a chuckle to the judge when anyone called him that.

"What's going on, Judge Williams?" Jovan asked.

He pushed his glasses up on his beak of a nose and coughed. "From what I gather, someone broke into the Brockman home."

"That's the third break-in this month."

"I know."

"Why the coroner? Don't tell me..."

Judge Williams lowered his head.

"Who?" she asked, her breath quickening.

"Sarah." Jovan crumbled to the ground. Judge Williams knelt, took her in his arms, and allowed her to cry. "I just talked to her yesterday," Jovan said. "She can't be dead."

Judge Williams kissed the top of Jovan's curly brown mane and sighed. "They have an alarm system that can wake the dead. How the hell did this killer get inside the house and no one hear it?"

Slowly, Jovan stood and brushed off her bottom. She wrapped her arms around herself. "I'm guessing there are no suspects?" she asked.

Judge Williams shook his head. "I'm thinking an inside job."

Jovan faced him. "Come on, now. You calling Mark a murderer? I mean everyone in the neighborhood figured he was sniffing up under skirts, but killing Sarah? I don't see it."

"Hon, that's because, despite what you write about, your mind is very idyllic. You don't want to think there's a world where husbands kill wives over things as *little* as infidelity."

Jovan shivered. Questions of her own husband's infidelity swirled inside her head. "I guess I do sometimes," she mused. "Nothing wrong with being idyllic."

"No, but it sure makes it tougher to deal with things like that." The two watched as the coroner escorted a black body bag from the house. A somber Mark walked behind the gurney.

"Sarah told me Mark was out of town," Jovan said.

"Supposedly, he came back a little over an hour ago from California. He found her."

Mark looked up and noticed Jovan and the judge. Jovan wanted to yell out that she was sorry. She wanted to run to him and wrap him in a hug. Instead, she offered a slight smile and held a hand over her heart.

She shook her head, turned, and rushed back toward her home. Before entering, she ventured one last glance toward the Brockmans' home. In the sea of detectives, paramedics, and lookers-on, Jovan noticed Cordell. She watched him step away from the scene and walk down the street.

"Where's he going?" she asked, shutting the door behind her. She didn't give herself time to worry about that.

Sarah was dead. The person she had monthly lunch dates with, the person she complained about Cordell to was dead.

Sarah and Mark were the very first people to welcome Cordell and Jovan into the neighborhood. Sarah, being a good ten years older than Jovan, often advised her in what *not* to do in her marriage. Sarah knew what it was like to live with a powerful, bull-headed man. She knew what it was like to question her husband's fidelity. Jovan slid to the floor and rested her back against the door.

"I can't believe this," she muttered. She wiped tears from her face with the back of her trembling hand. "You didn't deserve this, Sarah."

Just last week, while having lunch, Sarah told Jovan she was close to finding proof about Mark's affair. "When I saw the e-mail," Sarah had said, "I read between the lines. Something's going on. I just need more time to figure out what." Sarah's time was out. Jovan refused to let her time run out before learning what was going on with Cordell.

She stood and took a breath. "What a morning," she mumbled. She hugged herself tight. "Let's see if I can make this day worse."

With reluctance yet a strong determination, Jovan walked toward Cordell's office, hoping to be proven wrong about her suspicions.

Deadly Intentions. Double Jeopardy. The Sinister Chronicles. Murder on Hilltop Lane. Knocking on Death's Door.

It was only a matter of time that writing novels about death and suspense would cause Jovan to conjure up her own violent tendencies; it just took a bastard of a husband to bring it out of her. In fact, as she co-wrote with her twin, Cheyenne, what was soon to be their sixth bestseller, *Deadly Vows*, Jovan could only think about how she and Cheyenne decided to kill the husband in their book with a shot to the head. She wouldn't mind putting one clean shot into her *own* husband's mindless head.

Jovan leaned against the doorway of her home office, watching Cheyenne chat with their agent, Elyse. Cheyenne laughed. Jovan was jealous of her twin's happy, lighthearted nature. Cheyenne slumped casually in one of the red, high-backed chairs that faced her desk as her thin fingers stroked her beloved dachshund, Riqué.

Jovan couldn't hear the conversation in her office for the buzzing in her head. Her eyes burned with the sting of tears that begged to fall. She clutched her lower belly and moaned. Ever since her painful morning interlude with Cordell, her stomach had cramped. She had worn a pad for the first part of the day until the light bleeding had stopped.

Quietly slipping into the hallway, Jovan leaned against the wall and raised her hands to her face. It hurt her to relive any part of the day, but try as she might, her mind refused to let her forget.

Why did I go into Cordell's office, Jovan thought. She knew why. Sarah. That's how Sarah found out about Mark.

Jovan had never bothered with anything that pertained to Cordell's work. She never felt the need, but this morning, the urge was too strong *not* to look.

Not too long after learning of Sarah's death, Jovan found herself sitting in Cordell's stiff, black leather chair. The last thing she wanted to be was the type of wife who nagged or complained. She knew what it was like to be busy, to be successful. She and Cordell never really knew what a vacation was, and ever since she and Cheyenne penned their first novel five years ago, their lives had been in fast-forward.

After debating with herself for several moments, Jovan began to dig into Cordell's desk, opening drawers, riffling papers. There was nothing. She almost breathed a sigh of relief until she turned on his computer. It rocked her to see Cordell's indiscretion so blatantly placed on the desktop of his computer, in a folder marked "Alisha".

It was as if Cordell thought that he could keep his lies and secrets to himself for eternity, or he just didn't care if Jovan caught him. Jovan's eyes widened and her jaw dropped as she opened the folder to find hundreds of e-mails and correspondences between Cordell and his assistant.

"I can't believe it," she had whispered. There were e-mails and letters in the folder that dated back three years, making her cry harder in the realization that she had been deceived for almost half of her seven-year marriage.

Magically, with a strength Jovan didn't know she had, she turned off Cordell's computer, making sure to clean it of her intrusion. She almost broke when she saw the dark reflection of her face on the computer screen. Throwing up her protective shield, Jovan made the decision not to come forward with this information just yet. She couldn't.

She needed time to figure out exactly what to do before Cordell got wind of her knowing about his affair. She and Cordell had been cold toward each other for the past several months except for those times in the middle of the night when Cordell would roll over and demand sex. It wouldn't be hard to fake a cool personality toward the man she had vowed to love 'til death did them part.

When he came home for lunch and found her teary-eyed and despondent over Sarah's death, he told her to get over it. Before she could argue, he railed on her, not for the first time, for being a bit too fat in the waist and butt.

Jovan was startled at first by his words, finding Cordell to be more spiteful than normal. She studied the man that stood before her, his usually beautiful, chocolate face, contorted with frustration. There was a time when her fingers would explore that face, trace the fullness of his lips, the length of his lashes, getting lost in eyes that could easily draw you into the bedroom. *That* man was gone. He wasn't in the mean face that stared back at her in disgust.

Jovan had never questioned her weight, her body. She was average height and curvaceous, with a figure that most women, young and old, would kill to have. Jovan's hurt quickly moved to anger. Cordell had some nerve to yell at her for *anything*. He was the one who had left their marriage to satisfy his needs with another woman. He was the one who spent money as if they had it to burn, his and hers. Jovan never complained though, but now in her anger, it blinked in her mind like a neon sign. He was the one who came home several times a little more than tipsy.

"I will get through this," she said, her voice quivering. Taking a deep, cleansing breath, she wiped the stray tears from her face.

She reentered her office, welcomed by Cheyenne's lilting laugh as she said, "I know, El. I'm still looking for a man, too. I need to find me one like Cordell. Little Miss Jo is lucky to have met a wonderful man like him." Jovan took her seat behind her desk, her descent slow like an old woman with arthritic knees. Cheyenne laid eyes on her sister and stopped mid-sentence.

"El," Cheyenne said, her voice still bright and cheerful. "We have to run, but we'll be getting in contact really soon."

"Okay. Take care," El said. Cheyenne clicked off the speakerphone and gave her full attention to Jovan, watching the pensive expression on her face.

"Jo," she whispered, holding Riqué close as she rose from her chair to lean over Jovan's desk. "I'm sorry about Sarah. I wish I had known her as well as you."

Jovan shook her head. "It's not that," she said. "Well, it is, but…it's nothing." She turned her attention to her monitor. *Deadly Vows* stared back at her.

"Jo, come on. I can see something's wrong. Your eyes are bloodshot." With an unwavering voice, Jovan answered, "I want a divorce."

Cheyenne's bright, brown eyes widened in shock. With a grunt, she shifted Riqué from one arm to the other and sank despondently back into her chair, shaking her head.

"You're not serious, are you, Jo?" she asked, settling the chunky dog comfortably against her chest. "Are you really going to ask him for a divorce?"

Jovan leaned back in her chair and sighed. It was a quiet, drained sound filled with frustration and disappointment. Cheyenne read the pain reflected in her sister's eyes, and it broke her heart.

As she stroked Riqué's glossy brown coat, Cheyenne watched her sister pensively, noting the slow, almost painfully methodical way she shredded a piece of paper into tiny fragments, something she'd done since they were kids, and a gesture Jovan only did when highly upset.

"Sis." When Cheyenne spoke, her voice was soft and full of compassion. "Are you sure it's come to this? Maybe you're just having a rough time lately, and now with Sarah's death and everything, you only *think* you want out."

Alarmed by the burst of tears that sprang from her sister's eyes, Cheyenne placed Riqué on the floor and moved around the desk.

"Aw, come on, Jo, it can't be *that* bad..."

Jovan sobbed, gut wrenching sounds that wrung Cheyenne's heartstrings. She shook her head in utter confusion and sadness, wrapping her arms around Jovan even tighter.

"So what happened?" Cheyenne asked. Suddenly, the crying ceased; a blunt, chilly silence took its place. Surprised, Cheyenne released her twin. Jovan gazed past Cheyenne at some distant spot out the window.

When she spoke, her voice was quiet and cold. "He has another woman." Jovan bit the words off like bullets.

"No." Cheyenne sank back into the chair, her mouth partly open in astonishment.

"He's seeing some tramp from his office," she added. "Has been for the past three years. I found out this morning." Jovan turned her head and gazed into her twin's eyes with a flat, disgusted stare. "I want out."

Chapter 2

I've never met anyone like you before.

On Jovan's screen, this sentence grew large, almost breaking free from the monitor to wrap around her mind. But it was already there. She tried to block out her past, but the positive things, the things that made her love Cordell, kept creeping back in like, *I've never met anyone like you before.*

"Get up and move," she told herself. For days, she had stayed holed up in her home, trying to finish the manuscript, to avoid being in a world where death was literally near her front door. She went into her spare bedroom and changed into running shorts and a t-shirt. With her Reeboks on, she grabbed her mp3 player from the dresser and left the house.

She started off in a trot up the street, toward the blanket of trees that entranced the park. Her heart beat to the rhythm of her feet treading along the grassy ground. The sound of Marvin Gaye singing about grapevines couldn't push thoughts from her head.

Her mind carried her to a spot in time where she stood in snow, a bright smile plastered on her face. Her eyes wide as she watched Cordell profess his love for her. She remembered everything about that day. The sky was gray and overcast. Light sprinklings of snow covered the ground. It was just after New Year's—two years into dating, and they made their way across campus.

Unexpectedly, Jovan reached down, scooped up a handful of the crystalline powder, and blew it from her hands. When she looked up, she saw Cordell staring back at her, smiling. She looked at him and thought of hot cocoa—dark, sweet, and warming. She blushed.

"I've never met anyone like you before," he said, pulling her softly into his arms before kissing her.

"I bet you say that to all the girls, Cordell." She was

intoxicated by the heat that poured from Cordell's body, and for the life of her, she couldn't think of another place she would rather be.

"Only the girls I love. Like you." Cordell released her, and she felt the air cool her flushed cheeks. She shivered.

As she moved toward Cordell to kiss him, he picked up snow, balled it, and threw it in her face. She shrieked, smacking at him.

"Oh, you are so dead," she yelled after him, chasing him through the quad.

After that day, Jovan knew she couldn't be without Cordell. It was easy for him to pour his heart out to her, to tell her how wonderful she was, how beautiful she was, how he wanted to spend the rest of his life with her, and she believed him. She believed him all the way to the altar a year later.

"I hate you so much," Jovan panted out as she ran. She growled out her anger but was halted when someone grabbed her from behind.

She yelped as someone pushed her hard onto the ground. She fell to her knees and tried to get up. The person kicked her in the side.

"Stay down, bitch," a male voice yelled. Jovan did as she was told and kept her face down. Blood rushed to her head. The somehow familiar voice sounded muffled, like he had something over his face. Maybe a mask?

She tried to stay rational and not let her fear make her do something stupid.

"What do you—" Jovan began, but she stopped when the man straddled her back. She attempted to wiggle free. The man gripped her neck with both hands and pressed her face against the grass.

With one hand holding her head down, the other snaked around and ripped the mp3 player from its case.

"I don't have anything," Jovan whispered. "Don't hurt me."

Jovan wondered if Sarah had begged for her life during those last moments. With the thought, her breathing became erratic.

The man patted her down, and not finding anything else, he stood. Jovan tried to face him. As her body turned, he launched a powerful kick that connected with her side and flipped her onto her back. By the time she gathered enough energy to sit up, all that was left of the stranger's presence was the sound of branches breaking and his feet thumping the ground as he made his getaway.

Slowly, Jovan managed to get to her feet. She winced as she tried to breathe. The pain in her side throbbed. With small steps, she walked back down the street, her head moving from left to right, making sure she was alone.

Jovan saw Mark leave his house. He looked up the street and waved at her. He stopped mid-wave and then came running.

"Oh my God," he said, slipping an arm around her waist. When she cried out in pain, he moved his arm. "What happened?" He looked around. "Who did this?"

"Was jogging," Jovan said. "Woods. Someone grabbed me, hit me, and took my mp3 player."

"We have to get you to the hospital," Mark said.

"No, just get me to my house, please." Once inside, Mark helped Jovan to the living room and set her down. He sat on the chair opposite her and examined her face.

"No cuts or bruises," he said. "What did he do? Are you hurt? How's your side?"

"I'm fine," Jovan said, lying.

"I'm calling the police." "It's not..." Mark threw his hand up. His deep green eyes buried themselves into Jovan's brown eyes.

Jovan turned away.

After the call was made, the two sat in silence.

"I'm," Jovan began, paused. "I'm so sorry about

15

Sarah."

Mark's features darkened. He nodded. "Thank you. Between the police and the funeral, this is just so unreal. I never thought I'd have to do this."

"I know."

Mark reached out and touched Jovan's hands. She flinched, but Mark kept a tight hold on her.

"Look, I loved Sarah," Mark said. "I know I did wrong by her."

"Yeah, ya did."

"It only happened with the one woman—"

"Well, thank God for that," Jovan interrupted.

Mark let go of Jovan's hands. "I deserve all your anger, but you only know one side of this."

Jovan's mouth crinkled into a smirk. "One side, huh? What's the other side, Mark?"

Tears fell from Mark's eyes and off his chin.

Stunned, Jovan sat and watched for a few seconds before forgetting her pain and kneeling before him.

"I'll spend the rest of my life feeling guilty over not being home when this happened," he said. "But Sarah wasn't completely innocent in our marriage."

Jovan's first response was to curse Mark out for disrespecting Sarah now that she was dead. Instead, she leaned in and hugged him.

"It's going to be okay, Mark," she whispered through his silky, brown hair. "I'll help out if you need me to."

"What's going on here?"

They turned to find Cordell glaring at them.

"Cordell," Jovan said. "Don't go there. Mark and I were talking about Sarah."

"In your arms?" Cordell's nostrils flared as he came toward the pair. Jovan took her time standing and tried to get in the middle of the two men.

"Stop it, Cordell," she begged.

"She's hurt, man," Mark added.

Cordell pushed Jovan back into a chair as he lunged for Mark. Jovan grabbed her side and yelled out in pain.

Cordell turned to face her.

"Freeze!"

Two police officers stood at the opened front door, guns in their hands.

Jovan lay upon the sofa, her right hand resting on her belly. She took in slow breaths, trying to keep from agitating the pain on her left side.

She was so embarrassed. She definitely didn't want the police coming to question her about a mugging and ending up seeing her husband about to attack a recent widower. They had managed to convince the police that nothing was wrong.

But everything was wrong. To Jovan, anyway.

After the police left, then Mark, Cordell left Jovan in the living room, wondering what secrets Sarah had. All this time, Sarah was there to comfort Jovan and to dispel her own marital problems when she was part of her problem. Jovan wasn't sure whether to believe Mark. After all, Sarah couldn't defend herself—he could say anything. The question that resounded in Jovan's mind was if Mark was telling the truth, what did Sarah lie about?

With care, Jovan rose and walked over to the bay window that overlooked the garden.

"Maybe I'll go cut some flowers for the centerpiece tonight," she said to herself. She took hold of a few strands of hair and twirled them with her fingers.

The phone rang, and Jovan let the voicemail pick up. She knew it was Cheyenne. She had called at least 10 times. She knew Cheyenne was worried; she did just tell her that she wanted out of her marriage. She didn't feel like talking about

17

that or talking about the mugging. Besides, Cheyenne was due over that evening for a dinner that was to include Cordell and an associate from Anderson Technologies, the company that Cordell owned.

It didn't matter to Cordell that Jovan was banged up. They had planned this dinner over two weeks ago.

"You can do it," he had said. "Throw some heat on your side. You'll be okay." Jovan pressed her palms against the window.

"I wonder if he'll even show up," she said, sighing. She kneaded the small of her back. She turned back toward the sofa and picked up the remote for the entertainment system.

The sexy guitar riffs of Santana's came through the speakers.

Jovan threw the remote and screamed.

"God," she yelled. A wave of turbulent emotions hit her, almost erasing the physical pain. "I loved him. I shared my body with him, my life with him, and he threw it all away."

With bundles of raw nerves, Jovan jumped from the sofa and paced the living room while she mindlessly hummed a duet with Santana. Reaching the bay window, Jovan spun around, stopping when her eyes fell upon the framed wedding picture of her and Cordell on an end table. She gripped the frame in her hands.

"I can't believe I used to be *that* happy." Jovan viewed the picture of her, in white, smiling up at her husband, the man she adored more than life. People often said it was quite a coup for Jovan to find a man like Cordell to settle down with. Not only was he ambitious and a sure-fire go-getter, but he was also extremely attractive. Looking at Cordell in the picture, smiling down at her, looking so in love, it was unfathomable that he would ever betray her trust and their marriage.

"Look at you," Jovan cried, staring at the picture, "looking like you love me. It was all a lie. You killed our relationship and my heart. You need to feel some pain, Cordell.

Maybe I should hurt you."

Jovan flung the frame across the room. It crashed and broke in a corner of the living room.

The front door slammed, alerting her to the arrival of Cordell.

"Why is he back now?" she asked.

"Jovan," Cordell yelled. "You here?"

He walked into the living room and spotted Jovan standing with her hands on her hips. He noticed the shards of glass glistening off the polished, hardwood floors.

"You okay?" he asked.

She nodded. "Just doing a little spring cleaning."

He sniffed and pouted. "Dinner's not ready."

"Well hello to you, too, Baby," she replied, a faint smile tugging the corners of her mouth. "You're back fast. Thought you had some things to take care of at work."

Cordell groaned before dropping his briefcase onto the cream-colored sofa.

Jovan studied him, the chiseled features of his face, how his normally deep, penetrating, brown eyes appeared unfocused. His normally dark, baby smooth skin housed a five o'clock shadow. Cordell loosened his tie and sat onto the sofa. "So...what's...going...on...with...dinner?" he asked again.

"I heard you the first time," Jovan answered between clenched teeth. "Dinner's not for another three hours. I'm making baked salmon with carrots and zucchini, per your request, and the ingredients are in the refrigerator. It takes 45 minutes to an hour to prepare, so I have time."

"Well what about you?" His eyes moved along Jovan, showing disgust at her attire, a baggy blue sweat suit. "It's going to take you a while to make yourself presentable. Maybe you should start now."

Inwardly, Jovan flinched. *There's nothing wrong with me*, she thought. *He's the lying, two-timing bastard.* "You know, there used to be a time when you loved how I looked and complimented me every chance you got."

"Well, there used to be a time when you did more than sit your ever-growing backside in a chair and just write."

"*Just* write?" Jovan said, seething. "I believe it was my *just* writing that bought this home we live in, among other things." "So now you want to play the *whose bank account is bigger* game?"

"Are you trying to pick a fight with me, Cordell?"

He sifted through papers in his briefcase. "Oh," she said mockingly. "So now you wanna play the silent game? I am too tired to deal with this today." Jovan shook her head. It seemed like forever since she had had a decent conversation with Cordell. "You know, you never told me where you were last night before you came and found me ready and willing," she said, receiving a wide-eyed look from Cordell. Cordell ran his hand over his face, his fingers coming together to smooth out his thin goatee.

"I was out," is all that he would say.

"Well that's obvious, Cordell, but where? As your wife, I think I'm entitled to know where..."

"As my wife," Cordell yelled. "You're entitled? Entitled to what?"

"What is wrong with you, Cordell? Have you forgotten how to talk to me, or just talk in general? Why must you argue and criticize me? Is it that I'm not..."

Cordell's eyes shot upward to glare at Jovan, his features hardening. "Not what?" he asked. "Finish what you were about to say."

Frustrated, Cordell stood and snatched his briefcase from the sofa. He tried to brush past Jovan, but his elbow connected with her side and she fell onto the sofa.

Jovan winced and attempted to sit up as she held her side.

Cordell looked at her and when she gave him a glance, she saw a flash of concern in his eyes. It was quickly replaced with something mean. "Jovan," he said, anger edging his attempt to sound sincere. "Are you okay?"

She nodded. She turned her face away as moisture sprang to her eyes. The phone rang, and both of them jumped. Jovan leaned over the sofa and picked up the receiver.

"Hello," she answered. Silence. Out the corner of her eye, she could see Cordell watching her, his jaw twitching. She gave two more hellos before hanging up. "Must be a wrong number," she said, with a shrug. "Anyway, Cordell, we need to talk about all this. Please don't walk off."

"I got business to take care of, Jo."

"You always got business, always holed up in your office, or at Anderson's, or...wherever...but here."

"I don't want to talk about this." He stepped away from her. "I'm sorry I pushed you. I didn't mean to, but I need to be alone right now."

The phone rang again, and Jovan snatched it up, giving a gruff greeting. The tight anger in her face dropped, in its place came deflated cheeks, downcast corners of her mouth, and eyes that grew glossier by the second. She coughed to clear her throat. She turned her head away from Cordell and thrust the phone in his direction. "It's for you," she said.

He took the phone and turned to head to his office.

"You'll have to talk to me sooner or later, Cordell," she said. "We can't keep arguing over nothing."

"You worry about dinner and trying to make yourself presentable tonight. Leave my business to me."

Jovan watched Cordell disappear around a corner. Closing her eyes, she whispered, "I hate him. Lord, help me, but I hate him."

In the kitchen, Jovan tossed pots and pans onto the island as she prepared dinner. She jumped when her cell phone vibrated in her pants pocket.

"Yeah," she answered.

"You haven't returned my calls."

"Didn't feel like talking, Chey."

"Um, okay. Dinner still on?"

"Unh huh."

"You ain't tried to kill him yet?"

"Chey, shut up. We're gonna try to have...Hello?"

"S...i...s?"

"If you hear me, Chey, I'm calling you back on the house phone."

Jovan hung up her cell and picked up the phone hanging on the wall. There was no dial tone.

"I think she knows," Jovan heard Cordell say.

"What difference does that make now?"

Jovan placed her hand over the receiver as Alisha's voice leaked from it.

"Well, nothing, but—"

"I want to see you."

"I want to see you, too, Baby," Cordell said. Jovan's heart shrank in her chest. She could hear the love in his voice, a sound that had been absent to her for a while now. "But you know I can't see you tonight."

Alisha's soft, whiny voice filtered through the phone in what had to be a pouty sigh. She wanted her man. Jovan's man. "God, I can't wait for you and her to be over," Alisha said. "I want to be Mrs. Cordell Anderson. She has to be the most stupid woman on the planet to think you still want her."

Yes, I am, Jovan thought. She swallowed hard.

"Forget about her," Cordell said with no emotion in his voice. "Soon, you and me, forever, 'Lish. You're the only woman I need."

Jovan clicked the phone off just as her cell gave a weak

22

ring. She looked at the house phone, thankful she had hung up before her cell phone rang.

"Hey," she answered. "My cell is dying, and—"

"What's wrong?" Cheyenne asked.

"Nothing, just that I was trying to call you on the house phone."

"Jo, you're all stopped up. You've been crying."

"I'm fine, really."

"Jovan?" Jovan snatched a napkin from the roll in the dispenser, wiped at her eyes, and blew her nose.

"I was trying to call you on the house phone, but Cordell was on it."

"With who?" Cheyenne sounded ready to put her boxing gloves on and fight.

Jovan let a low whimper slip from her mouth.

"No, she did not call that house," Cheyenne roared into the phone. "Please tell me she didn't."

"I won't."

"I should strangle that bastard. I'm gonna give him a piece of my mind tonight when I come over there."

"Sis, no. Please. Don't cause a scene."

"Are you for real? Jo, he has his mistress calling your house. What did they say? Did you listen?"

"No," she lied. "I didn't hear anything. Dinner is still on, and I need you on your best behavior. For me, okay?"

Cheyenne sighed, but replied, "Only for you."

"Thanks. I'll see you later. Love you."

"Love you, too."

Jovan hung up her cell and plopped into a chair. "Did I ever know you, Cordell?" she asked to the empty kitchen. "It couldn't have all been a lie, could it?"

Chapter 3

"*E*verything's gonna be all right." Jovan sat at her vanity, whispering those words repeatedly. She watched herself in the mirror as she brushed her hair, smoothing her naturally curly hair into thick waves that fell over her shoulders. She could feel the brush vibrating against her scalp, indicating the shakiness of her hand. Every move she made was mechanical. She dusted her cinnamon skin with powder, trying to cover the faint lines from where her face made contact with the ground earlier. She applied eye shadow and lipstick.

"I have to play the loving wife tonight," she reminded herself. "I can hate him later." On top of her anger was confusion. She still wondered what was going on in Cordell's life, in his mind. What made him stop loving her? It was obvious he had a whole other existence where Alisha was his mate, and it seemed that it was that relationship he truly wanted, which left Jovan out in the cold.

Her almond-shaped eyes fluttered upwards as she mentally wrote a list of all she had done that afternoon. She looked down at the black silk pantsuit she wore, with black pumps and a pair of diamond studded earrings she had treated herself to when she and Cheyenne's first book was published. With her hair coifed just perfectly and her makeup minimal but effective, Jovan allowed herself the opportunity to smile, albeit a small, hesitant smile.

"Breathe, Girl," she whispered.

Jovan heard Cordell walk into the bedroom from the bathroom. He stopped as he caught her sitting at the vanity. Her anger reddened her face, and she tried to keep her eyes from him, but she was drawn to him, and she wanted to beat herself for feeling that way. She looked at herself in the mirror, and her eyes bounced back to Cordell.

The silent stare between the two ignited a slight warming in Jovan's heart. *Once upon a time,* she thought. There stood her husband, dressed in black slacks and a black pullover shirt, looking casual and sexy. Her mind strolled back in time, remembering how Cordell would try to woo her over to the bed while she was trying to dress for this or that event. Now, if they even kissed during those times, she considered it heavy foreplay.

With trepidation, Jovan rose from her vanity, accidentally dropping the brush onto the glass vanity top. Pushing the chair in, she smoothed her pants and hand-brushed along her blouse for any remnants of her hair brushing. Cordell continued to view her, as if mesmerized, his stare causing Jovan to feel jittery, nervous.

"Do you need anything?" she asked.

Without a word, Cordell rushed to her side and slid her into his arms before dropping a soft, lingering kiss on her lips. She grimaced from the hot pain that shot into her side, but she kept in her scream.

"I love you, Jovan," he whispered in her ear, holding her tightly.

Jovan shook, not able to hold back the confusion. She tried to push away from Cordell, but he refused to release her. The look in his eyes was intense. She felt her hard anger softening.

"Cordell," she whispered, moving her face away to look at him. "What's wrong? Do you know how long it's been since you've kissed me...for no reason?"

You love Alisha, remember, her mind screamed as she sought an answer from Cordell.

He didn't give her one. Instead, he kissed her again, this time, guiding her back, closer to the bed until they both tumbled onto it. Jovan's mind was reeling. Here she was just thinking about how she and Cordell used to do this very thing, and now here they were. She wanted to enjoy it, to revel in it, but it felt so fake. Besides, pain in her back and side throbbed.

Cordell's hands roamed over the contours of her body as he kissed her lips, cheeks, neck, ears. He moaned.

"You feel so good," Cordell said into her right ear, causing her to shiver deep within herself. She could feel her body responding to the warmth of Cordell's touch.

"You feel so good, Alisha," Cordell said.

Jovan quickly went rigid.

It was as if they were both frozen in time, neither able to move. Jovan moved first as she slithered from under Cordell and stood, smoothing her pants along her thighs. With a deep breath, she steadied herself and blinked back tears. She tossed her hair and took unsteady steps toward the bedroom door.

"Jovan," Cordell croaked out. The doorbell rang. "A man has needs, Jovan." Jovan spun around, her eyes red, tears streaming.

"And I didn't supply you with what you needed, Cordell?" she asked. "Is that what you're saying?"

"I haven't been happy for a while now," he stated simply, still lying back on the bed, an arm over his face.

"So why couldn't you leave me? Did you ever think that maybe *I* would want to move on, be with someone who could give *me* what *I* needed? You ever think of that?"

The doorbell rang.

Cordell sat up and opened his mouth to speak, but Jovan interrupted. "Of course you didn't because it's always about Cordell Anderson. You come home, insult me, and make me feel like less of a woman when there are plenty of men in this world who would feel damn lucky to have me in their lives.

"You make me feel like crap 24 hours a day, seven days a week, and you expect me to just give myself to you until I dry up and blow away, used and unloved. Is that what you think? I may have been trustworthy, believing in and living the wedding vows we said before God and our family, but I am *not* stupid."

"Jovan, let me explain."

"There's nothing to explain." She took a deep breath and let the air rattle inside her. "If Alisha is what you want, knock yourself out. I'm through. I can't give of myself to you anymore. I can't and I won't." Jovan turned back toward the door. "Now wipe the stunned expression off and put on your happily married face," she said. "Show time."

Jovan took each step slowly, her body feeling heavy enough to tumble down the stairs. Before she reached the door, she saw it open. She threw a smile on her face just before Cheyenne walked in.

"What took you so long coming to the door?" she asked. "I was trying to use my dinner etiquette and allow you to open the door." She chuckled, but stopped when she saw the stone smile set on Jovan's face.

Jovan walked up to Cheyenne and hugged her hard. "You okay?" Cheyenne asked. Jovan took her by the hand and led her to the living room.

"I'm okay," she finally replied.

"Did he do something to you?"

"No," Jovan said firmly. "It's cool."

Cheyenne forced Jovan to turn and look her way. Her eyes closed into slits as she examined Jovan's face.

"What are those on your cheek?" Cheyenne asked, keeping her voice just below a rumble.

Jovan shook her head. "Hon, I swear it's nothing."

"Are those scratches? You trying to cover up a bruise?"

"No, Chey, it's not like..."

"I'll kill 'em." Cheyenne let go of Jovan and rushed the stairs. "Cordell, who the hell do you think..."

Jovan reached for Cheyenne and brought her back down the stairs. "Don't pay her no mind, Cordell," Jovan said.

Cordell appeared at the top of the stairs briefly to respond. "Like I ever do."

"Fuck you, Cordell," Cheyenne spat.

"Cheyenne, please," Jovan said, frustrated. "I'll tell you about it later. I promise, it has nothing to do with Cordell."

The doorbell rang, and Jovan looked toward the door, then back to Cheyenne.

"Can you go check dinner for me while I get the door?" she asked.

"Go ahead," Cheyenne muttered before stomping her way to the kitchen.

Jovan reached the door just as Cordell made it down the stairs. They shared a glance that meant nothing. She opened the door and took a step back.

She couldn't place the man that stood before her—tall and thin, with a face that resembled that of a rat.

"May I help you?" she asked.

"Yes, I'm Jimmy Devane, an associate of Cordell's."

Cordell slid in front of Jovan and shook Jimmy's hand.

"Hey, man," he said. "Come on in. This is my wife, Jovan."

"Nice to meet you," Jimmy said with a hard New York accent.

Jovan shook his hand and looked from him to Cordell.

"Nice to meet you, too, Mr. Devane."

"Jimmy, please."

"Jimmy."

Cordell patted Jimmy on the back and told him to make himself comfortable in the living room.

"We'll be right there," he added.

Jimmy made his way down the foyer and Cordell moved in close to Jovan, his face hard, almost menacing.

"What?" she asked, feeling scared.

"Be nice," he said. "Be cool. Let's be on our best behavior."

"Look who's talking."

"Jovan."

She threw her hand up to Cordell.

28

"I don't want to hear it. You're the last person that should be telling me about behavior and manners. And Jimmy Devane? An associate? What dealings are you into with him?"

"The kind that keeps us living well," he replied and left her standing at the front door.

"No," she corrected. "*I* keep us living this well."

After dinner, Jovan took her time as she poured creamer into a small, silver container and the hot, just percolated coffee into a matching pitcher. She was biding time, trying to collect any nerves she had left. Cheyenne wasn't having any of that.

"After I beat your ass for not telling me about your mugging," she said, "I'm going to go in there and take on your husband."

Jovan placed the sugar bowl alongside the creamer and the coffee on the silver tray and leaned against the counter top.

When she finally looked up, she noticed the worried expression etched across her sister's face.

"This," Cheyenne continued, "this charade of a night is over. I can't sit out there and pretend to be fond of your husband when I know what he has done to you, Jo. And who the hell is this Jimmy Devane character anyway? I know he doesn't work at Anderson Technologies."

"That's because he doesn't," Jovan answered. "Cordell thinks I'm too dumb to realize this. Good ol' Jimmy is probably a gambling buddy."

Cheyenne inched her fingers through her sleek, burgundy-streaked hair, tugging gently at the ends. She groaned.

"I wouldn't trust him as far as I could throw him," she said. "Him or your husband."

"I know."

29

"Sis, I can't stand to see you like this."

For a fleeting second, Jovan's soft, facial features wilted, but she steeled up quickly. "I'll be okay."

"What are you going to do about this?" Cheyenne asked. "You can't stay."

Jovan settled into a chair in a nook of the kitchen and sighed.

"Chey, it's such a mess. I can't be here with Cordell, not anymore. He hurt me, and I know that if I stay here, he and I will both regret it."

"Then get out, Jo. Come home with me tonight."

Cheyenne sat down beside Jovan and held her hands. "You can stay with me for as long as you need. We can figure this out together." Jovan tried, but the tears demanded to leak from her eyes.

"I love him," she cried. "I love that bastard, God help me. But I hate him, too. I want him to feel the pain he has made me feel. Sitting out there tonight, smiling and pretending to be hopelessly in love with one another when I know he would prefer to be with...with...her. I can't tell you how low I feel. Like there's rock bottom, and I'm beneath that."

"Well, then you have—"

"Jovan," Cordell yelled from the other room. Cheyenne and Jovan stared at each other until Cordell came barreling into the kitchen.

"Jovan, I know you heard me calling you," Cordell bellowed. "What the hell is taking so long?"

"I'm talking to my sister."

"You can do that later. We have a guest, and we're waiting on coffee."

Jovan pleaded with Cheyenne with her eyes to stay in her seat, to not speak.

"Cordell," Jovan said. "Could you be sweet enough to take the tray out and serve *your* guest?"

"Didn't you say you were going to come in here, fix the coffee, and bring it in for us all to have?"

"You know what?" Cheyenne asked. She stood and moved in Cordell's direction. "You have some nerve to be in here acting all high and mighty, Cordell."

"This has nothing to do with you, Cheyenne," Cordell responded. "So just stay out of it."

"Nope, can't do that. You see, Jo is my blood. You mess with her, you mess with me. So how about you just take the coffee in, and Jo and I will be right out."

"I want her to do it, and I want her to do it *now*." Jumping from her chair, Jovan sidled up to Cordell, tears glistening in her eyes.

"I really don't know why you hate me, Cordell, I don't," she began. "I have tried to give you everything you could ever want. Obviously, it wasn't enough. You want someone to be your go girl, your slave? Then go get your mistress and leave me the hell alone."

Jovan pushed past Cordell and ran out of the kitchen.

Silence stifled the room. Cheyenne glared at Cordell, leaned to one side, and folded her arms.

"Enjoying yourself?" she asked.

"Cheyenne," Cordell turned away, "Don't even—"

"You are such a bastard, Cordell." She stepped close to him, close enough to smell salmon on his breath. "You don't deserve Jo. You don't deserve anything but to live a miserable life."

Cordell laughed in her face. "Don't you think I'm doing that now with your sister?"

Cheyenne's upper lip began to twitch, and before Cordell had time to react, she pulled back and gave him a hard slap to his right cheek.

"You think you're miserable now?" she growled, pushing him hard from in front of her. "Wait until *I'm* through with you."

31

Chapter 4

At the top of the staircase, Jovan glanced down across to the living room where she saw Cheyenne grab her purse and storm down the foyer, out of the house. She turned and walked into the bedroom that she frequently occupied. She walked through the bathroom that adjoined the bedroom and her office, and sat down on the window seat where the full moon was basking in all its glory.

"Damn him!" Jovan said as she made finger smudges along the window. "What did I do?"

Closing her eyes, she began moving backward and forward through her life with Cordell, trying to find the defining moment that made him hate her. She couldn't find it. *He* pursued her in graduate school; *he* asked her to marry him; *he* asked her to wait until they were both accomplished before children were brought into the marriage. *He* wanted to have a home custom-built in the pristine, historic area of Reisterstown, Maryland.

Even though it was Jovan's money that paid for the four-bedroom home, with luxuries such as a Jacuzzi, mud room, sauna, sunroom, and five private acres to frolic in, Cordell always managed to take credit for the home...calling it his castle, his sanctuary. Now Jovan sat at her window seat in her office, feeling like she was locked away from the world...in the one room she really felt was hers.

Deep in thought, she was startled when her office phone rang. She picked it up and hastily whispered, "Hello?"

"It's me, Jo."

"Chey." She sighed into the phone, settling back onto the window seat.

"Girl, get out of there now and come to my place."

"Did he do something to you when I left the kitchen? I swear to God if he—"

"No, he didn't; but I got one good slap of his disgusting face before I bolted. I hate people who feel they can just hurt others and not get punished for their actions."

"What kind of punishment could he get?"

"I know my slap wasn't enough. Him hurting you is like him hurting me, and you know how I get when I'm angry."

"I know."

"I'm worried about you."

"Need to be worried about us. I told El we would have the manuscript to her in a week's time, and if I up and leave right now, that will be disrupted."

"Are you serious? I'm talking about *you* right now. Jovan the person, my sister, not Jovan the writer. If you're crying and miserable every day, what good is that going to do you?"

"I dunno." Jovan paced her office. "I thought this was going to be forever, you know? I don't have the storyline for this situation, Chey."

"I know. I'm sorry. I'm worried about you. I love you."

"I love you, too."

"Will you come over here for a while?" Cheyenne begged. "Just until you figure out what you want to do?"

"Just give me tonight, okay? I'll get up early, pack up a bag, get some stuff together, and I promise to be at your place by brunch."

"Jo, if noon strikes and you're not here, I *will* come there and drag you out, regardless of how Cordell feels about it."

"I promise you, Chey," Jovan said, her voice hushed. "Come tomorrow morning, Cordell won't care if I'm here."

Showered and dressed in her blue cotton pajamas, Jovan glanced at herself in the medicine cabinet mirror while she brushed her hair and tied a black silk cap around it. As if exploring, she raised her fingertips to her face, allowing them to creep along her clear, cinnamon face, over her closed black eyes, the slight fullness of her nose, down to her full lips. Her eyes opening, she wiped at the tears that began to fall.

"I don't think I'm ugly," she whispered to her mirrored reflection. *I'm 31. I still look good.* She reached for a tissue on the back of the toilet to dab the tears from her eyes and cheeks.

Just the other day, someone mistook me for a student when I gave that writing lecture at the college. I could stand to lose a pound or two...I guess.

She went to the full mirror behind the door and examined her profile. Her full bosom that still managed to stay at attention.

Curves in all the right places.

Shaking her head, Jovan groaned. "It's not you. It's Cordell."

She turned the light out in the bathroom and dragged herself into the bedroom, falling onto the bed. By the time on the clock that sat upon the nightstand, it was well after midnight.

The phone rang, and Jovan reached quickly over to the nightstand to answer it.

"Chey, I told you—"

"It's not Cheyenne."

"Hi, Mark," she said.

"I know it's late. I'm sorry. I just wanted to make sure you were okay."

"I'm okay."

"Truly?"

Jovan closed her eyes. Tears leaked from the slits and onto her pillowcase.

"More or less," she said. "You?"

"Tired. Family been in and out, helping with arrangements. The funeral is in two days."

"Do you need help with anything?"

"No, but thanks. You know, I never noticed how quiet it is when you're all alone."

Jovan listened, and silence spoke to her.

"I understand."

"I'm sorry to be going on," Mark said. "Just wanted to make sure you were okay."

"I appreciate it, Mark. You can call me anytime. Get some sleep."

"You, too."

Jovan hung up the phone and flicked off the nightstand lamp before nestling herself under her thick comforter and pulling it up under her chin. Sighing, she took long, deep breaths, listening to hear if Cordell would magically come to her side, apologize for tonight, for everything, and beg her to forgive his indiscretions, his lapses in judgment, and try to work this out between them. Jovan eventually drifted off to sleep, with no appearance from her estranged husband.

Many nights, Jovan slept without a toss or turn, but on those nights when she would argue with Cordell, her body would stay awake while her mind slept. This was one of those nights. With a fluid ease, Jovan slid from the bed, walked straight to the door, and opened it. A sharp right turn, followed by a sharp left, and she was walking down the hallway to the master bedroom she shared with Cordell.

Her face was full of sleep, but her body, having moved in every hall and room of the house, knew the contours of it like a second skin. When her hand reached out to touch the knob of the master bedroom, she stopped. She frowned slightly and small lines etched themselves into her forehead. Without touching the knob, Jovan turned and walked back from which she came.

Jovan stretched and rolled off the window seat. "Ouch! What the hell?" She got up on her hands and knees and looked around. Her computer, desk, bookcase.

"All I want is some sleep," she whined. She crawled over to her desk and used the chair to get up.

The clock on her desk said 3:30 a.m. She rested her head on the desk for a while, and then muttered, "Pills."

Her sleepwalking episodes had been legendary as a child. Her mother told her of the time she went to check on her, and she found Jovan opening the bedroom window and trying to climb out, while asleep. Then, there was the time she walked all the way downstairs, out the front door, and started walking up the street before Cheyenne noticed Jovan was gone and called out to their parents. Some nights, Jovan started out in her bedroom, but she would wake up on the kitchen floor. Over the years, the episodes were handled with medication and stress-reduction exercises, but no amount of exercise or pills could help with the deterioration of her marriage.

Jovan marched into the bathroom, reaching into the medicine cabinet for a bottle of prescribed sleeping pills.

"It's been a while since I've needed you guys," she whispered. "Do your stuff." Running a cold glass of water from the sink faucet, she downed two pills. "Maybe some reading will help put me to sleep."

She stumbled back into her office and scanned her bookcase. Her eyes rested on a white- and red-laced album that had a picture of her and Cordell on the cover. *Through the Years* was scripted above the picture. Jovan picked up the thick album and made it back to bed.

She rubbed her hand over the soft lace and the picture.

Cheyenne had designed the album, collected the pictures, and presented it as a gift to the couple for their fifth year anniversary, a more pleasant time in Jovan's marriage. She remembered how Cheyenne was a shutterbug and loved to carry around her camera and snap shots of things, the way others liked to breathe. Their parents had thousands of pictures tucked away in albums and boxes, all of them, they said, too precious to throw away because Cheyenne took them.

The first picture in the album made Jovan's insides crunch in on themselves. It was a picture of Jovan sitting on the stoop out front of the brownstone she lived in while in graduate school. Her elbows rested on her knees and her chin rested on her fisted hands. It was spring. Jovan could remember that because she wore a pale blue cotton dress with white sneakers in the picture; back then, one of her favorite spring dresses.

She looked sad, so unbelievably sad, and Cheyenne somehow managed to capture the down sweep of Jovan's curly lashes, the shadow of her bowed head upon her dress, her flyaway mane, curled and blowing in the spring breeze. In that picture, Cheyenne caught a girl in love. A girl in love with a boy she had never said hi to. What struck Jovan most was what wasn't in the picture.

Cheyenne always had the ability to show up at the right time, and this time was no exception. Jovan had been waiting out on the stoop for Cheyenne to show up, and just as she did, Cordell had walked by and changed Jovan's mood from anticipation of her sister's arrival, to longing for a boy she couldn't say hi to. Cordell had lived a block from Jovan's brownstone, and he traveled just about everywhere by foot or his bike for the exercise. It was true that Cordell pursued Jovan vigorously about six months after that picture was taken, but it was Jovan who fell in love first. Despite the pain of it all, Jovan laughed. Even in a picture that showed how much she loved Cordell, he wasn't around. She closed her eyes and said a prayer for the heart of the girl in that picture.

By four a.m., she was out cold.

Jovan sat in the third row of an amphitheater, wringing her hands.

She thought, briefly, about pulling a tissue from her purse to shred, but she didn't want to make a spectacle of herself.

"It's okay, Jo," Cheyenne whispered in Jovan's left ear. Jovan turned to her sister. Just looking into Cheyenne's hopeful face made her realize that things were okay.

The feeling solidified itself when she felt warm hands surround her trembling ones. Jovan looked down and smiled. Cordell's hands collapsed themselves around hers and gave them a gentle squeeze.

"Chey's right," Cordell said before dropping a kiss onto Jovan's cheek. "This is your night...you and Chey's. Nothing to be nervous about, Honey."

Both Jovan and Cheyenne took deep breaths and held them in as the presenter read the nominees for the NAACP Image Award for Outstanding Literary Work - Fiction.

"We could win, right?" Jovan asked.

Cheyenne chuckled. "We have a one in five chance, Sis. Odds are good we could."

"And the NAACP Image Award for Outstanding Literary Work - Fiction goes to," the presenter read before opening the envelope, "and I don't think we should be too surprised by this...the wonder twins, Cheyenne Parham and Jovan Parham-Anderson."

The audience erupted into applause as Jovan and Cheyenne leapt to their feet and hugged one another. Jovan faced Cordell and he pulled her into a hard embrace before dropping a kiss onto her mouth.

"Congratulations, Baby," he whispered on her lips. "You deserve this."

Cheyenne took Jovan's hand and began to walk to the stage. Jovan turned to Cordell, who was still standing, and said, "Just tell me this isn't a dream. No one could be this happy."

Cordell shook his head no and laughed. "No dream, Jovan. You're getting everything you want."

Jovan and Cheyenne drew laughs from the audience as they took the steps two at a time, even in their flowing gowns. They hugged the presenter and reached out to receive their statuettes. Jovan pulled her statuette to her chest, feeling on top of the world.

"Thank you," she began, "thank you all. Man, if this is a dream, please, do not even bother to wake me up."

"Thank you," Jovan whispered just before waking up. She looked at the clock and groaned. After using the bathroom, Jovan walked to the master bedroom. The dream had to mean something. The awards were great, but it was that Cordell was there, being supportive that she remembered most. He actually loved her, and Jovan knew there was a time where Cordell did love her. It couldn't have all been a lie.

When she reached the door, Jovan placed her hands on it and sighed. "Don't turn me away," she said and then opened the door.

She used the dimmer lights so she could see into the room. Her eyes grew large as she viewed her husband curled up in bed, under their white comforter, as if he was asleep. But this wasn't a sleep Cordell would awaken from. Up around his head, the comforter was drenched with blood. Jovan screamed, running toward Cordell, but stopped as she saw the bullet hole that pierced his skull.

"Oh my God! Oh my God!" she wailed as her knees buckled and she fell to the floor. Her eyes scanned every corner of the bedroom in fast, short movements.

Jovan climbed from the floor and leaned against the bed, her hands seeking out Cordell's. "You're not dead, Baby," she whispered, blinded by tears.

Cordell's hands were cool to the touch. His fingers didn't curl instinctively around hers, and the realization that Cordell was not *there* anymore hit Jovan as she let out a gut-wrenching cry. She fell back to the floor and grabbed her stomach, the waves of nausea unable to stay dormant.

Chapter 5

Cheyenne's car came to a screeching halt outside of St. Agnes Hospital. With tears in her eyes, she got out of her car and ran for the automatic, double doors. A burly security officer moved in front of her and threw his hands up.

"Ma'am," he said. "You cannot park here."

"Look, I don't have time to move—"

"You'll get a ticket, and you will be towed."

"God! Tow me then. Just move!" Cheyenne pushed past the officer and made quick steps to the information desk.

"May I help you?" asked the elderly white woman with feathered, cotton candy hair.

Cheyenne closed her eyes and pressed her baseball cap tighter to her scalp. She gripped the desk as her knees began to go weak.

"Yes," she croaked. "My brother-in-law, Cordell Anderson, was brought in. He was shot."

The receptionist flipped through her logbook and her soft, angelic face crumpled. She looked at Cheyenne and her blue eyes read death.

"I know," Cheyenne replied softly. "Could you tell me where I might locate my sister, Jovan Parham-Anderson? She came in with him."

"Uh...um, yes, I can do that," the receptionist stuttered. "Dr. Jacobson said that Mrs. Anderson went to the chapel. Down this hall, and then make the third right."

Cheyenne tried to smile, but the thought of it would not connect with her face muscles. Her tennis shoes were loud as they smacked against the marbled floors. When she reached the door to the chapel, her hand gripped the cool, brass knob, and she swore she could feel the energy of God soothing her pain. She opened the door and found Jovan in the front pew, her face illuminated by the rows of candles in front of her.

Cheyenne removed her cap and pushed the bill of it deep into her back jean pocket. By habit, she ran her hand over her hair.

Cheyenne proceeded up the red-carpeted aisle. She reached Jovan and sat beside her. She noticed Jovan's silk cap on her head; she still wore her pajamas. Jovan pulled tighter on her trench coat, shivering as if she was freezing.

"Sis," Cheyenne spoke. "I'm so sorry." Jovan didn't turn. She shook as tears zigzagged down her rounded cheeks.

"Please talk to me, Jo." Cheyenne blinked back her own tears as she viewed the vacant look on her sister's face. Jovan stared at Cheyenne, but it was almost as if she was seeing through her, instead of looking at her.

"Sweetie," Cheyenne tried again, as she nestled Jovan into her arms. "Talk to me, please. I am so worried about you." She kissed Jovan's forehead while she smoothed down the wiry curls that broke loose from under her cap.

"Cor..." Jovan choked, sobbing.

"I know," Cheyenne cried. "I know, and I am so sorry. God, I cannot believe this."

"Mom...Dad...I...they...call..."

"I called them before I came, Honey. They'll be here tomorrow morning. Don't worry about them. We're all thinking about you right now." Jovan slid her arms around her sister, the two clinging to each other, weeping.

Cheyenne cradled Jovan's face into her hands, batting away the tears. "What happened?" Cheyenne whispered. Jovan shook her head.

"I lost my husband," she replied. She looked toward the small stained glass window of Jesus raising his hands up to a golden, clear sky. "He's gone."

Jovan looked down at her trembling hands.

"I touched him," she said. She wrung her hands. "I just knew he wasn't dead. I knew it." Her hands created a soft,

41

vibrating motion as she rubbed her face. "But he was cold. Empty."

She collapsed into Cheyenne's arms.

"I'm just glad you weren't hurt," Cheyenne said into Jovan's ear. The chapel door opened and Cordell's family came in. His mother, Margaret Anderson, rushed Jovan, stopping mere inches from her.

"What happened?" she screamed into Jovan's face. Jovan flinched. "Why is my son dead?"

"Mrs. Anderson," Cheyenne said, trying to intervene. Dean Anderson, Cordell's father, took his wife by the arm and added space between her and Jovan.

"Don't Mrs. Anderson me," Margaret cried. "My son is dead, and I demand to know why."

Jovan's eyes wavered from Margaret's scrutiny and fell upon Timothy, Cordell's brother. Jovan rocked back on her legs, almost falling to the floor. Timothy could have been Cordell's twin if they weren't five years apart. His face was broken into shattered pieces of pain, and Jovan wanted nothing more than to hug him and to make them both feel better.

"Well?" Margaret asked. She eyed Jovan, top to bottom, circled her like a vulture eyeing its prey. "You don't have a scratch on you. But my son is…" She buried her face into her husband's shoulder.

"I don't know," Jovan spoke. "I don't know how it happened. Or why."

They were pitted, three against two, the Andersons versus the Parhams. A stalemate. Margaret threw hatred to Jovan through the wet slits of her eyes.

"I loved him," Jovan said. "So much. I just can't…" She shook her head, her face full of confusion as she tried desperately to remember something, anything. "I don't know why someone would hurt him."

Timothy broke down, his strong shoulders jumping up and down as his father took him into his free arm. His face was dry, emotion and pain thick in his eyes, but he didn't let it travel outside of his mind, his heart. He stood, like a formidable oak as he tended to his mourning family.

"This is a time for us to come together," Dean spoke, his voice hard, authoritative. When he spoke, everyone listened. "We need each other. Let's not fight."

Gently, he slipped his arm from his wife and reached it out to Jovan. She wiped at the tears that tracked her face and walked to her father-in-law. His and Timothy's arms clutched her, and she could feel, hear the heartache rattling inside Dean's heart.

"Mrs. Anderson?" Jovan and Margaret turned simultaneously, answered, "Yes?" to the person who had managed to slip into the tension-filled chapel. "Mrs. Jovan Parham-Anderson?" he asked again. The man cast a tall shadow in the candle lit chapel as he walked up the aisle and stepped to Jovan. She reached back for Cheyenne, and Cheyenne took her hand, holding it tight.

"I am she," Jovan answered. She had to crane her neck to take in all of him. He was at least 6'4". She felt small as she looked up into sable-colored eyes.

"I'm Detective Ian Davenport," he said, removing his badge and identification. "I've been assigned to your case." He eyed everyone in the chapel. His jaw, first tight, slackened. "I'm sorry for your loss. I know this must be a difficult time for you."

"Yes," Jovan answered. "Thank you."

"Is it possible that I might ask you a few questions?" Ian asked. He dug his fingers into his curly brown hair and scratched.

"Um, okay," Jovan replied, looking at Cheyenne and then Timothy who kept his focus between Ian and Jovan.

"It's okay. Just a few routine questions for now, okay?"

Jovan nodded. She looked up to find Dean opening his arms. She took turns hugging him and Timothy. Margaret still looked on coldly.

"We'll talk to you soon," Dean said.

"Okay," Jovan replied. "Thank you."

"Mr. Anderson, correct?" Ian asked. "I will need to talk to you and your family as soon as possible." Seamlessly, he reached into his jacket pocket and pulled out a business card. "Please call me tomorrow."

Dean nodded before taking Margaret and Timothy's hands and leading them out of the chapel.

"Let's sit," Ian said as if a host at a party. The twins sat in a pew together, and Ian sat in the pew in front of them. He turned their way and paused.

"What?" Cheyenne asked.

"Twins," he said. "Captain told me about you, and how you were practically detectives for the precinct." Ian shook his head. "I'm sorry. Rambling. You just look so much alike. The hair is different, but still."

Despite the situation, Cheyenne laughed, and then gave a prayer to God for forgiveness. "Yes," she said. "Twins do that from time to time."

Ian turned to Jovan. He noticed a faint bruising just under her cinnamon-colored cheek and decided to keep that information for now.

"Mrs. Anderson," he said. "How are you? You sure you can handle this right now?"

Jovan nodded.

"Okay. Can you tell me about last night? Did your husband seem worried, nervous about anything?"

Jovan played with the belt of her trench coat.

"No," she answered, shaking her head. "He seemed his normal self."

"Do you know if your husband had any enemies?" Ian noticed a twitch in Cheyenne's right cheek and her eyes rolling.

44

"May I have a piece of paper?" Jovan asked, eyeing Ian's pad.

Ian raised an eyebrow as he looked at Cheyenne, then Jovan. He ripped a sheet from his pad and handed it to her. Jovan began to tear the sheet into thin, even strips.

"I don't know if my husband had enemies," she answered. "I didn't know much about his work at Anderson Technologies, or the people he interacted with."

"Did you two have mutual friends?"

"Not many."

While scribbling on his pad, Ian snatched glimpses of the twins. On the surface, it was obvious they were twins, but Ian was known for being able to read people with just a look into their eyes, a few sentences uttered through their lips. He could see the vulnerability of Jovan through the way her shoulders slumped forward, the way her head wobbled, as if too heavy to stay up, the way her eyes skittered around and never fully looked at a person for very long. He was sure, on the other hand, that Cheyenne had something simmering just beneath her exterior. He could feel it and see it. He wasn't sure what was simmering, but he jotted a note to find out, especially if it had to do with the case.

"Your husband was shot in your bedroom, yes?" he asked, giving his full attention to Jovan.

"Y..es," Jovan stammered out. "Our bed."

"And where were you, Mrs. Anderson?"

Jovan shredded the last piece of paper and then balled the strips up into a tight, compact ball. "Down the hall in a guest bedroom."

Ian's eyebrow rose at Jovan's response. "Oh?" he prompted. Jovan eyed Cheyenne, who took her hand and massaged it.

"We had a fight," Jovan said. She bit her lower lip. "I slept in one of the guest rooms."

"Physical?"

"No," Cheyenne answered. "I was there. Just a marital spat, period. Just like the ones millions of other couples have every day."

"Did you witness the spat?" Ian asked, intrigued that Cheyenne would answer for her sister.

"Yes, I was there. It was nothing, but things were said. Feelings hurt."

"How did you react to seeing your sister upset, Ms. Anderson?" When Ian's eyes hooked on to Cheyenne's, something sparked between them and for a few moments, a deep silence shrouded the trio.

That fire in her probably streaked her hair, Ian thought. He was the first to break contact, resting his eyes onto his pad.

"I was upset, understandably," Cheyenne replied. "I hated seeing my sister so distraught over what that..." Cheyenne looked away.

"Was this a normal occurrence in your marriage, Mrs. Anderson?"

Jovan lowered her head and placed her hands onto her lap. Tears fell from her eyes and made dark, wet circles on her coat. "We used to be so in love," she uttered before falling against Cheyenne.

Cheyenne hugged her sister as her jaw flexed and her eyes glinted with anger.

"It's okay, Sis," she whispered. "It's going to be okay."

Ian watched the raw love of Cheyenne penetrate Jovan. It touched him, and he immediately distanced himself from the pair. *Until there was a suspect, everyone was a suspect.* He reached into his pocket and handed Cheyenne a card.

"I'll be in touch," he said. "I'm going to talk to the M.E. now. Once again, I'm sorry for your loss." Jovan nodded, and Cheyenne replied, "Thank you, Detective." Cheyenne held Jovan as she watched Ian walk up the short aisle and leave the chapel.

Jovan looked into her sister's reflective eyes.

"You did good," Cheyenne whispered before kissing Jovan's forehead. "You did real good, Sis."

Chapter 6

*J*ovan sat in the guest room, crying uncontrollably. "I hate him!" she screamed into a pillow on the bed. Cordell had the audacity to yell at her for wanting to talk to her sister, to try to find some solace from the horrible evening she was having with her sister, husband, and his associate.

"I am so tired of this, of him," she continued to cry, her breath coming hard and fast, as she became blinded not only by her tears, but also by the anger she had toward Cordell.

For months now, Cordell had treated her like a second-class citizen, criticizing her, spending his nights away from home, doing every and anything that would cause Jovan to leave him, but she didn't. She sat around hoping and praying to make her marriage work. After all, her parents had been married for over thirty years, and she had always dreamed of finding that soul mate to settle down with, pursue her dreams with, have children with. Instead, all she had was her loving twin, Cheyenne, her adoring fans, and her writing. If she had never met Cordell, that would have been enough. But she had fallen in love with him, given herself to him, and now, she wanted more than her career. She wanted love, a marriage, and small Cordells and Jovans running around the house.

"He took all of that away from me," Jovan seethed. "I gave him me. I gave him my money freely, and he just didn't give a damn, screwing that tramp, cheating on me, and he thinks, he thinks I'm going to let him get away with it. He is so wrong."

Jovan marched into her office and went to her window seat. She threw the pillows across the room and then lifted the wooden top, revealing the .38 caliber she bought. She swore she would never use it, but that was months ago, and now, after tonight, she refused to allow Cordell to breathe one more breath in this house, or in the world.

The phone rang once...twice, and the answering service picked up taking the call.

"Jo," it was Cheyenne, "if you hear me, pick up...okay? If you want, come to my house tonight. I smacked your jerk of a husband, and I just don't trust him. I don't. So please, call me back or I'll be there in the morning to come and get you out of there. Love you, Sis. Call me."

Jovan had already planned it out. She would plead insanity, and at this moment, she felt out of her mind with craziness, gripping the gun and feeling its coolness, newness. She wasted no time making her move. She knew Cordell's habits like clockwork. She heard him escort Jimmy out of the house, make his way upstairs, and she let an hour and a half past, knowing that he would be sound asleep. Jovan rose from her chair and slipped out her office, making the deadly walk down the hall to the master bedroom she and Cordell shared.

With quiet ease, Jovan opened the bedroom door, the darkness of the room broken by the glow of the hallway light. There slept Cordell, not stirring, his back toward her. She could see the white comforter hugging along Cordell's body as he slept.

"I loved you," Jovan whispered, tears blinding her view. She made slow steps toward Cordell, the barrel of the .38 pointed at the back of his head. Briefly closing her eyes, she prayed to God for her soul as she fired the gun.

"NO! NO!"

Cheyenne came rushing into the bedroom. "Honey, wake up," she said as she shook Jovan. Riqué hopped onto the bed, waking Jovan with licks to her face.

Jovan's eyes sprung open, terror etched into them.

"Chey," she cried. "Oh my God, I...oh my God."

"What?" Cheyenne asked, wiping the tears from Jovan's face and staring into her eyes. "What's wrong?"

"I killed Cordell." Jovan wept, her head falling onto her sister's shoulder. Cheyenne felt her blood run cold as she held Jovan.

"Killed him? Honey, why would you even say such a thing? You didn't kill him."

Jovan shook her head, continuously running her fingers over her hair, trying to calm herself.

"No, No," she said. "I did. I remembered it in my sleep. I was in the guest room, so angry at Cordell, and all I could see was red."

Cheyenne sat beside her.

"I went into my office and you called," Jovan continued, "but I didn't talk to you. I let the answering machine pick up."

"That's not true. I called you, you answered the phone, and talked to me. Said you would be coming over in the morning, but of course, that never happened."

"No, I saw it. I saw it, Chey. It was so clear. I pulled out a gun from beneath my window seat, I went down the hall...and... killed...and...I...God!" Jovan jumped from the comfort of the bed and began pacing around the bedroom.

"Sis, listen," Cheyenne yelled, desperation in her voice as she watched Jovan so beside herself. "Just *think* about what you are saying. You don't own a gun. Never had a gun. It was just a dream."

"Maybe I took your gun?" Jovan's voice raised an octave.

Cheyenne turned her eyes away from Jovan as her hands gripped the bed sheets.

"No, Jo," she said. She took Jovan by the hand and led her into her bedroom. She pulled open the bottom drawer of her nightstand and lifted a .38 from the drawer. "See, my gun is right here where it always is."

Jovan coiled back. A wave of nausea hit her belly. She clutched her stomach and raced out of the room, leaving Cheyenne holding the gun.

"Oh God." Jovan's cheek cooled on the seat of the porcelain toilet. With the lid closed, she flushed the toilet twice and laid her head back onto the seat. Her stomach still jumped and twitched; she took deep breaths to calm herself.

"You okay?" Cheyenne walked into the bathroom and knelt beside Jovan, placing a hand in the middle of her back. She rubbed her there, then up around her neck. Jovan nodded and added a groan for good measure.

"Sis," Cheyenne added. "You know that you didn't kill Cordell, right?" Jovan breathed in and out with no words passing her lips.

"You told me what happened last night after I brought you here. Remember?" Cheyenne was almost pleading. "I came to the hospital. We talked to Detective Davenport, and I brought you here."

Jovan looked up from the toilet. Her eyes were closed, and her face appeared full of thought. "Kinda," she muttered.

"You went upstairs after the blow-up with Cordell in the kitchen. You cried, you talked to me, and you tried to go to sleep but couldn't. You got up, took some sleeping pills, flipped through an album, and fell out...you woke up and then...well, then you found Cordell."

"I know I told you that, but how do we know it's true? This was so real."

"Jovan, you had a nightmare. Stop this. I mean it."

"You know I get into those sleepwalking spells. What if I killed him while I was sleepwalking?" Cheyenne gripped Jovan tightly about the shoulders and shook her.

"Stop it," she yelled. "Do you remember going to the bedroom and finding Cordell?"

Jovan's placid expression changed to one of horror as her mouth gaped open and she let out a piercing scream. Cheyenne caught her limp body and watched as her sister cried out Cordell's name.

"It was so horrible, Chey. I prayed, prayed for him to be alive, but he wasn't. He was…dead."

"I know, Baby," Cheyenne cooed, holding Jovan tightly in her arms. "Cordell is dead, but you did not, I repeat, did not kill him. Detective Davenport and his crew are going to find who did this."

"The dream…was so real. I could smell the death in the bedroom before I even pulled the trigger."

Cheyenne shuddered, just thinking of her sister having murdered Cordell. She knew Jovan could never harm anyone, no matter how tortured she felt, but if anyone heard Jovan go off like she just had, there was no way they would think she was innocent.

"Jo," Cheyenne whispered, "honey, you have to promise me you won't tell this dream, your thoughts, to anyone else." Jovan looked at Cheyenne with fear in her eyes.

"I'm scared, Chey. My mind is playing tricks on me. What if I slip? What if I say something that could incriminate me?"

"As long as you have me, you don't need to worry about that. Talk about Cordell, yes. Anyone else, fine. But don't talk about the dream, your sleepwalking. That could lead to Lord knows what."

Ian sat in his car outside of Anderson Technologies, flipping through his small notepad. His pencil beat the rhythm of Marvin Gaye's "What's Going On" against the dashboard.

"Devane," he said. He had just questioned a slew of Anderson employees, asking them about Cordell's character, his friends, possible enemies, any problems at Anderson. Everyone attested to Cordell being a great boss with an optimistic personality. However, some couldn't help but to whisper their thoughts of a relationship going on between Cordell and Alisha Stewart. Alisha knew the entire goings on of Anderson Technologies and of Cordell, probably in the most intimate of ways.

Ian was eager to see Alisha, but when he had asked to speak with her, he was told that she had been out of the office all day, grieving, the employees said. As Ian slid his key into the ignition, he watched a black jeep roll up to the front of Anderson Technologies. He couldn't see the person driving through the jeep's tinted windows, but when the door opened and the owner stepped out, a small grin fell across Ian's lips.

"Devane," he said, remembering the description he had received from the precinct on Jimmy after talking to Jovan and Cheyenne. He quickly stepped out of his car and dropped his pad and pen into the pocket of his jacket. He looked both ways before zipping across the street. Jimmy hit the alarm on his jeep and headed toward the entrance of Anderson Technologies.

"Devane!" Ian called out. "Jimmy Devane?"

Jimmy eyed Ian up and down before responding. "Yeah, that's me. Who's asking?"

Ian whipped out his credentials and presented them to Jimmy. "Detective Ian Davenport."

Jimmy's face slacked. "Look, Detective," he said. "It's legal to park here, so no thanks with the ticket."

Ian laughed. "No, I'm a *homicide* detective. Wanted to talk to you about the death of Cordell Anderson."

Jimmy frowned. "You mean the murder of Cordell, right?"

"You know something I don't?" Jimmy glanced around,

taking in the people who walked the sidewalk. No one was paying him or Ian any mind.

"This ain't the best place to be talking, know what I mean?" Jimmy asked.

"Just a few questions here...or down at the precinct." Ian crossed his arms. "I'm not choosy."

"What do ya want to know?"

"How did you know Cordell?"

Jimmy took in the pad and pen that Ian pulled out. "I'm an associate," Jimmy responded.

Ian leaned back and gave Jimmy a once over. "An associate?"

"Yeah, of the business and friend variety."

"Care to explain?"

Jimmy leaned against the building and took out a pack of cigarettes and a lighter.

After sucking back a long drag, he replied, "Anderson and I have been friends for almost two years now. Occasionally, we hang and go to hot spots like Atlantic City and Vegas to gamble. Sometimes, I have a tip for him that can help him out with Anderson Technologies."

"What, you got a degree in computer technology?" Ian asked. They both laughed.

"One of dem smart ass detectives I see," Jimmy said, taking another pull. "No, I don't, but I have street smarts and common sense, and I always have my ear to the pavement, listening for anything that might help my boy get his dues."

Ian nodded. "I hear ya," he said. "What about the night he died? I heard that you were invited to his house for dinner? You, Anderson, his wife, and Cheyenne Parham?"

"It's true. Nice dinner, too. Cordell's wifey can cook up a storm, and everything was quite quaint...if you include the chilliness between the lovebirds."

Ian looked up, his interest piqued. "Between Cordell and Jovan Anderson?"

"Yep," Jimmy said, nodding. "They had the smiles down pat, but no love behind them. I figured they must have had a spat before I arrived. I had pretty much forgotten about it until Jovan blew up at Cordell, and Cheyenne smacked him."

Ian shook his head and tried not to act too excited or surprised by the news. He scribbled in his pad, *Girls need to give up the dirt*. "Okay, details," he said. Jimmy coughed before dropping his cigarette butt onto the ground and smashing it under his expensive leather shoes.

"Not much to say," he began. "Cordell was yelling at his wife because she wasn't doing something fast enough for him."

Bastard, Ian thought.

"After a minute or two," Jimmy continued, "she yelled at him to go to his mistress and leave her alone."

"Mistress?"

"That's what she said," Jimmy answered, shrugging. "She ran off, and Cheyenne, damn that one is a firecracker, smacked him, and told Cordell that he wouldn't know pain until after she got through with him."

"Until she got through with him?"

"Yeah. After that, she left, and then I said my goodbyes. I felt really embarrassed for my man, and I knew he didn't want to talk about it. So, I just pretended nothing happened and told him I would talk to him tomorrow."

"But tomorrow never came."

"Naw." Jimmy looked up at the sky. "I know you might be thinking Cordell was a bad guy...and yeah, he was a little bitchy to his wife that night, but he wasn't all bad."

Ian nodded and wondered how bad was *not all bad*. Of course a guy like this would back Cordell's precarious ways, Ian thought as he added a couple more question marks to Jimmy's name on his pad.

"Well, thanks," Ian said. "I may be getting back in contact with you soon. Do some follow up questioning."

Jimmy nodded. Ian backed away from Jimmy, taking in Jimmy's calm, laidback air. He nodded his pad toward him before turning around and heading to his car. He'd come back for Alisha later. For now, he needed to talk to a pair of ladies.

Chapter 7

Jovan nibbled on a piece of bacon as she sat at Cheyenne's dining table.

She groaned, rubbing the tears from her face. "I am so tired, but I don't have time to be tired. When Dean called last night, he said that they were gonna try to have the funeral as soon as the body is released. I need to get myself together for that."

"I still can't believe how Margaret treated you at the hospital," Cheyenne lamented as she poured more orange juice into her cup. "And then they wouldn't let you help in the funeral? Margaret's not sure you're innocent? That's just crazy."

"Their son was murdered. At least Margaret didn't hit me. Lord knows what Cordell had been telling them about me."

"Well, you lost a husband. They should have been more sympathetic."

"I just need to make it through the funeral. I'm sure we'll be able to grieve together and share our pain and …"

Jovan and Cheyenne peered at each other as they heard a knock at the front door. Cheyenne walked to the door and opened it, coming face to face with Detective Ian Davenport.

"May I come in?" he asked. Ian took an eye tour of Cheyenne, from the top of her head down to the green terrycloth robe she wore, finally resting on her bare, French-pedicured toes.

Riqué ran between Cheyenne's legs, growling. With a disgusted sigh, Cheyenne gave Ian the evil eye for checking her out.

"My bodyguard says no," she said, looking down at her beloved pet. "But you're here, so you might as well come in."

Cheyenne led him to the table where he gave a sitting Jovan a nod and soft smile.

"How are you doing this morning, Mrs. Anderson?" he asked.

"Please have a seat, Detective," Jovan said.

"Sorry, how rude of me," Cheyenne said.

Ian glanced her way, not believing her sincerity. He offered Cheyenne a smile that could have sweetened any cup of coffee and came back with, "Yes, how rude."

Once Ian was settled into his seat, Jovan finally answered. "I don't know how I am, Detective. How well can a person be at a time like this?"

"I understand," Ian said. "You have my sympathy."

"Thank you."

After sitting down beside Jovan, Cheyenne responded with, "So what brings you here this morning, Detective Davenport? I don't recall leaving my address with you yesterday."

"Well, I am a detective," Ian replied. "If I can't find out where you live, then I shouldn't be the detective on this case."

"Hmm," Cheyenne came back with. "Maybe." She and Ian stared down one another before Cheyenne added, "So, why are you here?"

"Chey," Jovan chastised.

"Sorry."

Ian took in the atmosphere, watching Cheyenne and Jovan closely. Both were clad in nightwear, eyes red; they had apparently been crying. Had Jovan been up all night crying to her sister, confessing to the crime, he wondered. Did Cheyenne keep Jovan awake with her own tale of murder?

"As the head detective, I'm trying to get as much information as I can about your husband so that I can solve this case in a prompt manner." He gave Cheyenne a chilly stare. "That *is* my job."

Jovan reached out and patted Ian's hand.

"I'm sorry, Detective," Jovan said. "It's just very hard to talk about. My mind can't wrap around this whole drama."

"I understand, Mrs. Anderson, and if you want me to come back at another time, I can do that. I just want to continue with my questioning while I'm on a roll."

"A roll?" Cheyenne asked. "We're not the first today?"

"This early in the investigation, it's premature to discuss what I know and don't know."

"Bullshit." Cheyenne stood and leaned over Ian. Ian's eyes, the color of cognac, bore into her stomach before sliding up to her face. Her face was tight and full of anger. "My sister's husband was murdered. She deserves to know any and everything that you can tell her."

The room turned as silent and hot as the sun rising at dawn. Ian cleared his throat and turned away from Cheyenne to face Jovan.

"I promise that if anything important comes up," he said, "I will tell *you*, Mrs. Anderson. But for now, in this early—"

"I understand," Jovan replied calmly. "I just want to get this over with." Cheyenne sucked her teeth and sat back down.

"I need to know everything that you know about Cordell," Ian began. "From the time you first met him, up until yesterday. I have talked with a majority of Anderson Technologies' employees, and they all pretty much have the same story to tell. I didn't get much information about possible enemies or the like."

"Did you talk with Alisha Stewart?" Cheyenne asked.

"She wasn't there, but I will be talking with her, yes. I did happen to find Mr. Jimmy Devane there."

"And?" Jovan asked.

"He told me that he was friends with Cordell, that they were gambling associates. And he told me about the dinner."

Jovan's eyes fell to the table while

Cheyenne turned her chair to study Ian's profile. "We could have told you about dinner, *Detective*," she gritted out.

"And you will," Ian stated. "But I need all sides of the story."

"And what's his?" Jovan asked.

"I want to know yours, Mrs. Anderson."

"We told you yesterday," Cheyenne jumped in. "They had an argument and Jovan slept in a guestroom."

"I need to know what was said, who said what, and who did what. I need specifics." Ian turned to Cheyenne, then faced Jovan. "Jovan, I need to know what you remember from the time you woke up that morning."

Jovan trembled and bit the inside of her cheek. She didn't want to remember. She didn't want to think about the things she found out about her husband. She didn't want to remember him calling out *her* name while he kissed her onto the bed. She shook her head and groaned from the pain she was causing to her cheek.

"So hard," she whispered. "Painful."

Ian sat back and tried another approach. "I checked back with the M.E. this morning," he started. "Your husband was a healthy, young man, aside from the bullet wound he sustained. The bullet wound that killed him." Jovan held herself tight as if afraid she would fall into pieces. Cheyenne opened her mouth, but Ian continued. "The M.E. states that from the entry wound, the shooter had to be in close proximity to the bed. Perhaps only a few feet, three at the most, and he or she was looking down at Mr. Anderson."

"Are you trying to paint us a picture?" Cheyenne asked. Ian looked at her and saw traces of wetness around her eyes.

"I spent a good part of last night at the crime scene," he added as he listened to Jovan weep softly. "I combed through the bedroom, along with my team, and though we can't say this conclusively, we feel confident that the perp is someone you know, Mrs. Anderson."

Jovan's neck snapped as she shot her eyes over to Ian. "Someone I know?" she murmured.

"Someone had to know the combination or know how to tweak it to gain entry without you knowing. Who has access to your home?"

"So what are you saying?" Cheyenne asked, her voice elevating. "Are you trying to accuse us of doing something?"

"Why would I accuse you?" Ian countered. "Did you do something?"

"Are you serious? Why? What reason in the world would I have to kill my sister's husband?" Cheyenne questioned. Her nostrils flared.

"I don't know," Ian replied. "When Mr. Anderson yelled at his wife, your sister, how did you respond?"

"I left." Cheyenne's voice came out weak.

"Is that all?"

"I was mad, okay! I was furious. Do you know how much it hurt to see Jovan crying? To see her husband treat her like garbage?"

"Did you threaten Mr. Anderson?"

Cheyenne opened her mouth to respond, but Ian faced Jovan and asked, "And what happened to your face, Mrs. Anderson? I noticed the bruising, but I didn't want to hurt you further last night. Did that happen at the dinner, too?"

"No!" The twins yelled at the same time.

"No," Jovan repeated. "I was hurt before dinner."

"By Cordell?"

"No," Jovan answered. She sighed. "It's so complicated."

"Why don't you know this already?" Cheyenne asked, agitated. "Jovan called the police about the incident after it happened."

All three jumped when the doorbell rang. Cheyenne excused herself and answered it, finding her mother and father on the other side of the door. Instantly, tears sprang to her eyes as Gerald and Daphne Parham rushed through the door, enveloping their daughter in their arms.

"Baby," her mother cried out. "Where's Jo?"

Ian watched a somber Jovan walk toward her parents as all four shared a grief-stricken family reunion.

"I'm so sorry, Honey," Jovan's mother whispered into her ear. "So very sorry."

Slipping his pad and pen into his jacket, Ian quietly rose from his seat.

"Mom, Dad," Cheyenne said. "This is Detective Davenport. He's in charge of the case."

Ian eyed the tall, thick man as he shook his hand. He was awestruck at the similarities between the twins and their parents.

"Detective Davenport, hopefully you're here with good news, yes?" Gerald said.

"Unfortunately, no," Ian replied. "But it's still very early yet, and we will do everything we can to find out who did this."

"Well I hope you find something soon," Daphne whispered, holding her daughters close to her chest. "Whoever did this could be after my girls, and I will not have them in danger."

"Rest assured, Mr. and Mrs. Parham, your daughters' safety will be a major concern for us." With a nod to the parents, Ian moved toward the front door, Jovan following.

Opening the door, Jovan said, "Thank you for all you are doing, Detective Davenport."

"It's my job." He looked toward Jovan's parents and found Cheyenne shooting him the ugliest of looks. "Is it possible for you to come into the station tomorrow and talk with me?"

"Okay," Jovan replied. "Cheyenne, too?"

"No, I want to talk to you alone, and then your sister. Say eleven tomorrow morning?"

"I'll be there." "Take care, Mrs. Anderson." Ian shook Jovan's hand and left the home while Cheyenne's eyes fired daggers at his retreating back.

Chapter 8

God, I remember my first time in one of these, Jovan thought as she entered the police precinct. Her curiosity getting the best of her, even as a child, Jovan had wandered away from her mother while at the shopping mall. She remembered crying for her mother and running in and out of boutiques to no avail. Several hours later, a tear-streaked mother, holding tight to her other daughter, ran into the precinct to place a missing child report, only to find her daughter sitting on a bench beside an officer. She was sniffling and sucking a lollipop at the same time. Though scared, Jovan eventually found comfort and her mother that day. She had a strange feeling in the center of her gut that today would be different.

She took in the frantic electricity that reverberated in the small, tight area. Desks almost sat atop each other, and men and women hustled about. She and Cheyenne spent a lot of time here, researching their books, noseying in on various crimes. Oftentimes, they were considered meddlesome, but the captain liked their spunk and never banned them from the place.

Jovan slipped her sunglasses off and placed them on the V of her white t-shirt. She shoved her hands deep into the pocket of her khaki slacks as if fighting off a chill. No one looked up long enough for Jovan to say hi, let alone have a conversation with. She reached out and gently grabbed the arm of a young, white, male officer, someone she didn't recognize. "Excuse me," she said.

"Yeah?" He took his eyes away from his report. His mouth opened slightly and shut back up. "You're Jovan Parham."

Jovan nodded. The officer maintained his excitement and collected himself. "I'm sorry about your loss, Ma'am," he said. "What can I do for you?"

"I'm looking for Detective Davenport."

"Last office down, Ma'am."

Jovan thanked him and made her way to Ian's office only to be called back by the young officer. She turned and said, "Yes?"

"Can't wait for your next book," he replied sheepishly. Jovan walked away. Since the media broke the news of Cordell's death, she and Cheyenne were awakened to media vans outside Cheyenne's apartment and calls from reporters wanting the inside scoop. She had to leave the apartment like a wide receiver this morning, breaking tackles and zipping through slight openings to get to her car.

Jovan saw Detective Ian Davenport stenciled on the glass of the door in front of her. She raised her hand to knock. Someone gripped her shoulder from behind, and she yelped. "I'm sorry." She spun around and found Ian standing beside Captain C.D. Michael. "That was stupid of me," the captain said.

"It's nothing, Captain."

The two hugged. "You hanging in there?"

Jovan nodded. "Trying," she responded. "Have you heard anything about who might've mugged me?"

Captain Michael frowned and answered, "Not yet. Hard, seeing that you have no idea what the mugger looked like. Thinking he might have something to do with the break-ins in your neighborhood."

Jovan's eyes widened. "Really? Sarah Brockman's death, too?"

"Maybe," Captain Michael replied.

Jovan noticed a shared look between Captain Michael and Ian. "And Cordell's?"

Captain Michael patted Ian's shoulder and said, "We're still looking into things, Jovan."

"I understand," she whispered.

"Ian, take Jovan in. Come see me once you're done."

"Will do," Ian said. He opened his door and ushered Jovan inside. "Mrs. Anderson," Ian began. "I want to apologize for insinuating the worst about your bruising."

The two settled into seats before Jovan responded. "It's okay. Considering the situation, I can see how you might assume."

"Well, I was hoping you could shed some light on your marriage for me."

"Like what?" Jovan began to wring her hands and wiggle in her seat. Ian offered her a sheet of paper from his stencil pad. She smiled a bit, took it, and commenced to shredding.

"Was it a happy marriage?"

"I thought so," she replied honestly. Her 30th birthday was a moment that instantly popped into her mind. Despite her growing success as a writer and her happy marriage to Cordell, Jovan didn't want to turn the dreaded 30. For weeks leading up to the day, Jovan moped, and it took a lot for Cheyenne to get Jovan in the mood to write or to do anything. Jovan had begged everyone to forget her birthday, to pretend it was just another day on the calendar. Her wish didn't come true, but she did overcome her sadness at turning 30. She was home, flipping through magazines, lying on the sofa, and vegging. She hadn't showered or gotten out of her favorite striped pajamas. She just wanted to eat Ben & Jerry's, watch soap operas, and read fashion magazines—in that order. Cordell came home from work, and the smile that lit his face hit her before he even dropped down beside her and planted a full kiss on her lips.

"Get up," he said.

"Nope." She stuffed a spoon of Chocolate Fudge Brownie into her mouth. When she swallowed, he kissed her again, replying, "Mmm, sweet." She hated herself for laughing.

"If you won't get up," Cordell said, standing up, "then I'll pick you up."

"I'd like to see you try." She laughed. Without another

word, Cordell bent down and swept Jovan up and over his shoulder, smacking her behind for good measure.

"You," he said, "are celebrating your birthday. What's left of it anyway. First, we have to give you a bath."

"Shut up." Jovan popped him upside his head. Though she wanted to forget her birthday, Jovan felt all her angst over the big 3-0 evaporate with the steam of her bath. She succumbed to Cordell's hands as he bathed her from head to toe, before washing her hair. His first gift to her was a sparkling, black gown that hugged her full curves and showed off the hourglass figure Cordell had fallen in love with. She began having fun, rushing mousse through her hair before pulling it into a loose bun atop her head, tendrils kissing the smooth skin of her shoulders.

"Where are we going?" she asked. Cordell only smiled as he dressed in a tux. Within two hours, Cordell whisked Jovan out of the house to the airport, where they flew to New York to take in a musical and spend a week at the Country Inn The City. For seven days, Cordell catered to her every whim, and by the time they touched down in Maryland, she couldn't remember why she was upset about turning 30.

"I fell in love with him first," she said to Ian after her trip down memory lane. "But he was a close second, Detective Davenport. I *know* he loved me."

"I know this might hurt, Mrs. Anderson, but I have to ask."

"Okay."

"Did he stop loving you?"

Jovan blinked quickly, her long lashes fluttering. She wouldn't cry. She was tired of doing that, and her eyes were too dry to produce a drop.

"I don't know," she replied. She coughed, slouched back in her seat, and hugged her arms tightly around herself.

"Do you think he did?"

He was sleeping with Alisha, she thought. He cheated on her. Could it have been some meaningless fling that would eventually end and bring him back to her? It was too late to even ask that question.

"Up until the night he died," Jovan answered, "I thought he loved me."

Ian eyed Jovan closely. He could see she was steeped in emotions. He noticed the way her bottom lip poked out and trembled, the way a slight twitch formed beneath her right eye, and the way her hands shredded the paper into tinier slithers.

"The day before..." Ian paused. "Tell me how that day went."

"I was home. I cleaned, and then I cooked dinner. Really didn't want to go through with the dinner, but—"

"Why not?"

"Cordell's associates usually bore me with their computer talk. Anyway, Cordell came home. We both got ready for dinner."

"No argument? Fight?"

Jovan closed her eyes for a brief moment and in the darkness, she saw Cordell push past her when Alisha called. She felt his searing kiss just before dinner. She heard him call her Alisha. She shook her head no.

"What happened after dinner?"

In a detached, robotic voice, Jovan explained to him the argument and leaving the kitchen. She explained sleeping in the guestroom, not being able to sleep, taking sleeping pills, and flipping through a photo album before crashing. She told him she woke up and went to Cordell, hoping they could talk.

"What time did you fall asleep, do you know?" Ian asked.

"Maybe three or four. I can't remember. The pills are fast acting, and I'm usually out within an hour."

"Okay." Ian scribbled something on his pad and asked,

"Did you see your sister leave that night?"

"I saw her grab her purse and leave."

"Do you know if words were exchanged between them?"

Jovan shook her head. "No, I don't."

"Did your sister like Cordell?"

"She is my sister, Detective. I loved him, and she was okay with that."

"Is that a no?"

"She got along with him. When I married Cordell, everyone thought it was such a big deal. Cordell was a catch." Jovan moistened her lips with her tongue before adding, "I never imagined he would be gone." Her voice became a hush in the office. "I thought we would be married forever. I never thought..." She gripped the sides of the chair, trying to do anything to keep from crying.

Ian could tell Jovan was on the edge, but his mind burned to know the answer to his next question.

"Mrs. Anderson, I have one more question for now, okay?" She nodded. Ian averted eye contact with Jovan and asked, "Do you know if Cordell was participating in any extracurricular activities? Besides the gambling, that is?"

He watched Jovan's eyes well up and overflow with tears.

She didn't speak.

"You mean was he having an affair?" she finally asked in a strangled voice.

"Yes, Ma'am."

"I don't even want to think of that." Jovan shook her head as she whispered the word no. "Why would you ask me that, Detective?"

Someone softly knocked on Ian's door. A female officer poked her head in.

"I'm sorry, Detective," she said. "Cordell Anderson's parents are here."

"Thanks," Ian replied. When the door closed, Ian stood and went to Jovan. "The last thing I want to do is upset you further."

She didn't respond. She stood and shook Ian's hand.

"I will be in contact, okay?"

"Thank you," Jovan said. She wiped at her eyes before shielding them with her sunglasses.

Ian opened the door and Jovan came face to face with Cordell's parents. Ian could see the animosity directed toward Jovan from Cordell's mother.

"Hello, Jovan," Dean said, opening his arms. Jovan slid into them and let out a deep breath when they hugged. She looked to Margaret, but she turned her face away from Jovan. Feeling like a scolded child, Jovan gave a quiet goodbye to Ian before heading out of the precinct. Ian watched until Jovan's figure disappeared outside the door, blinding flashes from cameras sucking her shadow up. He gave a sympathetic smile to the Andersons and ushered them into his office.

Cheyenne examined the game of Scrabble that colorized her computer screen. Her Internet opponent, some guy in California, played a word she had never heard of.

I'm gonna kill you, she typed into the chat box.

He replied, *You wish.* ☺

Gnu is not a word.

Check and see, he typed back. Cheyenne opened up the word lister and sure enough, Gnu was a word.

"A large African antelope," she said, laughing. "Learn something new every day."

Whatever. Moving on, LOL, she typed next.

Someone knocked on her door, and she groaned. "Man, somebody messing up my Scrabble groove." She typed in, *BRB*, and ran to the door.

Cheyenne's face fell when she saw the culprit responsible for interrupting her game.

"It's you," she said.

"Good afternoon to you, too," Ian replied, smirking.

Cheyenne smelled his cologne as he stepped into her apartment.

"Mind if I come in?"

She glared at him. "A little late to ask, don't you think?" She followed him to her sofa and watched him sit. "Have a seat," she said, her words laced with sarcasm. Cheyenne took the overstuffed chair. "I talked with my sister."

"I'm not surprised. Where is Mrs. Anderson?"

"Went for a drive. Needed to clear her head."

"I always thought you two were joined at the hip. Genetically speaking, of course." Ian cracked a smile at his weak attempt at humor, but Cheyenne stayed solemn, almost mute.

"I'm surprised Captain Michael would give this case to you, what with you being all new and everything."

"I'm no rookie."

Cheyenne grinned. "Okay."

"Captain thought this case needed someone who didn't know you all in a friendly manner."

"Then he picked the right person." Cheyenne pulled her feet up onto the chair. Ian watched the effortless way her legs slipped up under her. "Gonna give me the 20 questions now?"

"Miss Parham," Ian spoke. "I'm just trying to do my job as I have told you before. I've talked to several people within the last few days, and as Mrs. Anderson's twin, I would think you would want to talk to me so that I can solve this case."

Cheyenne sighed. She didn't want to get caught up in an argument with Ian. Despite the sadness of the situation,

Cheyenne felt a kick start in the pit of her stomach the minute she opened the door to Ian. She would have to be deaf, blind, and mute not to see how attractive he was, but she had to remember, this was about something more important than the attractiveness of Ian.

"Okay," she stated. "Ask away."

Ian pulled out his pad and pen before asking, "What was your relationship like with Mr. Anderson?"

"We didn't have a relationship. He's my brother-in-law. I thought he was a pretty good guy. He treated my sister well."

Ian took in the way Cheyenne cracked her knuckles.

"So you liked him?"

"Yeah." She chewed on her bottom lip. "He was okay."

"Many people have said he was more than okay," Ian said.

"Like who?" Cheyenne sat up in the chair, eyes focused on Ian.

"Mr. Anderson's employees thought he was a great boss and a nice person, overall."

"Really?"

"Said he was very dedicated to his work and to his marriage."

"Dedicated my ass," Cheyenne said, standing up. "The way he tried to rule over my sister the other night—"

"The night he died?" Ian asked. Silence. "Either you or your sister is going to have to tell me about that night. I have a few inconsistencies."

Cheyenne moved over to the sofa and sat down beside Ian. Their hands touched for a second.

"Inconsistencies?" Cheyenne asked.

"Did your sister leave you in the kitchen alone with her husband?"

"The night of the murder?" Ian gave her a look. "Yes, I was alone with him."

"Did you have words with Mr. Anderson?"

71

"I told him what I thought of him."

"Which was?"

"He was a bastard for treating my sister like dirt."

"Anything else?"

Cheyenne stared at Ian long and hard, hard enough for him to catch aflame. He didn't back down; he stared back at her with the same intensity. "What are you trying to insinuate, Detective Davenport?" Cheyenne asked.

"Did you say anything else…or do anything to Mr. Anderson while you were in the kitchen with him?"

Cheyenne threw her hands up, exasperated. "Do anything? Are you insane? How in the hell am I supposed to remember what I said anyway?" she asked. Cheyenne went from calm to angry in six seconds. "I was infuriated. I could have said anything."

"Anything like what?"

"That I would kick his ass, something. I don't remember, Detective Davenport. You're over here grilling me like a common criminal. I know you talked to the employees, but did you check out or ask about the inner workings of Anderson Technologies?"

Ian was both attracted to Cheyenne and repulsed by her digs into his ability to work this case. He decided to play dumb. "What would I learn about AT?" He eyed Cheyenne. Momentarily, his mind left his staunch detective persona as he looked Cheyenne's way. He examined her poised air, how even in a state of bereavement, she was still quite beautiful, just like her sister, but different, too. Ian could feel the fire that appeared to be a strong trait in Cheyenne. Under different circumstances, he might have asked her out, gone out on a date, enjoyed her company, but, he inwardly sighed. He didn't do suspects.

"Isn't that your job, to find out?" She gave him a sly smirk. "It's almost common knowledge that Cordell spent money like it was the latest fashion, and Anderson

Technologies is thriving, but it's not Microsoft. Jovan and I make pretty good money, and she's been known to spend her funds on behalf of Cordell, but we are not extravagantly rich as some would assume. Where would he get the money to spend so freely?"

"Good question," Ian answered. He stared at her and threw her a replica of her sly smirk.

She grimaced. "Have you talked to Alisha Stewart yet?" Cheyenne asked, receiving a raised eyebrow from Ian.

"Why?"

"Well, she is, was Cordell's assistant and close confidante at Anderson Technologies," Cheyenne answered, with a bit of a snarl to her voice. "If anyone would know about the ins and outs of Cordell and Anderson Technologies, she would."

"Hmm." Ian pretended to consider Cheyenne's suggestion.

Out the corner of his eye, he could see her steaming. He stood, and Cheyenne followed suit.

"Thank you for your time, Miss Parham," he said as he walked to the door.

"That's it?" Cheyenne looked at Ian with questions in her eyes.

"For now." Cheyenne opened the door for Ian and before he left, he stated, "The M.E. found a slight hand print on Mr. Anderson's face." He watched Cheyenne flinch and then her eyes widen as his hand came up and feathered down her cheek. "He suspects from a slap. Do you have any idea where he might have gotten that from?"

Chapter 9

"Why did you stay with him?"

The night before Cordell's funeral, the twins lay in Cheyenne's bed, talking, both too drained, yet too wired to sleep.

"I don't think you would understand, Chey."

"Try me."

"I'm not sure," Jovan said, and it was 100 percent true. "I loved him."

"There are millions of men you could have loved."

"Spoken by a woman who has never been in love."

Cheyenne smacked at Jovan's thigh and rolled away from her.

"Okay," Cheyenne said. "I might not have had that great romance, but I do know that if you love someone and he treats you like shit, you split. Period."

"It wasn't always like that though." Jovan went silent. She couldn't explain it to Cheyenne. For as much as they looked alike and had similar qualities, Jovan knew when it came to being smart in love, Cheyenne had that in spades. Jovan was an intelligent businesswoman and wonderful writer; but when it came to the heart, especially her recent problems with Cordell, she often withdrew herself from the pain of it all, writing or thinking of happier times and situations, and often found herself wanting to stay within her thoughts as opposed to making an appearance in the real world.

"When I saw Cordell," Jovan finally said after a lengthy silence, "I fell for him. It wasn't even his looks. I just felt something inside his soul, and even when I found out about him and Alisha, I kept thinking that he would flip back to his old self and would love me again." Jovan dug her head into a pillow while Cheyenne rubbed her back.

"I'm so sorry," Cheyenne whispered. She bit down on her bottom lip to keep it from trembling. "Do you need anything?"

Jovan wanted to scream, *Cordell*, but instead, she replied, "I just want to be alone."

"You sure?"

She nodded into the pillow before sitting up. She gave Cheyenne a hug, slid from the bed, and walked to the door.

"Tomorrow is going to be rough," Jovan said. "I just need to think for a while. I'll be okay." Cheyenne gave her a look. "Promise," Jovan added.

Jovan sat up in bed, alone, trying to prepare herself for what lay ahead. But how do you prepare yourself to bury your mate? Jovan thought about that as she cuddled in a corner of the bed. If this had been a little over a year ago, back before the animosity between Cordell and her had grown, back to when she was too naïve to think he could cheat on her, Jovan could grieve, really grieve. Now, after all that had passed, her mind was playing tricks on her. One minute, she wanted to cry and rant and wonder how something so horrible could have happened; the next minute, she felt a calm enter her, almost wrap around her securely, lovingly, reminding her that now she could maybe be happy.

Sleepy eyed, Jovan checked the time on her watch—1:00 a.m. With a heavy sigh, she slipped herself under the comforter and closed her eyes. The darkness of closed lids gave way to a bright, vibrant blue sky, and the transparent blue waters of the Virgin Islands. For a year before the wedding, Cordell and Jovan saved their money, he building computers, her as copy editor at the local newspaper. Every penny was kept in order to have their honeymoon in the Virgin Islands. Jovan often wrote of the peace and tranquility of the blue waters of the Islands in her poetry, and once she told Cordell of her poetry, he wanted her dream, her thoughts to come true.

Every year after their marriage, they vacationed the week of their honeymoon at the same spot in the Virgin Islands, Cordell wanting the two to never forget how special that time was for them. Just nine months ago, they were in the Islands, celebrating their sixth anniversary, and even though things were already beginning to sour, Cordell had made their week perfect, being the ever-attentive husband to Jovan. Now, Jovan laid in bed, pillow pressed close to her chest as she swore to have smelt Cordell's Gray Flannel cologne on it. Breathing deeply, she let her tears soak the pillow.

"I did love him," she whispered. "We could have worked this out. We could have gotten counseling, something, if he had just told me about Alisha."

Clutching the pillow tighter, Jovan blinked tears from her eyes, squelching the thoughts of Cordell professing to love her, while more than likely whispering the same words to Alisha. Instead, she let her mind ride the wave of the Blue Island waters as Cordell loved her, and she loved him, unaware of how he would come to hurt her.

Though she entered sleep on the tranquil waters of the Island, her slumber was bombarded with questions and fear. How did one prepare herself for an invasion of privacy from the media and the police as they investigated her husband's murder? Her nightmares told her that her life would never resemble normalcy again. She tossed and turned all night, begging God to give her the strength to deal with all the obstacles that would come to her through this most horrific journey. She knew she couldn't do it alone, and she would need a bigger strength than that of her family to endure this.

Her first test of strength came the next morning as she encountered Cordell's parents at the church just before the services. Jovan had always gotten along famously with Dean and Margaret Anderson. They had deemed her the perfect choice for their son. But their son was never murdered before, never had a wife that could have been the trigger person behind the murder. Over the past year, Dean and Margaret gave excuse after excuse as to why they couldn't come to visit.

Jovan assumed Cordell had told them some terrible lies about their relationship and made her poison in their eyes.

Jovan, escorted by her family, made her way up the aisle of the church to the front pew. She stopped cold in her tracks as she felt the icy stare of Cordell's mother, but her heart skipped a beat when her eyes rested on Timothy. Jovan blinked away tears as she watched sorrow circle around the chiseled features of Timothy's face. He looked her way and then bowed his head. *God, he hates me, too,* Jovan thought.

"Sis," Cheyenne whispered in her ear. "I know. It's okay. We're here for you." Bracing herself, Jovan masked her fear and crept up to them.

"Mom...Dad," she said, not sure if she still had the right to call them that any longer. Margaret glared at Jovan while Dean seemed sympathetic, caring, like he had the few times she had seen him over the last week. Timothy's eyes glistened with tears, but no hate appeared to be in them. Jovan offered the slightest smile in his direction.

"We are so sorry for your loss," Daphne Parham interjected, stepping between Jovan and the Andersons to offer her condolences. The twins watched as the parents conversed with one another. Jovan's hand went to her throat, stroking it, feeling the intensity of the church begin to choke her.

"It'll be okay," Cheyenne whispered in Jovan's ear as she wrapped her arms around Jovan. The Parhams took their seats, leaving their daughters to the pained stares of Cordell's parents.

"Your parents say you had nothing to do with Cordell's death," Margaret said.

"I didn't," Jovan whispered, wiping the tears from her face. "I swear—"

"Don't you *dare* swear in this church!" A pregnant pause hung in the air. "So help me *and* you if I find out otherwise." Margaret took Dean's hand and marched away.

"I didn't...I didn't..." over and over Jovan repeated the phrase as mourners watched Cheyenne guide her over to the pew to sit.

"Jo?"

Jovan turned around and found Timothy standing before her. "Yes?" she responded, her eyes pleading for acceptance. Timothy opened his arms, and Jovan hugged him.

"Mom and Dad are in pain, Jo," Timothy said as he stroked up and down Jovan's back. "They don't hate you. None of us hate you."

Jovan looked into Timothy's face and gently wiped his tears away. For a brief second, she saw Cordell's face, but she knew she would never see him again.

"Thank you for saying that," Jovan said. Timothy stared into Jovan's eyes until they both became slightly uneasy. He kissed her forehead, and Jovan jumped slightly, remembering a time when Cordell would offer such a small drop of affection.

Timothy stepped back from Jovan and asked, "Are you doing okay?"

Jovan shook her head no, but replied, "I'm hanging in there. How about you, Hon?"

"My brother's gone," came his reply. Jovan nodded, hugged him again. When they parted, Jovan sat with her family and glanced over at Dean and Margaret. Margaret's eyes were full of spite, for Jovan, and partially for Timothy for offering the olive branch.

The second round began at the gravesite as Jovan listened to the Pastor read Psalm 23. Above the mourners, a helicopter could be heard. In the distance, the media stalked the cemetery, zooming in their lenses to get shots of Jovan and Cheyenne in mourning.

Jovan took heavy steps up to Cordell's casket where it hovered above its final resting place. She laid a rose upon the casket before bending her head to kiss the cool, smooth surface.

"I love you," she managed to choke out. Despite all the hell she had been through, all the pain and lies, she did still love him. With shaky steps, Jovan stepped back from the casket, turning to rejoin her family only to find Ian a few rows back, his eyes taking in everything. He gave her a nod of acknowledgment before appearing to look away.

Before reaching her family, she heard someone call her name. Out of the corner of her eye, Jovan caught sight of Alisha Stewart approaching her from the left as Cheyenne marched toward her from the right. Jovan took in the bloodshot look of Alisha's piercing blue eyes, the stream of tears that steadily fell from them, the pain and hurt of someone who desperately mourned a passed loved one.

Before Jovan could protest, Alisha had her in a tight embrace, whispering, "Cordell was a wonderful man."

Jovan shot her an incredulous look as Cheyenne came up, snatching her from Alisha's hold.

"You would know all about that, wouldn't you, Alisha?" Cheyenne whispered. "Stay the hell away from my sister."

A numb Alisha watched Cheyenne escort Jovan away to a group that had gathered to pay their respects.

DEATH AT THE DOUBLE INKWELL

The background suited Ian. Even as a youngster, he preferred to blend in to the paint on the wall and watch and hear everything that went on around him. So far, his keen awareness of his surroundings hadn't helped him one bit to try to solve this case, and he had to admit that it troubled him. Though it had only been a little over a week, Davenport had a reputation for solving cases in lightning speed, and usually, within no time, he would have something tangible to snoop out, but in this case, nothing.

Despite his feelings of Jovan's innocence and his rule to scope out everything before saying *he/she did it*, Ian had the Parham twins at the top of his suspect list, followed by Jimmy Devane and Alisha Stewart though he hadn't talked to her yet. She was out, taking personal days to grieve. Well, she didn't grieve at home; Ian had checked. From his information, Alisha had been by Cordell's side since the creation of Anderson Technologies, practically his right hand woman some employees suggested. Ian was sure Cordell used more than his right hand on this curvaceous sexpot. After watching the coldness that Cheyenne exhibited toward Alisha, he knew that something was going on there, and a visit with Ms. Stewart would be happening soon.

Now Jimmy Devane? He was a character in a category all by himself, Ian thought as he eyed Jimmy sitting with a couple of heavyweights in the computer industry in Maryland. Players with money most definitely. Ian was never one to prejudge a person, but by the black, shoulder-length, greased up, slicked back hair and the slender face, pointy nose, and beady black eyes, Jimmy Devane didn't appear to be the type of person who would be schmoozing with the likes of Cordell Anderson, or the men he sat with at the cemetery.

He had listened and paid attention to Jimmy when he talked to him outside of Anderson Technologies. He seemed

"What?"

Jovan shook her head. "Nothing, it's just that no one has ever been hurt before. Why hurt someone now?"

"First break-in, no one was home. Second one, the Hendersons were asleep. Slept right through the robbery."

"And Sarah?"

Mark swallowed hard. "I found her in the closet. Like she was hiding."

"God." Jovan bit down on her bottom lip.

"That had to be so devastating for her." Jovan lifted a hand and pushed a loose lock of Mark's hair from his forehead. Mark looked straight into Jovan's eyes, and she watched as his eyes switched from green to ocean blue.

"You're going to get through this," Jovan whispered. "We both are."

Mark nodded. "I know."

Jovan opened her mouth, and then closed it.

"What?" Mark asked. He removed his hand from Jovan's. "I know you still have issues with me because I had the affair, but—"

"That's not it." Jovan chewed on the inside of her cheek before asking, "What secret did Sarah have?"

"We don't need to get into that now."

"Please." Jovan sighed. "I'm so tired of lies and half-truths. I can take whatever you have to give out, Mark. Just tell me, please."

Mark stood and took a few steps away from Jovan. With his back facing her, he said, "Sarah was having an affair."

"What?" Jovan jumped and raced toward Mark. She gripped his arm and turned him around. "Why would you say that, Mark?"

"Because it's true. Had been for a while."

"No." Jovan's hands dropped to her sides. Her fingers pinched at the black, silk fabric of her dress. "You're lying."

"Why would I lie, Jovan? I'm not a complete bastard."

"She was good to me," Jovan muttered to herself. Her face scrunched up in confusion. "She gave me advice. Helped with Cordell." She wished for a piece of paper, a napkin, something as she faced Mark. "Who?"

Mark shook his head no. "It doesn't matter," he said.

"Who?"

"Jo?" Cheyenne stepped out into the backyard. "Hey, Mark."

Mark looked at Cheyenne and tried to smile. "Hi, Cheyenne."

Cheyenne stared at Jovan, then Mark. "Everything okay out here?"

"What's up?" Jovan asked, ignoring the question.

"Okay, Mom and Dad think we should go out and talk to the media. They don't think the vans will leave until we say something."

"She's probably right," Jovan said. "I'll be right in, Chey."

Cheyenne stayed around a beat longer before going inside the house.

"So are you going to tell me?" Jovan asked, hands on her hips.

"Jovan," Mark said. "It's not important. Not right now."

Jovan groaned. She pointed to Mark and said, "You will tell me sooner or later." With that, Jovan turned and walked into the house.

Jovan and Cheyenne's parents looked at them with worried eyes. The buzz outside heightened As the twins marched to the front door and opened it, the buzz outside heightened. There was no need to search for a microphone. Within seconds, one was pushed into Jovan's face.

Questions flew out of the mouths of the reporters. *How are the girls holding up? How is the investigation going? Are there any suspects? Are you both suspects?*

"Um, hello," Jovan began, straightening her back and taking a breath. "I heard several questions, so let me begin by saying that Cheyenne and I are doing as well as can be expected. Today was an extremely painful and heartbreaking day for me, for all of us. Now, we need to worry about taking care of each other and picking up the pieces."

"What about the investigation, Jovan?" a reporter in the back yelled.

"Unfortunately, there aren't many, if any, clues as to who might have done this. We are cooperating with the police to make sure they catch the person who is responsible for..." Jovan stopped. For killing my husband, she heard her mind say. Batting away tears with her hands, Jovan continued, "We're hoping something will develop soon, so we can put an end to this hor...horrible experience."

"And to answer your other burning question," Cheyenne added, stepping to the microphone, "neither I nor my sister had anything to do with this unfortunate incident." Out in the mass of reporters, Cheyenne spotted Ian listening attentively.

"We were both shocked and devastated by this, and we will do any and everything the police need us to do in order to bring this situation to its rightful conclusion.

"To all who have sent your sympathies to my sister and the families, we thank you from the bottom of our hearts. Now, if you don't mind, like my sister said, it's been a painful day, and we wish to be with our family now."

With those closing words, Cheyenne glared at Ian before leading a tearful Jovan back into the house.

DEATH AT THE DOUBLE INKWELL

Jimmy Devane turned the TV off after watching Jovan and Cheyenne talk to the media. "I still can't believe Cordell bit it," Devane said.

"This is a complex situation here," Jameson Burke voiced.

"Now that Anderson is gone, something is going to have to be done with Anderson Technologies. This is the opportune time to jump in and try to get our hands on the company while the getting is good. Make an offer to Anderson's attorney and have him draw up some papers so that we can get the business under our control."

"You don't waste any time, do you?" Devane asked. His face was a picture of disgust. "Besides, you're one of Anderson Technologies' biggest competitors. Do you really think they will sell to you?" Jimmy inched his fingers through his black, slick hair.

"Cordell has been a naughty boy." Burke chuckled. "By the time his wife airs out all his dirty linen, she will be begging us to buy it from her...to rid Cordell from her life."

"In the meantime," Jimmy said, sighing, "I need to keep Davenport away from me. He caught me at Anderson the other day and asked me all these questions about my relationship with Cordell and about the night of his death."

"What did you say?" Burke asked. He sat behind his desk and gave Devane his full attention.

"I told him the truth," Devane answered. "I told him that I was friends with Cordell and that he invited me to his house for dinner the night before he died."

"He didn't ask where you were?"

"He did, in a roundabout way, but he seemed more interested in my relationship with Cordell and what type of associate I was."

"Hmm." Burke sat back in his chair and closed his eyes.

Devane paced around the office. "I need your help," he said. "I know he's going to come back for me, and I need to prove my innocence."

"But you *are* innocent," Burke insisted. "You're blowing this out of proportion."

Devane ran his hand along the stubble on his chin. Burke's cool assurance wasn't enough to curb his growing anxiety.

Burke shook his head and grunted. Digging in his bottom drawer, he retrieved a small square package wrapped in brown paper. Devane locked his eyes on the package and immediately stopped pacing and moving. Burke tossed it to him, and Devane caught it.

"Take that," Burke said. "Calm yourself down."

"Thanks Boss. I need this."

"The problem with you, Jimmy, is that you worry too much. I will handle whatever Davenport throws our way. You're innocent. He will know this."

Devane smiled, balled his hands – with package – into his coat's pockets and exited Burke's office.

Chapter 10

"So they've heard nothing?" Elyse asked.

Jovan shifted in her office chair. "No," she answered.

"And I'm starting to feel antsy, El. Detective Davenport placed officers outside the house."

"It's that unsafe for you there? If that's the case, then you should go back over to Chey's."

"This is my home. I'm not going anywhere."

"I know, but if it's unsafe for you, Jo, then maybe—"

"No, so next subject."

"You are so stubborn."

"I know."

"I'm sorry I couldn't make it to the funeral," Elyse began. "Things have been pretty hectic, and the funeral came so quickly."

"Cordell's parents," Jovan explained. "As soon as his body was released, they had the funeral already planned. They controlled everything. It felt so odd having his mother hating me."

"For her to even think you had anything to do with this is just plain stupid."

"It was her eldest son. I try to look at it from her point of view."

"To me, she doesn't have a point of view, but you've always been the understanding type. How did Timothy act toward you?"

Jovan sat back in her chair. She smiled briefly.

"He almost made up for the way his mother acted. He was so sweet, and he came over after Margaret blew up at me, and he gave me this big hug. For the first time since all this happened, I felt like things might be okay."

"You guys were always close."

"Been with that boy through a lot of craziness." Jovan's

mind replayed the media attention brought on by Timothy's battle with drugs. Being the brother of a prominent, black businessman had made Timothy's situation headline news.

"It had been a while since I last saw him," Jovan added. "You know he was in rehab for almost seven months. I went to visit a couple of times. Cordell never wanted to go. I think he felt responsible for Tim's drug habit."

"Why would he feel responsible?"

"Because he was the big brother. I guess he thought he should be looking out for Tim."

"Well how is he doing now? He look okay? Doing okay?"

"He's been out for five months," Jovan answered. "And, he looked real good, the spitting image of Cordell…a little tired, but under the circumstances, I can…"

The doorbell interrupted them. "Be right back, El, somebody at the door." Jovan trotted down the stairs to the door. Ian greeted her on the other side.

"Detective, hi. How are you?"

Ian offered Jovan a smile that brought out the beautiful, yet masculine features in his face.

"I'm doing well, Mrs. Anderson."

"Please, call me, Jovan."

"Um, okay. Jovan, I was hoping I could check out Mr. Anderson's office again." Ian followed Jovan to the foot of the staircase. Jovan chewed on her bottom lip and looked away. Instantly, she thought of the Alisha file and Cordell's lies. A pain shot deep into Jovan's belly, causing her to slump on the bottom step. Ian knelt in front of her. "Are you okay, Jovan?" he asked.

Jovan nodded. She wondered if her fingerprints would be found on the computer. She remembered wiping the monitor, keyboard, CPU button, and desk off, but one could never be too sure. She squeezed her knees together, her fingers gripping them.

"I'm okay, thanks," she muttered. "What do you hope to find?"

"I don't know." Ian sat beside Jovan on the step. He examined Jovan's face and found it devoid of any emotion. "This is okay with you, isn't it?"

Jovan stood and turned her back to Ian. "Sure," she replied. When she faced Ian again, all trepidation was gone. She gave him her best smile before adding, "I'll be in my office if you need me." The doorbell rang. "Or I'll be right here." Jovan's breath caught in her throat when she opened the door to find a familiar face staring back at her.

"Cordell," she whispered, her hands reaching out to him.

"Timothy."

Jovan shook her head and focused her eyes back onto Timothy. She let her head drop, and Timothy stepped to her and pulled her into a hug.

"It's okay," he said as he rubbed her back. "Light hits a certain way, people see him in me. Mom can't stop crying every time she sees me."

"I'm sure she does," Jovan said, her voice muffled in Timothy's shoulder.

"Probably wished it was me instead."

Jovan stepped back and took Timothy's face into her hands. She stared into his sharp, brown eyes, and said, "Don't ever let me hear you say that again, Timothy. Your mother would never think that."

"I know, it's just that..."

The two stood, a foot apart, looking at the other. Jovan moved first, reaching out to touch Timothy's hand.

"What brought you by?" she asked. When Timothy failed to respond, Jovan said, "Talk to me. What's going on? You doing okay, right?"

Timothy nodded.

"I needed to feel connected to him, you know?" he said.

"Yeah. I do."

"You're the closest thing I know to him."

"You're welcomed here anytime, Babe."

"Thanks." Timothy kissed Jovan's forehead. She stepped from his loose hug and remained silent.

"Elyse!" she finally said.

"Huh?" Timothy asked, confused.

"Come in. I'll be right back." Jovan jogged up the steps and into her office. She snatched the phone up and blew out, "El, I'm so sorry. Detective Davenport came, and then Timothy showed up."

"No problem," Elyse replied. "Was about to get worried when five minutes past."

"Sorry."

"Don't be. Go handle your business. We'll catch up later."

Jovan hung up and raced back down the steps before falling beside Timothy on the sofa. "God, I'm so tired." She huffed. "Running around, getting things done, trying to be sane."

Timothy slid an arm over Jovan's shoulder and gave her a squeeze. "Take it easy, Jo," he said. "Take everything one day at a time."

Jovan rested her head on Timothy's shoulder before letting out a ragged breath. "I wished I had taken that one day at a time approach while Cordell was still here."

"Am I interrupting anything?"

Both Jovan and Timothy turned their heads to find Detective Davenport eyeing them. Jovan inched away from Timothy and stood.

"No, Detective Davenport," she said, running her hands over her jean clad hips. "Is everything okay?"

"We need to talk," came Ian's deadpan statement.

"About?" Jovan's throat went dry. She coughed. Ian looked at Timothy and back to Jovan.

"I think it would be best if we talked in private," he stated.

Jovan steeled herself for what was about to come. She had never really thought about the computer since Cordell's death or what might be found on it. Hell, she thought Cordell might have guessed she knew and disposed of the evidence, but sure enough, the secret was out and a light bulb popped off in her mind as she read what had to be on Ian's mind.

Damn, she thought. *Prime suspect, Jovan Parham-Anderson.*

Cheyenne pulled open the doors to her walk-in closet. She shifted through pantsuits, skirt suits, casual attire, and dinner attire as she tried to organize her closet. She was too stressed to write, and after writing, Cheyenne's favorite thing to do was clean.

Cheyenne pulled out the luggage at the bottom of her closet. Riqué came bounding into the room, finding solace on Cheyenne's bed, right on top of her black silk pantsuit.

"No, no, no, Baby," she said, collecting the dog into her arms and settling him onto the floor. "Momma doesn't wear fur…especially dog fur." Placing the luggage atop the bed, Cheyenne took a deep breath before she opened the roll-on bag, wanting to air them all out before she restored them to the closet. From the roll-on bag alone, she pulled out several matching bra and panties sets.

"Now see," she said. "I bought these again thinking I left them in the hotel." In the zippered compartment, Cheyenne spotted photographs. Sitting beside the bag, she glanced at one picture, smiling. It was of her and Jovan, last year, at the Mystery Writers' Association convention in Atlanta. They were all smiles, barely looking 18 in the picture. With a sigh, Cheyenne rubbed along her forehead. "Feels like a hundred years ago."

"She's my heart. Of course I'll look out for her." That's what Cheyenne told their parents just that morning as she dropped them off at the airport. Both were reluctant to leave, wanting to stay and help Jovan through this painful time, but Cheyenne reassured them that it wouldn't be necessary, that she was there for her sister, and would never let anything happen to her. She couldn't stop being there if she tried. She earned the title of *Watcher* at a young age as she watched out for the more naïve, more gentle Jovan.

Since Cordell's death, Cheyenne had been worried that Jovan would fall into a depression or would let guilt overcome her. She didn't want anyone, including Detective Davenport, assuming that Jovan had anything to do with the murder of Cordell. She was less worried about herself. She knew she had the *oomph* to get past anything, but Jovan wouldn't be able to take too much more turmoil in her already fragile condition.

Falling back onto her bed, Cheyenne sighed before closing her eyes. "I got my sister's back," she whispered. "I won't let anything happen to her. Even if that means going toe-to-toe with Davenport."

Davenport. That was another issue altogether for Cheyenne.

During the most horrific day of her sister's life, she had to meet *him*, the enemy. That first glance into his eyes was almost her downfall. She had never seen eyes so sensual and telling in all her life, and they would have to be set into a face that could only be described as beautiful.

In the last two years, Cheyenne could count on half a hand the number of men she even said hello to, and they were in the publishing industry, so it was always work related. That first glance of Ian had ignited or awakened something inside her, and she checked it quickly, realizing that it wasn't the time to explore any romantic interests, especially with a man who was looking for the killer of Cordell…and eyeing her and her sister.

"Figures." She sighed, rising from her bed. "First fine man I meet in ages, and I'm pegged a murderess." With a dry laugh, Cheyenne dropped the photographs on her nightstand and headed out her bedroom, down the hall to her office. Shutting down her laptop, she placed it in its bag, along with other papers, and zipped it up. She was due over Jovan's house shortly, and punctuality was never a strong point of Cheyenne's.

After a short shower, Cheyenne rambled around her bedroom, slipping on a white tank, tan capris, and her Reebok Classics before snatching up her laptop bag and heading out her door.

"Damn," she cursed as the phone rang. She wrangled her keys from her pocket, opened the door, and raced to the phone before the machine picked up. "Hello," she answered out of breath.

"Cheyenne."

"Jo, what's wrong?" Cheyenne could hear the shakiness of Jovan's voice on the other end of the phone, and it made her heart race as fear crept into her.

"Come to the house, please."

"Girl, I was on my way over there now. What's wrong? Are you okay?"

"Detective Davenport is here." With a hushed voice, Jovan added, "Please hurry."

Cheyenne hung the phone and with lightning speed, bolted out her apartment, trying to figure out in her mind how to curb the disaster that was forthcoming.

Ian's eyes moved toward the sound of the front door opening and slamming shut. He blinked as the fire called

Cheyenne rushed into the living room, her body and demeanor hard, emotions scattered over her face.

"How convenient that she has a key," he said, taking in Jovan, then Cheyenne. "So I guess you had a key the night of Mr. Anderson's murder."

"How dare you imply..." Cheyenne seethed as she walked right up to Ian.

Despite the seriousness of the situation, Ian couldn't help but take in the smooth cinnamon skin of Cheyenne's shoulders and chest, her cleavage snug in her tank top. He eyed the bleeding heart tattoo on her left bicep and the small pair of red lips on her neck. He felt his face grow warm when he thought about kissing her there.

While Ian tried to keep the embers from flaring, Cheyenne glared at him, hands on hips, breathing labored. Even hostile and in danger of being arrested, she was beautiful, he thought to himself, quickly slipping that information into an *unnecessary* file.

"Let's just be civilized, please," Jovan whispered. She took Cheyenne's hand and sat her down on the sofa alongside her.

Jovan sat back, watching the visual words being tossed back and forth between Ian and Cheyenne. It wasn't until Ian coughed and shook his head as if trying to remove a thought that he snapped away from staring at Cheyenne.

Cheyenne turned to face Jovan and began wiping the wet stains from her cheeks. "I'm sorry, hon," she said. "You okay?" She hugged Jovan.

"No, I'm not." Jovan cleared her throat. "I've been sitting here the last fifteen minutes, wondering what Detective Davenport has to say. I couldn't bear to hear it alone." Jovan faced Ian and asked, "What did you find?"

Cheyenne took Jovan's hands into hers and gently massaged them.

"I found a file in your husband's file cabinet," Ian said.

Jovan calmed herself. *Did he check the computer*, she thought as she tightened her own grip on Cheyenne's hands.

"A file?" Jovan asked. "What was in it?"

"Correspondence between Mr. Anderson and Mrs. Sarah Brockman." Jovan's face paled.

"What kind of correspondence?"

"From what I gather," Ian began, "he was having an affair with Mrs. Brockman for at least a year."

"Oh my God," Cheyenne whispered.

"No," Jovan said. She stood, licked her lips. She tried to find specific points in the living room to focus on: the sofa, the entertainment center, the paintings on the walls. None of them kept her from falling to the floor.

Cheyenne raced to Jovan and gathered Jovan up into her arms.

"She was my friend," Jovan cried out. "She talked to me about Cordell. Told me to face my marital problems." Cheyenne turned to Ian and glared at him.

He shrugged and lowered his head. "I'm so sorry to have to tell you about this, Jovan," Ian said. "I found more."

Jovan laughed, the sound chilly and hysterical. "What else could there be?"

"I turned on Mr. Anderson's computer, and I was surprised he didn't have a password or something on it."

"Why?" Cheyenne asked.

"A business man," Ian said. "Important documents. Wouldn't want just anyone knowing what was on it."

"It was just he and I here, Detective," Jovan said, her voice shaky. "His business was his, just like my writing career was mine."

"So you never went onto his computer?"

Jovan sat up and batted the wet streaks from her face. "No," she answered, simply.

"So then you didn't know about Cordell's affair with

Alisha Stewart?"

Alisha's name rang in Jovan's ears. She remembered Cordell whispering Alisha's name in her ear by mistake just weeks ago.

She remembered the file on the computer, right there on the desktop as if to taunt her. She remembered the phone call she overheard between Cordell and Alisha. He said he loved Alisha. Wanted her. Loved only her. Not Jovan. And now there was Sarah, too? Jovan pressed her hands against the sides of her head, hoping to stop the pounding that increased in her temples.

"On the computer," Ian said, "there is a file marked Alisha with several e-mails and letters written to her."

Jovan raised her face and wiped at her eyes. The shock of Sarah and Cordell momentarily dissipated as she said, "I found out recently about him and Alisha."

"You told me you didn't know about any affair," Ian said. "You lied to me."

"I was embarrassed, Detective Davenport. Unfortunately, people know me around here, and the last thing I wanted was for people to know that Cordell had been cheating on me through half of our marriage. I was hoping that he and I could work through our problems, resolve the animosity." And partially, that was true. Despite what she heard on the phone, what Cordell told her, Jovan couldn't help but to remember the day he told her that he loved her. They were married. They had built something between them. Though the hope was growing fainter each day, Jovan still believed things might work out.

"Obviously, you didn't read the entire file," Ian said.

"No, I didn't," Jovan said dryly. "A few of the e-mails was more than enough."

"What was in the file?" Cheyenne asked.

Ian walked the length of the sofa and back to the other end, pacing in front of the twins. He wanted to see their reaction to the news, but he also frowned because he didn't want to hurt Jovan any more. However, his motto was to always speak the truth. He wouldn't renege on it now.

"According to the e-mails," he said, "Cordell didn't have a reconciliation in mind between you two." Jovan swallowed hard.

"He said specifically that he was going to leave Jovan?" Cheyenne asked. Ian nodded. "That son of a bitch. I can't believe he would do that to you, Jo. I thought maybe, maybe you two could talk about this."

"He really didn't love me," Jovan whispered, lost in her own thoughts. "All that time."

"Mrs. Ande…Jovan," Ian said. He knelt before her, sympathy in his eyes. He didn't want to believe she was a good actress, despite what it might have looked like. He couldn't help blurting out, "Are you surprised by this?"

Jovan stared at him, hard. "What do *you* think?"

"Did you know that Mr. Anderson kept a journal?"

Jovan stared at Cheyenne and back to Ian.

"A journal? No, I didn't."

"I found one in the bottom drawer of his file cabinet."

Jovan didn't want to know any more. She knew all she needed to. Cordell never loved her, never planned to make their marriage work. A decade of her life had come and gone, and it was all a lie.

"I don't care," she said, standing and walking the length of the living room. She rubbed through her ivory silk tee at the small of her back. "What, did he write that he hated me? That he didn't love me?"

When Ian remained silent, Cheyenne asked, "Well…what's in the journal?" Ian noticed the calm that rested on Cheyenne's face.

"For starters, he claims that you were unstable," Ian said.

"Unstable?" Jovan responded.

"He wrote about this one time that you came barging into the bedroom and you were sleepwalking." Jovan stopped pacing and looked at Cheyenne.

"What's so weird about that, Detective Davenport?" Cheyenne asked.

"Well, nothing, but he says that she threatened to kill him while in her sleep."

"I *never* did that!" Jovan yelled, racing up into Ian's face. She reached out to grab his lapels, beg him to believe her, but she stopped. "I never threatened to kill him."

"But you did come into the bedroom...sleepwalking?" Ian asked.

"Yes." Jovan chewed on her bottom lip. "I suffer from sleepwalking. It doesn't happen every night, but it does happen when I'm under stress."

"And what happened that night?"

"I don't remember." Jovan shrugged. "I never remember what happens while I'm in a walk."

"So you could have threatened to kill Cordell?"

"But I didn't," Jovan said, pleading.

"But you *could* have?" Ian repeated.

Jovan nodded. Cheyenne cut an evil stare at Ian that made him lower his eyes momentarily. Jovan sniffed as a few tears tumbled down her cheeks. Cheyenne handed her tissues from the box on the coffee table.

"So what else does Cordell lie about in his little journal?" Cheyenne asked. Ian gave her a look as if to say he was sorry for being so rough. Cheyenne continued to cut her eyes at him.

"Well," Ian began, looking from Cheyenne to Jovan. "He writes that you were obsessing over your latest book, particularly the death of the husband."

Jovan lowered her head in her hands.

"That bastard," Cheyenne spoke. "She was never unstable, Detective Davenport. She didn't act out our book on

Cordell. I don't know what kind of game Cordell was playing, but that's a bold-faced lie."

"How *did* the husband die in the novel?" Ian asked. Both sisters sat quietly on the sofa. "How?"

"He was shot in the back of the head," Cheyenne answered after a long pause. "But so what? It's a book...it's fiction."

Before Ian could speak again, she added, "Is any of this going to result in my sister being taken downtown?"

"I don't know," Ian responded.

"Look," Jovan said, pushing into the conversation. "I don't know anything about what Cordell wrote in his journal. I wasn't obsessing. I rarely talked about my writing with Cordell, just like he didn't mention Anderson Technologies to me. He may have heard Chey and me talking about the book, but I never obsessed over the murder of the husband in the book. That's just absurd, Detective."

"What you need to do is go check out that tramp, Alisha," Cheyenne said. "Instead of confronting my sister like she's a criminal."

Facing Jovan, Ian said, "I'll be back with some officers to pick up Cordell's computer and check around his office some more. Please, don't go in there." With a nod to Jovan, Ian made his way to the door, Cheyenne close behind him. As he opened the door, he turned back, his face breaths away from her.

"Just so you know," he said, his voice low, his breath warming Cheyenne's face, "I'm not here to make your life or Jovan's life a living hell." She looked at him with suspicion.

"You're not?" she asked.

"No, though I can tell by your face, you don't believe me." She shrugged. "I want to believe your sister is innocent. My gut says that she is, but if at times the information leads me to you two, don't curse me out. I'm just doing my job."

Cheyenne eyed him—the softness of his eyes, the

sincere sound of his words—and briefly let a sour smile touch upon her lips.

"What about me?" she asked. "Are you sure about me?" She swallowed a lump of disappointment as questions clouded the clarity of Ian's eyes. "It's okay. I'm considered the bitch of the family. It's only natural you would assume it. But I swear, I didn't kill Cordell. Jovan's my heart, and I would never do anything to hurt her."

Ian took in the Jovan qualities of Cheyenne, noticing that behind her tough veneer, she was just as scared about this situation as her sister. Mustering up a smile, Ian added, "I'll be in touch," before turning to leave.

Cheyenne leaned against the doorway, watching Ian trot down to his car and leave.

"Does he believe me?" she asked, shutting the door and clamping down on the emotions that fluttered in her every time she came into the presence of Detective Ian Davenport.

When Cheyenne finally left, Jovan sat on the sofa for hours, letting her mind wander through everything she had learned. Cordell had a journal. Jovan didn't even know he liked to write. Cordell was intent on leaving her for Alisha. A decade of her life was for nothing. Though she tried to get her mind around these things, her brain couldn't stop thinking about Sarah. She trusted Sarah. She trusted every word that came out of her mouth. The lunches they had. The confidences they shared. She couldn't figure out why Sarah would do this to her or why Cordell would have an affair with Sarah if he were so hell bent on making Alisha his next 'victim' for happily ever after.

Her skin felt prickly as seconds wore on and the thoughts exploded exponentially in her head. She jumped from the sofa and marched to the door.

Dark skies and pouring rain met her.

She didn't go looking for shoes. She didn't find a raincoat or an umbrella. She punched in the code to her alarm and shut the door.

She saw the lights on over at Mark's and made her way to his front door. The normal Jovan would rap on the door three times and wait an appropriate amount of time before knocking again. No, this Jovan was pissed, hurt, and beyond betrayed. She needed answers.

She banged on the door and continued to do so until Mark finally opened the door, screaming, "Who the hell is…" before silencing himself.

"Jovan," he said. He looked outside, from left to right, before focusing on a drenched Jovan. "Are you okay? Why are you banging on the door like a lunatic? Why are you out here without shoes on? Please, come in before you catch pneumonia."

Jovan let Mark usher her into the house.

"Stay right here," he said and he trotted away. He came back with a peach-colored bath sheet and wrapped it around Jovan's shoulders. "What are you doing out in the rain, Jovan?" he asked.

Jovan opened her mouth, but nothing would come out. She shivered but not from the rain, not from the chilliness of the air condition in the house.

"Why?" she managed to squeak out before tears mixed with the rain on her face.

"Why what, Jovan? Is this about Cordell?"

"Why?" she asked again. "Why didn't you tell me about Cordell and Sarah?" She began pummeling Mark's chest. "Why? I thought we were friends. Sarah was my friend. Despite whatever you may or may not have done toward Sarah, you and I were friends. Why couldn't you tell me?"

Mark grabbed Jovan's hands and pulled her into him. He wrapped her tightly in his arms, his right hand rubbing the back of her head.

"I'm so sorry," he whispered. "I didn't want you to find out. Losing Cordell was enough."

Mark walked her into the living room and sat her on the sofa. "Sit right here," he said. "Be right back."

Jovan cried as she looked around the room. She was the one who told Sarah to go for reds, pinks, and whites in the living room. She took in the pictures that graced the end tables and the fireplace mantle. Pictures of Sarah and Mark looking happy. A picture of her and Sarah, wearing Walk for the Cure t-shirts and matching white shorts and hats. A picture of both couples; she couldn't help but laugh at the arrangement. Mark had his arm around Jovan's waist, Jovan had her arm up over Sarah's shoulder, Sarah had her arms wrapped around both Jovan and Cordell, and Cordell had his arm around Sarah's waist. Jovan picked up the frame and studied the photo. She looked at Cordell's hand and how his fingers were splayed just beneath Sarah's breasts. She could see a slight bubbling of Sarah's t-shirt between Cordell's fingers as if he was holding her tightly, like she was his. She took in how Cordell's head tilted toward Sarah and Sarah's angled near Cordell's chest.

She stared at the photo so intently, she never noticed Mark return to the room. She snapped from her thoughts when Mark tried to pull the frame from her hands. She looked into Mark's sad eyes and asked, "Was it going on then?"

Mark nodded and managed to get a hold on the frame as it slipped from Jovan's grasp. He sat it back on the table before giving Jovan a cup of tea.

"Orange pekoe," he said. "Need to warm you up."
She sipped and let the warm liquid soothe the cold from her body.

"Is this why you started your affair?" Jovan asked. Before Mark could respond, she added, "I'm sorry. That was so tacky of me."

"Under the circumstances," Mark said, laughing though he knew not a damn thing was funny, "we should be nothing if not open books to each other now. Get all of this out in the open."

After sipping from his cup, Mark continued, "I knew about the affair from the beginning. Started about thirteen months ago."

"Why?" Jovan asked. "You two looked so happy."

"We were. For a while, then I wanted children, and Sarah didn't." Mark laughed again and shook his head. "So ironic."

"What is?"

"I think she started having the affair so she could forget about our issues."

"And so what's ironic?"

Mark sat his cup on the coffee table; Jovan did likewise. He faced Jovan and studied her round face, the tearful brown eyes, her wet hair now crinkling up into tight curls. She looked so innocent and so unaware. He knew this experience was shedding all types of new light into her life. He didn't want to add to it. Absentmindedly, he reached out and stroked Jovan's cheek.

She didn't flinch or move away.

"Tell me, please." Jovan sighed. "I really can't take anymore lies. We're open books, remember? Your words."

Mark dropped his hand and rested it upon Jovan's hands that lay clasped on her lap.

"Sarah was about two months pregnant."

Jovan sat up and hugged Mark. "I'm so sorry," she said. "I mean I know you and Sarah had problems and she about ruined my world, but that baby could have brought you two back together."

Jovan felt Mark go rigid in her arms. She leaned back and stared at him. "It wasn't my baby," he whispered.

Jovan's bottom lip trembled. "No," she said, standing. "It was not Cordell's."

"Unless she was having an affair with someone else," Mark said.

"Sarah was having Cordell's baby?" Jovan more said than asked. "I wanted children. But no, Cordell wanted to wait. He wanted us to be mega-successful first. He wanted to devote his life to his company and me before we brought kids into the picture."

"It's not your fault, Jovan," Mark said.

"I wasn't good enough." She shrugged. "Something about me. I don't know. I tried to be good."

"Jovan, stop it."

"So, why did he do it, then?" she screamed. "Why would he hurt me like that? What type of person would just betray his wife like that?" She pointed to Mark. "Or her husband like that?"

"I don't know," Mark responded.

"I really loved him, you know?" Jovan tried to suppress her tears. "Every time I tried, he would tell me I was ugly. Or I was fat. I just thought it was me. Like I did something wrong."

Mark walked toward Jovan and wrapped his arms around her. "It wasn't you, Jovan," he whispered into her hair.

Jovan buried her face into Mark's firm chest and slid her arms around to his back. For a long moment, they stood like this, holding each other and rocking slowly.

The storm that raged in Jovan's head quieted. She sighed but continued to hold Mark close. She felt his hands run over her what had to be Bozo like hair. She felt his hands move down her back and press against her lower back.

A short moan escaped her. She closed her eyes when she felt Mark staring down at her. She was beyond embarrassed. Despite the situation, her body betrayed her. It had been more than a while since someone really wanted to hold her, wanted to care about her feelings.

She felt Mark's warm lips against her forehead, and she opened her eyes. Before she could clear her mind and get back to any sense of stability, Mark kissed her. She sighed against his mouth as her hands moved up his chest, up to his stubbled cheeks, to his silky, dark hair. Jovan went airborne as Mark lifted her and pressed her back against a wall in the living room.

"Jovan," Mark whispered before kissing her cheeks, her chin. His hands wandered gently over her hips and bottom. "You're so soft."

Jovan panted as Mark found the sensitive spot on her neck, right below her right ear. Every nerve in her body pulsated, making her body hum with need.

Mark's kisses trailed from Jovan's neck to her collarbone. She cooed.

When Mark began grinding himself against Jovan, she felt his excitement for her and immediately pushed him away.

"I'm so...so," she stuttered. "Sorry." She took in Mark's slightly swollen, pink lips, his eyes that had changed from green to sea blue, the flush in his cheeks.

"Th...thank you for the tea. The talk." She stumbled to the door, opened it, and ran out into the pouring rain.

Chapter 11

*I*an wanted to finally meet this Alisha Stewart up close and personal and see what she was all about. Except for the funeral, Alisha had managed to be wherever Ian wasn't. This time would be different. He had someone tail her and let him know the minute she showed up at work.

As he stepped off the elevator onto the third floor of Anderson Technologies, he took in the modern look of the lobby where a pretty, young receptionist sat. He smiled at her, and she was happy to give him a warm smile in return.

"Detective Davenport," she chimed. "Wondered when I might see you here again."

"Oh really?" He leaned against the oval desk and closed the space between him and the receptionist. She blushed. "Is Miss Alisha Stewart in, Mallory?" he asked.

"You remembered my name." Mallory's eyes widened and drank Ian in.

"It's my job," he replied.

Mallory sat up straight, pushing her small, yet perky breasts in Ian's direction. "I'm sure she's in Mr. Anderson's office," she said, with the roll of her eyes. "Down the hall, take a left…last door on your right."

Giving a nod and a smile to Mallory, Ian questioned the air of irritation she exuded from him mentioning Alisha. As he began his walk down the hall, Ian heard Alisha's name being whispered and he slowed his stroll. Listening, he heard three women cattily talk of Alisha and her apparent ego trip since Cordell Anderson's death.

"I swear, Mr. Anderson passes away, and she acts like the Queen of Anderson Technologies."

"I know. She had the nerve to ask me to fetch her some coffee this morning."

"Well, she *was* doing the boss…now she's reaping the benefits of all her *hard* work."

After one of the women burst into laughter, Ian coughed and made his way around the corner. Startled, the three women jumped, their eyes wide. Their mouths dropped.

Ian strolled past the women and stopped just short of Cordell's office. Peeping in, he saw the small, attractive figure of Alisha Stewart pacing, hands in the air.

"Keep him on the down," she spoke into a headset. "Everything's going to work out perfectly. Just give me some time to smooth things out."

Ian stepped into the office, leaning his tall frame against the door opening. He cleared his throat, and Alisha spun around, looking like a deer in the headlights of a semi. Her red hair swirled about and fell upon her shoulders.

"I'll get back to you with the information you need," she added. "Thank you for bringing your technological needs to Anderson."

Ian watched Alisha use shaky hands to remove the headset and place it on Cordell's desk.

"Smoothing things out? Keep him on the down?" he asked, watching Alisha's porcelain skin redden. "Who's him? Something wrong with Anderson Technologies? I thought it was a thriving business—"

"Can I help you?" Alisha interrupted, flashing her blue eyes to Ian before sweeping her long strawberry locks behind her ears.

"Yes, I'm hoping you can help me." Ian pulled out his badge and ID, receiving a frightened look from Alisha. "You're a very hard woman to get a hold of, Miss Stewart."

"Is this about Mr. Anderson?" she asked. "A few employees told me you were looking for me."

"Yes, it is. May I have a seat?"

"Oh, please forgive me. Sit down…"

"Detective Davenport," he stated.

"Detective Davenport."

Seating himself, Ian stared across the desk, watching Alisha comfortably ensconced behind Cordell's desk. "I see you're fitting in at the helm of Anderson Technologies."

"Well," she began, fiddling with pens and pencils on the desk. "Since Mr. Anderson's death, I jumped in to take care of business until it's decided who will take over."

"It must be a tedious task to run the company during such a mournful time." Ian watched Alisha flinch, a sadness enveloping her face.

"Very tedious, but I have always been by Mr. Anderson's side, so I know all there is to know about the company and how he would want it ran."

"What about his wife, Jovan Parham-Anderson? Doesn't she have a say as to the running of the company?"

"No," Alisha said, taking a minute to calm herself. "Jovan doesn't have any involvement with the company."

Ian paused before stating, "Recently, information regarding you and Cordell Anderson has come to my attention."

"Really?"

"Yes. Do you want me to tell you, or do you prefer filling me in?"

"Perhaps you should tell me," Alisha replied, sitting back in the chair.

"Okay, I see we're going to play games, Miss Stewart. I'll go first. Rumor has it that you and Mr. Anderson had a three-year affair..." Ian let his words dangle in the air between them. "I must be frank," he added. "I know the rumors are true because I've read Mr. Anderson's journal as well as the correspondence between you two."

With her blue eyes darkening, Alisha yelled, "Damn him" before tears began to roll down her cheeks. "I told him to destroy all of that. I didn't want a scandal...just him."

"Where were you the night of April 14th, early morning of the 15th?"

"You can't possibly believe—"

"Everyone's a suspect, Miss Stewart. I wouldn't be a good detective if I ignored you."

"I loved Cordell more than that cold fish Jovan ever could. I never wanted Cordell to die—"

"Never wanted? So you just wanted him hurt? Wounded?"

"No!" she exclaimed emphatically. "I had no reason for Cordell to be harmed at all. We were planning to be married."

This news had Ian sitting straight in his chair. He knew that Cordell didn't want to be with Jovan anymore, but he never explicitly stated he wanted to marry Alisha. "Did it ever dawn on you two that he *was* married?"

"That marriage had been dead for years."

"Jovan didn't think so."

"Of course not." Alisha laughed. "She lives in her mind, thinking she and Cordell could work through their problems, but he had long since tired of her and their life, and I welcomed him with open arms."

Ian looked into the dampened eyes of Alisha and could feel her hurt and pain for Cordell's death, but at the same time, he knew how love and love's labors could make people do some unthinkable things.

He wondered if Alisha knew about Sarah. Alisha was so adamant about Cordell's love for her, Ian half-wanted to ask about Sarah and the baby she carried. See what Alisha's reaction would be. But he wasn't ready to share that piece of information just yet.

"I need you to give me a detailed timeline of where you were the night of Cordell Anderson's death," Ian said. He took out his pad and pen and waited for Alisha to begin.

As Alisha spoke, Ian couldn't help but to drift a bit.

There was Cordell. There was his wife Jovan and her twin, Cheyenne. There was the supposed love-of-your-life and mistress, Alisha. There was the next door neighbor and lover and mother of Cordell's unborn child, Sarah. There was, of course, Sarah's husband, Mark. There was the associate, Devane.

Ian was getting pieces to a puzzle that just wouldn't fit into the larger scheme of thing. If he were going to solve this case, he would have to flip the script and think beyond the logical, because so far, logic was nowhere near this case.

Cheyenne paid close attention to her quiet twin who took dinner plates onto the deck and placed them on the checkered-cloth table that was laden with pasta salad and honey-grilled chicken. Cheyenne sat the pitcher of iced tea down and watched as Jovan took a seat and began piling food on her plate.

"Um, Jovan," she said as she poured herself a glass of tea.

"Yeah," Jovan replied, glancing up quickly before focusing her attention on her plate.

"You never answered my question about the house. Would you please look at me?" Jovan looked across the table at Cheyenne. "What is wrong with you?" Cheyenne asked. "I called you like ten times yesterday, no call back, and today, you haven't said more than five words."

"Sorry. What's up?"

Cheyenne shook her head. "I asked about the house. If you plan to sell it. It's an awfully big house for one person."

"I love this house, Chey. I don't think I could leave, not right now." Jovan bit into a chicken strip. "Why don't you move in with me?"

Cheyenne halted her fork, speared with chicken, in mid-air.

"Are you serious?" she asked.

"Of course I am." Jovan's hands went animated as she explained. "The house is big enough for us both to have our own space...besides, I would love to have my writing partner back within shouting distance."

"Well, my lease *is* up in June..."

"Come on, you and I can start going through Cordell's things, putting away keepsakes and giving things away to the Salvation Army and Goodwill...make the space for you and your belongings, design a work space for you, and—"

Cheyenne held her hands up. "Whoa, slow down, Jo. What's up with this moving on, getting past, and trying to deal thing here? Didn't you just find out that your husband was having an affair with your supposed friend and next door neighbor?"

The first word that popped into Jovan's head was Mark.

She couldn't forget how his kisses seared deep into her frozen center. Or how she had avoided his calls and knocks on the door the day after.

"Why are you blushing?" Cheyenne asked. "One day goes by, and you done lost your religion."

Jovan put down her fork and said, "I have something to tell you."

"What?" Cheyenne dropped her fork and gave Jovan her undivided attention.

Jovan took a breath before rushing out, "Sarah was pregnant with Cordell's baby."

"What in the hell..." Cheyenne stopped. She didn't have any more words. She just looked at her sister, who sat as if she just told her to pass the bread.

"Not only was my loving husband having two affairs behind my back," Jovan said, "but he got Sarah pregnant, too. The bastard didn't want *my* children, but he could—"

"How do you know this?" Cheyenne interrupted.

Jovan blushed again. "Mark told me."

"Does Detective Davenport know about this?"

"I haven't told him."

Cheyenne opened her mouth to speak three times, before finally getting out, "I will talk to him about this. Sarah's dead. She was having a baby. Would Mark be angry enough to hurt Cordell over this?"

"No," Jovan spat out. "Definitely not. Mark couldn't hurt someone like that."

"Wasn't he cheating on Sarah?"

Jovan shook her head. "No. Well, only once and because of Sarah's affair."

Cheyenne leaned back in her seat. She watched Jovan and the rosy hue just beneath her cinnamon-colored skin. She took in the pile of napkin strips Jovan had made. She listened to the excuses Jovan stacked for Mark.

"Why are you defending Mark?" she asked.

"I'm not," Jovan said a bit too loud. "It's just that I know where he's coming from. We were both cheated on. Our freaking spouses cheated with each other and became pregnant. Of course I would feel sorry for him."

"Hmm. Okay. I'll buy that for now." She studied her sister a bit longer before adding, "I will come back to this discussion later."

"No doubt," Jovan said. Inwardly, she sighed. The last thing she wanted was to explain what she and Mark did. She couldn't explain it to herself.

"You were talking about packing Cordell's things up and giving them away," Cheyenne said. "Have you even talked to his family or his lawyer to see what Cordell wanted to have happen with his things?"

Anger flared up in Jovan. Her lip curled into a sneer as she answered, "First response is to say fuck him. He would be lucky I didn't destroy his memory in every trashy tabloid that would hear my story."

"And your second response would be?"

Jovan drank some tea and counted down from ten. "Last year," she began, "Cordell was adamant about us doing wills. He named me beneficiary. However, he gave just about everything to his parents and Timothy, as well as percentages to our children…" Jovan sighed "…which we didn't have, so those assets will become mine."

"What about Anderson Technologies? What'll happen to it?"

"Have to begin looking for an interim president or a permanent one. I haven't talk to Mel about the particulars."

"I'm sure Alisha is just too thrilled to be taking over the reins of the company while the search is on." Cheyenne sucked her teeth. "I burn up every time I think of Cordell and her together…what they did to you."

"I know you do, and I would be a liar if I said I didn't feel like kicking and screaming over the whole situation. I thought I was going to live happily ever after with Cordell." She tried to smile but failed miserably. "I guess I thought wrong, huh?"

Cheyenne reached out to take her sister's hands. "Jo, it's not your fault. You are a beautiful, smart woman. Remember that."

"I'm trying to not feel so much hate for Cordell and Alisha. For Sarah. I'm trying to remember I'm still a good person. I want to just be able to breathe again, let the past stay in the past, and move on with my life."

"And pray they find Cordell's killer before Detective Davenport places us behind bars."

Jovan sighed. "Yeah, that too."

The two sat for several moments in silence, enjoying the bright afternoon sun on a warm April day. After swallowing a bit of chicken, Cheyenne eyed Jovan and said, "Sis."

"Hmm," she replied, chewing.

"What do you think of Detective Davenport?" Jovan's eyes rose to meet her sister's, taking in the softness of Cheyenne's voice, the look of interest in her eyes. Jovan laughed, something she thought she had forgotten how to do.

"He's okay." She smirked. "What? Have you gone and caught feelings for our arch nemesis?" The look in Cheyenne's eyes was priceless. "You have, haven't you?"

"He's just so attractive." Cheyenne sighed. "Minus him thinking we're suspects, of course."

"Of course."

"It's been so long since I've found a man attractive, worth getting to know. And call me crazy, but I think he might be feeling me, too."

"I noticed. The way you two bite each other's heads off… it's love all right."

Cheyenne threw a noodle at Jovan.

"Well," Jovan said, "after I get charged for Cordell's murder and sent away to prison, I want you two to make me an aunt, you hear?"

Cheyenne frowned.

"I'm joking," Jovan added.

"It doesn't matter anyway. As long as I've been out of commission…one year, ten months, and 13 days—"

"But who's counting?"

"Exactly. I wouldn't know how to act around him one-on-one. That, and as long as this investigation is an investigation, he is totally off limits to me."

"Just don't shut the idea completely out. You never know how love is going to come at you. He could be your Mr. Right."

"I'd settle for Mr. Right NOW for now, thank you very much."

Jovan laughed, being silenced by the phone. She leaned over to pick up the cordless on the table and answered, "Hello?

Oh hi, Mel, I was just talking about you. Always good things about you, Dear."

Cheyenne watched the smile vanish from Jovan's face as she said, "Okay, I'll be here."

"What's wrong?" Cheyenne asked as soon as Jovan hung up the phone.

"Mel is coming over. He wants to discuss Cordell's personal and financial affairs…says there are some discrepancies he found in regards to Cordell's finances."

"Of course there are," Cheyenne vented. "He had two mistresses and a gambling habit. Don't stress, Jo. Let's just wait until Mel gets here and explains it."

Jovan nodded, but she couldn't stop the knot that settled in her stomach from tightening.

"Okay," Jovan said. "Explain this to me again, Mel. I just can't believe this."

Jovan and Cheyenne sat in stunned silence as Mel repeated his findings.

"Basically," he began, leaning back against the sofa as he ran his left hand through his disappearing gray strands. "Cordell had been using funds from Anderson Technologies for non-Anderson expenditures. On paper, Anderson Technologies looks to be a thriving company and under new direction, it probably still can be a huge success, but in reality, the company wasn't doing well, and it appears that at least six-million dollars has been taken from the company."

"How could that have happened without you knowing about it?" Cheyenne asked.

"Like I said, on paper, Anderson looked to be thriving, but after Cordell's death, I thought it would be only proper to closely examine all of his legal effects so that you and I could go over them, Jovan, and you could decide your next action. I found discrepancies—"

"Discrepancies?" Jovan and Cheyenne asked in unison.

"Cordell was very creative in how he covered for missing Anderson funds. He increased the numbers for promotional, marketing, advertising, and public relation activities that he was working to try to do something international, and only someone who was seriously looking to find something wrong would." Mel took a breath and noticing he had a captive audience, continued. "It only took a few phone calls and check receipts to know that Cordell had been taking money from the company.

"Once I had that information, I took a trip to Anderson, informing Alisha Stewart that I was handling Cordell's business affairs. She appeared mildly concerned but allowed me the opportunity to go into Cordell's office where I found his personal financial log."

He paused, taking a breath. "For the last year, Cordell had been making monthly deposits of $100,000 into a New York based bank account, and actually had a two-year lease on a penthouse in Manhattan. He also had another account in Maryland where he also deposited $100,000 a month."

"Damn him," Jovan whispered.

"For Alisha and Sarah no doubt," Cheyenne whispered.

"Smaller amounts were taken out over the year as well."

The twins sat in silence, each taking the news in different ways, Jovan wanting to be alone to cry, and Cheyenne thankful that Cordell was already dead.

"There are two other things." The girls glanced at him incredulously.

"What else could you possibly have left to say?" Jovan asked.

Mel hesitated before speaking. "A week before his death, Cordell had an insurance policy drawn up on you, and the amount was quite substantial. It had your signature on it, so I thought the matter was copasetic; however, with Cordell's recent passing, I thought there might be an oddity to the matter."

Jovan felt her hands shake and her heart beat swiftly in her chest.

"How much was the policy for?" Cheyenne asked.

"One million dollars." As if played frame by frame, Jovan rose from the sofa, taking painstaking steps around the living room.

"I didn't sign any policy," she stated simply, glancing over at her sister, who looked as confused as she felt. "I don't even know why he would forge my name on something so important."

"I don't want to scare you," Mel said, looking sympathetic, "but I felt that maybe he assumed you might have gained an enemy or two."

"That's ludicrous," Cheyenne exclaimed, her nostrils flaring. "How would an insurance policy help her? How about police protection? Why would he not tell her about it?"

"You said there were two things," Jovan cut in.

"Cordell also drew up an insurance policy for himself for the same amount."

"That's insane, Mel," Cheyenne ranted. Jovan continued to pace the floor as she massaged her temples and willed herself not to break.

"I know this is a lot to take in at once," Mel said. "But I think in terms of Anderson, you might have an out if you wish to choose it."

"An out?" Jovan asked, stopping in mid-pace.

"I have been receiving phone calls from Jameson Burke this morning. He spoke of interest in buying Anderson from you."

"Are you serious?"

"Quite. I didn't breathe a word about any problems at Anderson, but I did inform him that any decisions about Anderson would come directly from you."

With a sigh, Jovan found her way over to Cheyenne and plopped herself down on the loveseat. Looking over at Mel with tired eyes, she said, "I don't know. This is so much information to take in at once."

"I understand, Jovan. I just felt you should be kept abreast of everything."

"And I thank you for that, Mel. I really do. I need a day or two to digest all this, so if Burke calls you back, let him know that I'll be getting in contact with him in a few days through you."

"I sure will." Mel rose from the sofa, collecting his briefcase. Jovan rose along with him and guided him to the front door.

"Thank you for calling and coming by, Mel," she said, reaching out to shake his hand.

"It's what I get paid to do." With a soft smile and a reassuring pat to Jovan's hand, he continued, "I will be waiting to hear from you. Take care now."

"Thanks." As soon as the door closed behind Mel, Jovan had her forehead rested upon it. "What in the hell?" she muttered.

"You okay?" Cheyenne asked, walking up behind Jovan and resting her chin on Jovan's shoulder.

"Girl, I don't know," she answered. "How could I have been so stupid? How could I not know Cordell was taking money from Anderson Technologies? How could I not know he had a love nest for himself and all his women?"

"How *could* you know? It's not like he publicly advertised it. Mel didn't even know." Jovan turned, giving her sister a quick hug before walking back into the living room. "I know what you need to do," Cheyenne continued. "You need to go and talk to that tramp, Alisha."

"I'm afraid I might actually hurt her if I did that."

"Hey, a smack or two never hurt anybody. Besides, you need to worry about getting you through this."

"You're right about that." Jovan sighed, falling onto the sofa in a heap. "I'm going to go clean up our lunch, then shower and change…and make my way over to Anderson Technologies."

"Good," Cheyenne replied, sitting beside Jovan and pulling her into a tight hug. "You know everything is going to be okay, don't you?"

"Oh, who died and made you the optimist? Usually it's me who sees the rainbow after rain."

"Well, sometimes you lose your way, and I have to be there to help you see the light." With a kiss to Jovan's forehead, Cheyenne hopped up and snatched her backpack from the side of the sofa.

"Where you running off to?"

"Well, while you're off to talk to Miss Stewart, I need to go talk to someone about all of this information."

"Dream man?"

Cheyenne cut Jovan a dirty look before rolling her eyes. "Detective Ian Davenport."

"Same thing," Jovan tossed back.

"Whatever. He needs to know. I'm sure the highly intelligent detective is in the dark about all this."

"And I'm sure once you're through with him, he'll be knowledgeable on *so* many levels."

Cheyenne gave Jovan another roll of the eyes before turning and making her way out of the house. "He'll be more knowledgeable, yes." Cheyenne answered. "But what will he *do* with the knowledge?"

Chapter 12

Cheyenne stepped into the police precinct and sighed. It was steaming hot in there. Her cherry peasant blouse began to cling to her torso just from the initial wave of sweat that played tag along her body. Lines of perspiration slid down her chest into her cleavage. Wiping her forehead, she said, "How do they manage to solve a crime in heat like this?"

The precinct was buzzing. Cheyenne had always been a person who lived in the forefront of every situation, but she loved to take a step back and watch others do their thing; watch their mannerisms and behaviors as particular situations arose. The precinct was no different. She watched suits and uniforms conversing with one another, one detective talking about a dismembered body that was found in a dumpster behind a popular restaurant in downtown Baltimore. She cringed.

Cheyenne wrote about murder and mayhem every day and had made visits to other precincts and even to the morgue so she could get the feel for where she was writing about, but standing here, secretly hearing about the senseless death of someone made her nauseous.

Shaking off the uneasiness that swept over her, Cheyenne slipped her backpack onto both of her shoulders and began fiddling with herself, fixing her blouse and smoothing her hands over her matching, ankle-length skirt before halting herself.

Why do I feel the need to look presentable for him, she questioned. She chuckled to herself. She knew the answer better than anybody.

On the way to the precinct, Cheyenne had coaxed herself into breathing soundly, deeply, into not thinking about Ian. It failed. Miserably. "God, how can I be so smart and together and yet fall apart at the thought of seeing that man?"

"What man?"

Cheyenne spun on her heels to come face to shoulder with Ian. Her eyes took a lazy stroll up to his face. The full, dark pinkness of his lips made her want to kiss him. She secretly moaned at the deepness of his eyes, the light golden hue of his smooth skin.

"Miss Parham? Cheyenne?"

She continued to stand there, absorbed by the sheer beauty of a man who could still believe that she was a criminal. It wasn't until Ian softly shook her that Cheyenne awoke from her thoughts.

"Huh?" she asked, blinking her eyes a few times until she brought herself back into the here and now.

Ian smiled down at her, a perfect, gleaming smile. He could be an actor…model, she mused. "I asked what man were you talking about."

"A man?"

"Something about you falling apart over some man."

Instantly, Cheyenne's cheeks turned a dark red as blush rose to her face. "You must have misheard me," she came back with. "No one makes me fall apart."

"Is that right?"

"Yes, it is." They stood there, staring at each other.

"So, Miss Parham, what brings you to my hot and sticky abode?"

Running her fingers through her silky locks, she sighed. "I wanted to talk about the case. Some information came up that I think you're not aware of."

"Me? The greatest detective of all times?"

"Yes," Cheyenne replied, laughing. "Even you can make a mistake once in a while. You think me or my sister had something to do with Cordell's death…that's mistake number one."

"What's mistake number two?"

Being so damn adorable for starters. "No need to hash out all your faults. Do you have time to talk?"

"For you, of course. Follow me."

My pleasure, she thought, watching Ian's strides. Cheyenne could feel eyes on her, but she cared more about the view in front of her.

She could feel the blush, once again, returning as her eyes made a slow dissension down the back of Ian, from his short, curly hair, to his broad shoulders, to the way his khakis were worn low on his hips. And with his white shirt tucked in, it gave her a glorious view of what had to be a round, firm backside.

"Mmm," she cooed, before running into Ian's back. He had stopped abruptly, or was it that she was so lost in the back of him, she didn't realize they had gotten to his office.

Ian opened his door and hid a smile as Cheyenne bowed her blushing face and walked into his office. It was small and hot, with file cabinets practically around the entire room. He motioned for her to have a seat in the chair facing his desk.

Both seated, Ian rested his large hands atop his desk. "So," he began, looking into Cheyenne's sparkling eyes. "What did you want to tell me?"

Dropping her backpack to her side, Cheyenne languidly crossed her legs, taking a deep breath before beginning. "I almost don't know where to start," she said.

"Take your time. Just jump in."

"Okay. Just let me get it all out and then you say whatever you need to say, okay?"

Ian nodded, slightly amused by how Cheyenne's eyes skittered about the room and how she couldn't keep her hands still.

"I think you know that Sarah was pregnant with Cordell's baby though you didn't tell us. Well, we learned today that Cordell swindled about six million dollars from his company, set up a penthouse in New York, and opened two accounts that had big, monthly deposits."

Cheyenne watched Ian's eyes grow wide. His full lips curled into a smirk. "I did know about Sarah," he admitted. "Didn't know about the other things."

"You thought I was done?" Cheyenne asked.

Ian picked up a pad and pen and began scribbling. "What else?"

"Cordell had two insurance policies drawn up, one for himself and one for Jo, each a million dollars." Ian let out a low, long whistle as he wrote. "Jo's signature was on her policy, but she didn't sign it."

"You sure about that?"

Cheyenne gave him a stare before answering, "To top off the surprises, Jameson Burke wants to purchase Anderson Technologies."

"Damn, I see they don't even let the body cool before they start charging in—business as usual." Ian grunted.

"You got that right. I wondered why he would even want Anderson Technologies. He already has a long standing in the community with Burke International." Cheyenne's eyes wandered upward, and she stared at the ceiling.

"What?" Ian asked.

"Just thinking," she said. "Burke's not the cleanest person around."

"You mean the smuggling charges?" "There have always been thoughts that Burke dealt in drug trafficking. I'm surprised he would even think that Jo would sell the company to him."

"Well, to Burke's credit," Ian said, "none of the charges have ever stuck, so he is in the clear. I don't think your sister would judge him on that."

Cheyenne laughed. "Don't be too sure."

"Besides, Anderson has young blood...the entrepreneurs and moneymakers of tomorrow. Burke would be a fool to not want to spike his older, more established company with the intellectuals and computer whizzes of Anderson."

Cheyenne smiled, impressed. "You seem to know an awful lot about Anderson Technologies."

"Let's just say I make sure to keep on top of everything that interests me." Cheyenne wondered if that statement was to be taken figuratively, literally, or both. She watched the knowing smile of Ian's disappear from his face.

"What?" she asked.

"Was just remembering—"

"Remembering what?"

"How much should I even be telling you? Like you said, you and Jovan are still suspects. Should I be so freely giving out information?"

"I won't even go on my *we're innocent* spiel because you either believe or you don't," Cheyenne said. "I'm free with information, as is my sister, because we are innocent, and believe it or not, we trust you...and know you wouldn't wrongfully charge us... at least we hope not."

"I never mean to arrest someone wrongfully. Sometimes the evidence is too compelling to argue, even if the evidence is wrong."

"So based on what you know now, what's your verdict? Do you really think we're guilty? Either of us?" For a long moment, Ian stared into the dark pools of Cheyenne's eyes, and despite her fiery personality and ability to jump from sweet to hostile in 0.5 seconds, he believed her and Jovan to be innocent.

"My gut tells me you two are innocent, but—"

"Great," she said, smiling. "No buts. You think we're innocent, for now, so let's go with that. Come on, tell me what you were thinking a minute ago."

"Just remembering the funeral...and seeing Burke and Devane together."

"Interesting pairing. Burke and a known gambling associate of Cordell's?"

"Exactly. This man seems to hobnob with all the big people of Maryland, and it makes me wonder why they hang around him."

"You think Devane might know something?"

"He appeared upset over Mr. Anderson's death, but I don't know. He might definitely know about the money being swindled seeing that he told me that he and Cordell went on many trips to Vegas and Atlantic City."

"I would like to throw something out there to you."

"What?"

"I'm wondering if Jo's mugging and Sarah's death are related somehow. I know there have been a few robberies in the neighborhood, but there haven't been any in weeks, and Sarah was the only person killed. Though Jo denies it, I'm thinking Mark Brockman might have had something to do with his wife's murder."

"Thought that. He was out of the state when it happened. Air flight shows he landed hours after the murder."

"Could have paid someone to do it."

"Thought that, too. We've scoured the house, his job, his bank accounts, and found nothing so far."

"What about Cordell? I mean here he is, married, with two mistresses, one pregnant. Not like I go around doing bad things, but if I was trying to be DL with everything, a baby would not be a way to do it. Sarah couldn't possibly pass the baby off as Mark's. I mean Mark has a nice tan and everything, but he..."

Ian laughed. "I know," he said. "I never asked Jovan about the night Sarah Brockman died. Didn't know until I saw the file at Jovan's house that Sarah Brockman and Anderson were having an affair."

"Just throwing anything out there that might get at the truth and finally prove that Jovan and I didn't do anything."

Cheyenne took three tissues from the box on Ian's cluttered desk and dabbed at her neck and chest. She noticed how Ian struggled to keep his attention on her face; it strayed, and often, to her lip tattoo on her neck.

"I'm tired," she said, her eyes scanning the books, the cabinets, and mounds of folders that laced the circumference of Ian's office. "This is so hard on Jo, and I'm trying to keep reassuring her that this will end, and that we'll be okay."

"Is it working?"

Cheyenne shrugged. "More or less. She has her okay days and her bad days." Cheyenne leaned back in her chair, raising her arms to rest upon the chair's arms. "You know, not to make you laugh, but when Jo and I are writing a story, our initial suspect is usually the main character."

"Which would be you and Jovan."

"Correct; however, we already know," she said sweetly, smiling in Ian's direction, "that neither of us did it, so our next move would be to branch out. Either through other family members that would have a motive or to the people outside of the family that had motive for wanting someone dead."

"Hey, you think *I* could be a mystery writer?" Ian asked, his voice dripping with sarcasm.

Cheyenne's eyebrow rose, and she frowned. "I'm just trying to help, Detective."

"I'm sorry," he said. "I will admit that we both do things pretty similarly."

"See," Cheyenne said, slamming a hand down on the desk. "We *do* have something in common." Ian noticed how Cheyenne's eyebrow slid down and in place of the rough edges that showed along her exterior, a soft glow began to appear.

She really is beautiful, he thought. "Hopefully it's not the only thing," he said aloud, inwardly shunning himself for being so bold.

"Hopefully." Cheyenne looked indifferent, but in reality, she felt her insides bubble.

"Okay, so tell me this…who would be your next suspect?" Ian leaned back and twiddled his pen between his thumb and index finger.

"For Sarah's murder, Mark or Cordell. For Cordell's murder, Alisha or Mark. For Jovan's mugging, someone tied to this whole Cordell fiasco."

"What about Cordell's family?

"God, his parents treated him like gold. He was one of those kids that grew up with a little privilege, so they dreamt big, and at times, actually won big. Cordell and Timmy were best friends. You would think they were twins because they look so much alike. Just thinking about it now, I want to laugh because Cordell's family and ours are very normal, which in this day and age is a rarity."

"Okay, so who else?"

"Not to be a broken record, but the mistress, Alisha."

"Now, you wouldn't be saying that because right about now you'd like to throttle her into next week, would you?"

Cheyenne feigned being upset. "Wow, how did you know?"

"Hey," he answered. "I'm a detective. This is what I get paid to do."

"Okay, I want to hurt her, yes, but she would be the next viable suspect. She was having an affair with Cordell, obviously, something very serious for him to have swindled his own company for her."

"It appears he swindled for Sarah, too."

"Yeah, but Sarah is dead, and he didn't leave evidence that he wanted to be with her permanently."

Ian rubbed the bridge of his nose with his index fingers. "I spoke to her today."

"Alisha?" He nodded. "And what? So what did she say? What did you say?" Cheyenne bit the inside of her cheek to keep from moaning as Ian ran his tongue over his lips before answering.

"She tried to be professional, as if nothing had been going on between her and Cordell, but when I told her about the computer and the correspondence, she cursed Cordell for not destroying the evidence and being so nonchalant with the letters and e-mails. She also said that Jovan knew about the affair."

"What?" Cheyenne yelled. Ian could see the anger formulating on her face, yet the anger melded into her beauty, giving her a sexy, almost sultry appeal, especially in the eyes. "Jo did not know about the affair. Not initially. If she had known, I would have known."

"Alisha says that Jovan lives in her mind, believing that she and Cordell could patch things up when that simply was not the case. She also told me..." he hesitated, wondering how this piece of news would affect Cheyenne.

"What? Tell me."

"Miss Stewart informed me that she and Cordell were to be married." Cheyenne's expression fell flat. Gone were the anger, the confusion, and the spite, even the joy of being in Ian's presence. She was just stunned.

"Married? Alisha and Cordell? Without Cordell getting a divorce from Jo?" she asked, her voice a whisper.

Ian nodded. Cheyenne's mind began to spin. How could she tell Jovan this? It would crush her, more than she already was. A person who could marry one woman, continue to live a life with her, and at the same time, plan another life with another woman, or two...someone like that had many a skeleton in his closet.

"Shit!" Cheyenne groaned, rubbing her forehead.

"What? Are you okay?" Ian asked, jumping from his chair and circling his desk. He looked into the tired and dazed eyes of Cheyenne.

"Jo went to Anderson Technologies."

"When?"

"I came here. She went there. She and Alisha...this bit of news, I don't know how she will react, or how spiteful Alisha will be."

"Don't say any more," Ian stated, taking Cheyenne by her left hand and helping her from the chair. "Grab your backpack and we'll head over there now. I'll drive." Cheyenne opened her mouth to protest, but Ian shook his head. "No time to argue this time around, Chey. Come on."

There was no time for Cheyenne to revel in the fact that Ian called her by her nickname. Her vision was a blur as Ian whisked her out the precinct.

Chapter 13

The first late night at work.

How long can bliss last? For some, a lifetime, and for others, it's so fleeting, you second-guess yourself in wondering if it ever existed. Jovan had been riding that blissful train for what she thought was most of her marriage with Cordell. They managed to have spontaneous trips and vacations, candlelit dinners, bubble baths, public displays of affection, any and everything that people in love took part in. She had no reason to believe that Sarah or Alisha would ultimately be her marriage's downfall.

Cordell always made it a point to come home before six in the evening so that he and Jovan could spend quality time together, and only a handful of times did he have to break his routine.

This night, the first of many late nights, Jovan lit the whole house in votive candles, poured herself into a champagne-colored negligee that was a step above being nude. In three-inch, champagne-colored heels, she sauntered into the living room, from the kitchen, two champagne flutes and a bottle of Dom Perignon in her hands.

The anniversary of their first date. This was their celebration for tonight. Cordell initiated the night years ago, telling Jovan that every year they would celebrate the first date…the date that allowed them to spend the rest of their lives together. On the fifth anniversary, four years into their marriage, Jovan wanted to please Cordell in every way she could, and the setting of the candles and champagne and of her, lying in a come-hither position on the sofa, was what she knew Cordell would love.

8:00 p.m.

"Hmm." Jovan sighed, glancing at her watch. "He's usually home by now." With that, she picked up the phone and

131

dialed Cordell's office number. The voice mail picked up.

"Maybe he's on his way home," she concluded, still smiling and hopeful to spend the entire night with her husband.

10:00 p.m. Phone calls to the office, his cell phone, and his pager came up unanswered. Wigged out of her mind, Jovan dialed every hospital in the area, asking if Cordell Anderson had been admitted. She had also contacted the police station but to no avail. Wherever Cordell was, he didn't want to be disturbed.

1:00 a.m. Jovan lay upon the sofa, sleeping soundly. She didn't hear the swooshing, clicking sounds of a key going into the front door and someone entering the house. Cordell had stopped where the foyer met the living room and spotted Jovan on the sofa. He crept up to her and bent down before her, dropping a tender kiss onto her lips. Fluttering her eyes open, Jovan's focus came into view and she found Cordell kneeling beside her on the sofa.

"Baby," he began, kissing her lightly across her face, ending at her lips. "I'm so sorry about tonight."

"You didn't get my phone calls, pages?" she asked, her voice husky.

"My pager must have died, but I received the phone calls as I was about to leave Anderson. I had turned off my phone and cell while I was working on a project. You know I didn't want to forget our anniversary."

At the time, Jovan believed Cordell's lie. After all, she was quickly awakened by the soft moist kisses of Cordell, and then he helped her from the sofa and whispered in her ear, "Go upstairs, Baby, and I'll turn out the lights down here and... maybe we can celebrate at *least* once before we go to bed tonight."

When she went upstairs, awake and smiling, she had no idea that tonight was the initial meeting into the new relationship between Cordell and Alisha. She had no idea that he sent her upstairs to wait on him because he wanted to call Alisha, let her know that he made it home in one piece. If she only knew then, what she partially knew now, would she even be in this predicament?

Jovan wanted to look the part of a woman who wasn't falling apart, who did have everything in her life in order. After Cheyenne left, she showered and slipped into a cinnamon-brown linen pantsuit and matching pumps, her curly 'do looking crisp. She knew she needed the façade of sanity as the elevator door opened and she stepped into the lobby of Anderson Technologies.

She felt all eyes on her. They all pitied her. She lost her cheating husband to a gunshot while his tramp of a mistress was moving up in the company…and in life, evidently, with the penthouse and money in Manhattan.

Mallory stared at her with eyes full of curiosity, but Jovan gave her a curt nod and started her way down the hall to what used to be Cordell's office. Three more steps. You can do it, she coaxed herself as she neared the office's entrance. She had counted at least ten employees who had given her silent condolences with their stares; the others were merely being nosey.

At the entrance, there in her sight was Alisha, sitting in front of the computer, her fingers flying across the keys.

"You look so comfy in here," Jovan said as she stepped into the office and shut the door. Her fingers poised above the keys, Alisha slowly turned her head toward Jovan, her blue eyes flashing fear, yet victory. She had taken Cordell from Jovan, and now, she sat at the helm of Anderson Technologies, for the time being anyway. With a smile as full of sentiment as a Hallmark card, Alisha rose from the chair.

"It's been a while, Jovan," she said. "I've been worried about you since…well, since the funeral." Alisha opened her arms as she approached Jovan, but as she came eye to eye with Jovan's cold brown eyes, she halted, dropping her arms. "It's a rarity to find you here at Anderson," Alisha continued. "You've been here how many times before?"

In swift fashion, Jovan took in the svelte figure of Alisha, her hair pinned atop of her head in a fancy bun, her body clad in a fire engine red power suit, complete with matching pumps.

If the skirt were two, maybe four inches shorter, she would look like she belonged in this office, Jovan surmised.

"Yes, it's been a while since I've made an appearance," Jovan answered, passing Alisha as she perched herself in the chair Alisha had occupied. "However, I never really had a reason to be here before."

"And you do now?" Alisha asked, her lovely face contorting into anger as she watched Jovan glance at the computer screen, watched her fingers fiddle with loose papers on the desk.

"I would say I most definitely have a reason to be here today."

"And that would be? Don't leave me in suspense."

"Mel paid me a visit today."

As impossible as it was, Alisha's already pale, porcelain skin whitened. "Mel Stein?" she asked, knowing the answer. Jovan nodded the affirmative. "What did he want?"

"As you know, Mel was Cordell's attorney, and even after Cordell's death, he's been seeing to Cordell's financial affairs, and recently he came across some major discrepancies that he brought to my attention."

"Such as?" Alisha asked, as her weakened knees caused her to sit in the chair facing the desk, facing the amused, slightly angered face of Jovan.

"The penthouse in Manhattan, the account in New York, other monies taken from Anderson Technologies for various expenses...outside of Anderson."

"Jovan—"

"Jovan what?" she countered, her voice rising. "Please, don't even try to insult my intelligence by telling me something stupid. I know the account and penthouse were for you two.

I've already seen the e-mails and letters that were written by the two of you."

They sat in silence, Jovan weary, and Alisha leaning back in the chair, clearing her throat. "You know, I have a mind to jump across this table and wipe that fake-ass, distressed look from your face," Jovan said, keeping a calmness to her voice, despite the anger of her words.

Alisha looked startled; her red-painted bottom lip quivered.

"Do you know what they call women who screw around with married men?" Jovan continued.

"Do you know what they call women who can't face the fact that their husbands no longer want them?"

Jovan jerked back, as if stung across the face with a slap. That hurt, and try as she might, she couldn't deny that she was that woman.

"That's hardly the point," she stuttered, rising from the chair to lean across the desk into Alisha's face. "Cordell never asked me for a divorce. He never stated that he wanted to leave me."

"Hell, why would he?" Alisha laughed, a bitter, bellowing laugh. "His actions told you loud and clear. When was the last time he looked at you, I mean really looked at you and made you feel loved? When was the last time he kissed you, and you didn't smell my perfume on him?"

"You slut," Jovan exclaimed, lunging over the desk to grab at Alisha, but missing.

"When was the last time he made love to you, Jovan, tell me that? Why would he want to do any of those things with you when he was doing them to, for, and with me?"

Jovan kept her tears in check as she slowly crawled down from the desk and straightened her pantsuit out. With a deep breath and the strength of God, she managed to find a piece of tranquility and retook her seat behind the desk.

"I'm glad to see that you're so very unrelenting of your

hate toward me, Alisha."

"I don't hate you," Alisha said, still with raised voice, still spite-filled. "I pity you. He didn't love you; I'm not sure he ever did."

"See, that's where you're mistaken. I know that Cordell loved me in the beginning. I know this, and if he told you any differently, it was to get your silly ass into bed with him." Jovan set her mouth firmly, stiffly and looked straight ahead at Alisha. "But none of that matters now."

"Oh, it doesn't?"

"No, because you are right about one thing. I was a fool for staying with Cordell, but now…well, he's not here, so my new, better life can begin."

"I can't believe you." Alisha's big blue eyes filled with tears. "You are so cold. Now that Cordell is dead, you can live your life?"

"This is not even what I came for. You have no right to tell me about myself. You were simply a replaceable toy for Cordell. I was his wife. You were his whore."

"Whore?" Alisha leapt from the chair, her hands falling onto her slender hips. "I was the type of woman Cordell should have been with all along, dedicated to taking care of his needs, to serving and loving him."

"If Cordell wanted a slave, I'm glad he didn't want me because I've never been that type of woman. I wasn't born to take care of someone else, unless that was my child. I'm glad you felt you could give up your own life to get screwed into Cordell's. No pun intended."

"How am I screwed? Any day now the cops will be busting down your beautiful doors to arrest you for killing Cordell."

Jovan let a small, tight smile fall from her lips. "Things will be okay for me and mine." She pressed her hands together and nodded. "God knows I didn't kill Cordell. Eventually, the dark cloud in my life will be lifted, but will yours?"

Alisha laughed. "What are you talking about now, Jovan?" With respected ease, Jovan rose from the chair and walked around the desk before sitting on the edge of it. She faced Alisha.

"Cordell illegally took money from the company, for you and him. He covered his tracks by increasing the budgets for various activities in the company. You, as his right hand woman, would have known these things."

"No." Alisha jumped up, her face close enough to Jovan's to smell the floral scent she wore. "I knew nothing about—"

"Well, that will be determined after the investigation of Anderson Technologies," Jovan stated simply. "Whether or not you helped to cover the tracks, I know there will be something that proves you were in on the penthouse and New York bank account, I'm convinced of that. Cordell was only bright when it came to computers and technology, so I'm sure there's a slip up somewhere."

"You're lying about this, aren't you?" Alisha spat, her voice loud and ringing in Jovan's ears.

"I have asked the detective in this case to check you out thoroughly concerning my husband's death, and regardless, you will be disposed of from Anderson Technologies. I'll make sure you get your ass dragged into court for stealing money from this company, and you'll never work in this industry again. I would say that makes for a wonderful day for me."

"I won't let you ruin me, Jovan."

"All the people in heaven, hell and on earth couldn't stop me from doing this, Alisha. You took what was mine and helped to ruin my life. I will always despise you for that."

"You bitch," Alisha yelled, raising her hand to slap Jovan. Jovan blocked her hand, gripping it tight on the downswing. She raised her own hand in an attempt to give a good one to Alisha.

"What the hell is going on here?" Ian asked from the

doorway. By his side, Cheyenne stared wide-eyed at the dueling pair, a wicked smile on her face.

Jovan released Alisha's hand. "I was talking to Alisha," Jovan said, stepping to her sister to give her a hug.

"I see we made it just in time," Ian retorted. "Just before World War III."

"Never," Jovan said. "I was just giving Alisha the news that Mel delivered to us today."

Alisha turned to Ian and Cheyenne, her face flushed. "I told Jovan that I knew nothing about Cordell's swindling of funds."

"But you knew of the penthouse and the New York bank account?" Ian asked. Alisha nodded. "So it's reasonable for one to believe that you knew about the stolen funds."

Alisha remained silent.

"Of course she has nothing to say." Cheyenne laughed. "The guilty never do."

"Cheyenne…" Ian sighed.

"What? It's the truth."

"Miss Stewart," Ian began. "Jovan will decide whether she wants the Anderson drama to come to light, but my suggestion to you is to not leave this city. I'm not through with you."

Alisha nodded, tears clouding her vision.

Ian guided Cheyenne out the door and motioned for Jovan to come with them.

"Miss Stewart?" he asked.

"Yes?"

"Do you know a Jimmy Devane?"

Alisha shook her head. "No, I don't. Should I?"

"He's an acquaintance of Mr. Anderson, and I just wondered if he ever spent time around here."

"I'm sorry, but I don't recall Cordell mentioning him, nor do I remember meeting him."

"Okay, thank you."

Jovan slowly came from around the desk and passed Alisha. At the door, Jovan stopped and said over her shoulder, "You might have managed to get Cordell's love from me, but someone trumped even your lowest low."

"What the hell are you talking about, Jovan?" Alisha asked.

Yes, the entire situation was a mess. Yes, in normal circumstances there would be no laughing, but Jovan did exactly that—laugh. It rippled out of her like a geyser. Cheyenne stood behind Ian, hiding her own smirk.

After she calmed down, Jovan said, "Cordell had another affair. The woman was pregnant. Guess who was the baby's daddy?"

Ian grabbed both Jovan and Cheyenne by the arm and ushered them away from the office.

Alisha rushed to the door, closing it before sliding down to the floor, not caring if her suit wrinkled. She could hear Jovan and Cheyenne's laughter down the hall.

"I'm scared."

"Ain't nothing to be scared about."

"You didn't hear everything she said."

"I heard it from you…just now."

"Jimmy…"

"Alisha…" Jimmy sat on his bed, smoking a cigarette, making puff rings. For the last thirty minutes, he had listened to Alisha wail into his ear over Jovan. Stolen money, penthouses, bank accounts, pregnant mistresses. First thing that popped into Jimmy's head was how he could get a cut of the money. With Cordell gone, he had lost a lot of his business. *That bastard could spend a fortune*, he thought, chuckling.

"Nothing's funny about this, Jimmy," Alisha cried out. "Any day now, investigators will be all over the company, crunching numbers, and they will figure out exactly how much money was taken from Anderson and where it went. I can't go to prison, Jimmy. I just can't!"

"Alisha, calm down. We will figure this out. Don't worry about it."

"But it's not just the money, Jimmy. Cordell cheated on me. He got another woman pregnant."

Jimmy guffawed. "Um, Babe, under the circumstances, I don't think you should be crying over mistresses."

Alisha sniffed. "I'm not going to jail for anything. I didn't kill Cordell. I didn't know about the other woman."

"Then what is there to worry about?"

"Okay, you over there acting so cool about everything. How about this: Detective Davenport asked about you."

Jimmy's attention perked up with the mention of his name and the detective. He stumped his cigarette out in the ashtray and coughed.

"What did he want with me?" he asked. "He's already talked to me."

"He asked if I knew you."

"What did you say?"

"What do you think I said? I told him Cordell never mentioned you to me."

"You think he believed you?"

Alisha rubbed her left temple with her free hand. "I think he did, but you can never be sure. So what are we going to do? They are determined to place blame on us somehow, and I'm not going to prison just because Cordell wanted to spend money on me. We were in love."

Jimmy snorted, "Yeah, love, I know. Don't worry about it, 'Lish."

"What do you mean don't worry about it?"

"Just don't, okay? I'll handle this. You just continue to arrive at Anderson, bright and early, every day, as if nothing is wrong. I'll handle this."

"You promise?"

"Hey, have I ever steered you wrong before?"

Chapter 14

$\mathcal{F}$or weeks, Jovan forgot that she was a writer, that she had other interests besides being a widow and trying to keep from being a suspect in her husband's murder. Her confrontation with Alisha yesterday was still weighing heavily on her mind as she pulled out a pair of jogging shorts and a long-sleeved t-shirt. She decided it was time to start running again and to try to get back some of her life.

The first thing she noticed was that her shorts was baggy on her waist. She laughed. "I'm going to start pitching stress as the next great diet," she said at the reflection that met her back in the mirror. She sat on the foot of her bed and tugged on her shoes, then brushed her hair back into a ponytail. Before leaving the house, she grabbed her key and a pocketknife. She was ready to get back out into the world, but she was smart enough to know that crazy people were still out in that same world.

She set the alarm, locked the door, and opened the knife before sliding it up in her left sleeve and making tracks up the street.

She hesitated briefly before entering the park. She looked from side to side every few seconds as she kept a steady pace. A tree branch snapped behind her, and she spun around and stuck the knife out. "Don't make me hurt you," she yelled to nothing. She laughed at herself. "Pitiful, girl," she said.

"Jovan."

She screamed and turned to find Mark running up to her. He grabbed her hand with the knife in it.

"You trying to kill somebody?" he asked, panting.

"You scared the shit out of me, Mark."

"I'm sorry. Was about to go jogging, and I saw you leave the house. Thought I would come the other way and we'd meet in the middle."

Jovan closed the knife and with her free hand, punched Mark hard in the arm. "You still scared me," she said. "Jesus." She took a few, quick breaths before calming down.

"I'm sorry." He stuck his arm out. "Want to hit me again?"

Jovan grinned and swatted his arm away. "Shut up."

She took in Mark's slick, dark curls pressed against his forehead, his clean-shaven face, the spark behind his green eyes, his wet, clingy t-shirt, muscular, hairy legs. She swallowed hard.

"Haven't heard from you in a few days," he said.

Jovan looked at the ground. "I know."

"I called. Came by."

"I know."

"Jovan," Mark said as he slipped a finger under her chin and forced her to make eye contact with him. "It was wrong of me to take advantage of you the other night. We've both been through so much, and I needed to feel something other than pain, and you were there, and your face and your mouth, and I kissed you."

Jovan let Mark ramble on before adding, "I kissed you, too, Mark. You didn't take advantage of me. I'm not some damsel in distress that you just plucked from danger and had his way with."

Jovan stood, inches away from Mark, trying desperately to hide a blush that threatened to rise in her cheeks. She had to avoid Mark. She didn't want to admit that though her husband hadn't been dead that long, she had been devastatingly attracted to Mark. It was beyond inappropriate for her to act like some schoolgirl who finally got to date the hot, hunky senior.

Mark crossed his arms. "I didn't call you a damsel in distress, Jovan." He shook his head and smirked. "I'm just saying." He took a tentative step toward her. "Would it be wrong for me to say that I kind of missed you the last couple of days?" he asked. Jovan reared her head back and laughed.

"Very wrong," she said.

"Sorry."

Jovan moved a step closer and said, "Well, I kinda missed you, too."

Mark laughed. "Kinda?"

She held up two fingers about an inch apart. "About that much."

"I guess beggars can't be choosers." Mark's finger moved from Jovan's chin to her cheek and down her neck. "How are you doing?"

"I'm hanging in there."

Mark stooped a bit until he was face to face with Jovan. "Can I hug you?"

Jovan lowered her gaze briefly. She shrugged though she was unable to hide her smile. "If you want," she said as if she could care less. Mark grinned and slid his arms around her waist, pulling her into him. Before letting her loose, Mark dropped a kiss on Jovan's lips. Jovan reached out and touched Mark's face. Her fingertips traipsed over his smooth cheeks, his lips, his ears, his hair. With her fingers threaded into his thick hair, Jovan leaned in and kissed Mark hard.

They moaned simultaneously. As their mouths opened, Jovan broke the kiss.

She giggled nervously. "Something that feels that good can't be good for you," she said.

She turned and walked back the way she came. She heard Mark trot up alongside her. He playfully bumped her. She bumped him back.

They both stopped playing around when they exited the park's wooded entrance and saw a police car parked in front of an unmarked car outside Jovan's house.

The two jogged down and noticed Detective Davenport standing at Jovan's front door. Two policemen stood behind him.

Ian looked at the pair. "Hello, Mrs. Anderson," he said in a professional tone. "Mr. Brockman. Interesting seeing you two together. Looking chummy."

Mark nodded but remained silent.

Taking Ian's stoic cue, Jovan straightened her back and responded, "Detective Davenport. What brings you here this morning?"

"Mrs. Anderson," Ian began, his whole demeanor stiff and impersonal. "We received a tip this morning."

Jovan felt her knees buckle. Mark held her. Ian took note.

"A tip?" Jovan asked, her voice shaky.

"Do you mind if we talked in private, Mrs. Anderson?" Ian asked. Mark stepped away. "I'll talk to you later, Jovan," he said. "Okay, thanks." Jovan and Ian watched Mark walk to the sidewalk. Jovan unlocked the door, turned off the alarm, and invited Ian and the officers inside.

"What tip did you receive?" she asked as soon as she shut the door.

"It was anonymous," he said.

"Okay." Jovan hugged herself. "What was the tip?"

"Mrs. Anderson, do you own a gun?"

"No. I told you that weeks ago, Detective."

The phone rang, and Jovan sighed. She ran into the living room and answered, "Hey, Sis."

"Isn't that convenient that she calls right now," Ian said.

"Yes, Chey, it's Detective Davenport," Jovan said. "Yes, we're back to the full name now."

"Would you mind if we took a look in your office?" Ian asked.

"Hell, yes, she'd mind," Cheyenne screamed into the phone.

"I have nothing to hide," Jovan said.

"Jo, you don't have to show them a goddamn thing,"

Cheyenne said.

"I have to go, Sis," Jovan said. "If you want, come on over." Jovan hung up and led Ian upstairs and down the hall to her office.

"So what's this tip about a gun?"

Ian eyed Jovan and answered, "We were told that a gun might be located in your office."

Ian watched as Jovan's face contorted with fear.

"No," she said, shaking her head. "I've never had a gun. They scare me." Jovan's eyes bounced around the room, her desk, chair, the walls, her window seat.

"No," she said, repeating it two, three more times. Her mind instantly flashbacked to the nightmare she had after Cordell's death. It was a dream, she thought. She knew she didn't own a gun. She stepped back and allowed Ian space to check out the office. Officers began searching Jovan's bookcase and file cabinets. The office phone rang, and Jovan answered it.

"Jo, I'm on my way," Cheyenne said. "I'm going to call Tara."

"It'll be okay," Jovan said, not fully believing what she said. Her breathing began to come heavy. "What do I need our lawyer for? I haven't done anything." She walked to the window seat. She heard Cheyenne calling for her, but she couldn't respond. She looked down at the pillows and thought, *You're not in there.* She threw pillows and with shaky hands, she lifted the lid. Nothing. She began to cry, her chest heaving. Ian watched her kneel to the floor and drop her head onto the window seat. He wanted to go to her, give her a hug, perhaps some reassurance, but right now, he couldn't befriend her.

Ian went to Jovan's desk. He flipped through planners and calendars and stacks of typed pages around an illuminated computer screen. He opened the top drawers and sifted through the paper, and then he moved to the bottom drawers. In the bottom, right drawer, he lifted a wooden box carved with a delicate design. Something slid inside. When Ian opened the box, a rope of disappointment knotted itself inside his gut.

"Mrs. Anderson."

Silence hung in the air like a hand over a mouth, removing the oxygen from the room. Jovan lifted her head from the window seat and stood. "Yes," she said, afraid to turn around. Ian didn't respond, and curiosity got the best of her. For a brief instant, her eyes met with Ian's and she watched as conflicting emotions raised havoc in his eyes. With a blink of her eyes and a silent prayer to God, Jovan looked down into Ian's hands and saw the black, shiny .38.

"Oh my God," she whispered.

"What?" Cheyenne cried out over the phone. "Jovan, talk to me." She could hear Ian talking to Jovan, and she strained to catch a word or two. Fear penetrated her when the phone went dead. "Hello," she yelled.

Hitting END on her cell phone, Cheyenne broke numerous driving violations to make it to Jovan's in record time. She punched in the code to the security alarm and barreled into the house, yelling, "Jovan, you here?" After racing through each room, Cheyenne muttered, "Shit," and hopped back in her car.

Cheyenne hurriedly dialed a number on her cell phone as she raced to the police station.

On the third ring, a soft, feminine voice answered, "Hello?"

"Hey, Tara, this is Cheyenne."

"What's wrong, Cheyenne?" Tara asked. "You and Jovan okay?"

"No," she whispered, turning on her blinker before maneuvering onto the Beltway. "No, we're not. We need you to meet us at Precinct 3."

"Is this about Cordell?"

"I think so. I was on the phone with Jovan when the police arrived. We got cut off, and I just left her house and no one was there. I think they took her down to the station."

"Okay. I'll be there as soon as possible."

"Thanks, Tara," Cheyenne said before hitting END. As she dropped the phone onto the passenger seat, she felt the first rush of tears stream down her face. She had to get to the station and protect Jovan.

"She's not talking."

Ian glanced upward at one of the young officers who checked out Jovan's house. Ian figured he would let the other two officers go in and talk to Jovan. She had to be angry with him for bringing her in, but what was he to do? A gun was found in her home, the same caliber that killed her husband. He'd be stripped of his badge for sure if he hadn't brought her in.

"I'm not sure she's going to talk to anyone," the young officer added.

"Okay." Ian grunted, rubbing his jaw. "I'll go in, see if I can get her to talk." The officer nodded, and Ian rose from his chair, exiting his office, and leading the officer to the interrogation room. "Bernstein," he called out to the other officer who sat across the table from Jovan. "I'll take over from here."

"Okay, Sir," Bernstein said as he nodded toward Jovan and left the room, closing the door behind him. Ian glanced at Jovan seated at the table. Her hands were folded atop the table, and her eyes looked away from him.

"Jovan," Ian said. He sat opposite her at the table.

"Detective Davenport," she said, raising her eyes to his. "Shouldn't I wait until my attorney gets here before I speak with you?"

"Yes, you have that right, Mrs. Anderson."

"I don't know why I am here anyway. I told you that gun wasn't mine. I thought you believed I was innocent."

It was Ian's turn to look away. The pain that lived in Jovan's face was more than he could take. "What do you expect me to do?" he asked, lowering his voice. "We got a tip about the gun, and the gun was there. You told me you didn't own a gun. Something isn't right about this picture, Jovan, and I wouldn't be a good detective if I didn't follow up on each and every lead."

"Even when the lead is a lie?" Jovan asked. "Who is this damn anonymous caller anyway?"

Cheyenne and Tara Jenkins stood in the doorway.

"Yes," Cheyenne said. "Who *is* this anonymous caller?"

"Sir," Bernstein said, coming up behind them. "I told these ladies that you were in here with—"

Ian nodded. "It's okay, Bernstein. Let them in."

"Hello," Tara said, holding out her hand for Ian to shake. He did. "I'm Tara Jenkins, Cheyenne and Jovan's attorney." Ian watched as Cheyenne, clad in a short, green sheath dress, ran to Jovan. She hugged her and kissed Jovan on the forehead.

"You okay, Hon?" Cheyenne asked. Jovan nodded.

"Can you please tell me what is going on?" Tara asked. "Are you charging my client with anything?"

Ian shook his head no. "As of this moment, no, we are not. Truth be known, the higher ups want this case solved yesterday, but not at the expense of sending one of the sisters to prison without hard proof."

"Yeah." Cheyenne laughed sarcastically, tossing back her hair. "I guess the publicity would really harm the department if you all continuously harassed innocent people. Particularly those who are considered celebrities and *moral* celebrities at that."

"Cheyenne told me that you found a gun at Jovan's home," Tara interjected.

Ian's eyebrow rose questioningly as he stared at Cheyenne.

"And how would she know this?" he asked.

"Because I was on the phone when your little anonymous sting went down, Detective Davenport," Cheyenne retorted.

"Yes, but the phone was cut off before you heard what was found," Ian said.

Cheyenne's face flushed. "I *heard* you talk about the anonymous call, Detective Davenport. My sister wouldn't be down here if you hadn't found what you were looking for."

"Okay," Tara jumped in. "Can we talk about my client now?"

"The gun has been taken to the lab for testing," Ian said. "We will test it against the bullet taken after Anderson's death, run prints, and search for gun ownership. Jovan, if there is anything you want to tell me, now would be the time to do so."

Jovan looked outraged. "That goddamn gun is not mine," she yelled. "No test will prove that it is. I did not kill my husband. I couldn't kill anything or anybody, and no, I didn't snap and kill him on a whim either."

Ian half expected Cheyenne to let loose a string of profanities from her mouth, but she sat there, taking on the normally docile role of her twin.

"May I take my client?" Tara asked. "Unless you have further questions, or feel the need to retain her…"

"We're not going to hold her, but I do have a few questions," Ian said. "Ladies, please have a seat." When all parties were seated, Ian said, "Jovan, where were you the night of Sarah Brockman's murder?"

"Detective," Tara began. Ian held up his hand.

"Miss Jenkins, I'm not trying to insinuate anything. Please, let me ask these questions."

"I was home," Jovan answered. "I was writing, and then I went to bed."

"Where was your husband?" Ian asked.

150

Chapter 15

"I need a week-long nap." Jovan walked into her home, immediately kicking off her tennis shoes before padding to the living room and falling onto the sofa. Tara was in tow, taking a seat on the loveseat.

"I know you must be going through a lot right now, Jovan," Tara said.

"My life has been a roller coaster since Cordell's death. Actually, just before it, too. I just want all of this to be over."

"I wish there was more I could do for you, Jovan. It's all like a big waiting game."

"I know. We never thought something like this would happen. It feels like we're living in this horrible nightmare that will never end. Our work is suffering."

"I can only imagine how this has affected your writing," Tara commented.

"Writing?" Jovan asked, laughing. "What is that? I'm waiting for Elyse to call and inform us that the publishing house wants to forgo on our next novel."

"It's been that bad?"

"Not really." Jovan sighed. "Surprisingly, we're still on publication schedule, but with all this, I don't know when we'll get back on track with our writing."

"Jovan," Tara began, hesitant. "I don't want you to get angry with me for asking you this, but—"

"You want to know if I killed Cordell, don't you?" Jovan asked, calmly, expecting the question. Tara nodded. "No, I didn't," Jovan answered. "I swear I didn't."

"I believe you and because I do, I have a question."

"Go ahead."

"Would you and Cheyenne consider doing a polygraph test? I mean the results aren't admissible in court, but it might be a way to get your names off the suspect list."

Jovan sat back on the sofa and folded her arms. Her chest heaved and her eyes closed. She cracked her neck before replying with, "That's true. That's actually a great idea, Tara. The sooner we can get off that list, the sooner we can get some sort of life back."

"You want me to look into it?"

"Definitely."

For a minute, the two sat in silence until Tara said, "I'm truly baffled. It's not like Cordell was some Joe Schmoe, and he was murdered in his own home, a home with security and a wife in it at the time. How do they not know anything?"

"I know. I've rolled this around in my head so many times, I can barely see straight," Jovan lamented. "Everything they have points to me. It makes me question my own innocence."

"Don't do that," Tara warned. "Because the moment you do, it weakens you, and if, God forbid, this case goes to trial, prosecution will use that weakness to twist everything you say to their benefit."

Jovan closed her eyes, sighing. "Cordell really wasn't who I thought he was," she whispered. "In the last year or so, he changed so dramatically. I was so stupid not to realize that he had fallen out of love with me until a few days before he was murdered, and even then, I questioned trying to make it better even though it was obvious he wanted someone else."

"What?" Tara said, astonished. "Cordell was having an affair?"

"Yep. For some time, so I hear." A wistful expression floated across Jovan's face. The doorbell ringing jolted her from her sad reverie. "Excuse me," she whispered before making her way to the front door. On the other side she found Timothy.

It bedazzled her how much Timothy looked like his older brother, the chiseled looks, lean, athletic body, and penetrating brown eyes. He was dressed in a white, crisp Polo tee and a pair of jeans. She hadn't noticed his hair the last time he dropped by, but he wore it grown out a bit, in twists. Despite the sullen look to his eyes and the down curve of his lips, Timothy looked well, Jovan thought before stepping out on the steps and hugging him.

"Hey you," she whispered, planting a short kiss on his cheek.

He smiled. "Hey," he responded. "I was worried about you. Thought I would pay a visit."

"I'm glad you did. Come on in."

As they walked into the living room, Tara stood from where she sat, her purse clutched in her hand. "Tara, you remember Cordell's brother, Timothy?" Jovan asked. Timothy and Tara shook hands.

"Nice to meet you again," Tara offered, along with a smile.

"Likewise," Timothy said.

"I hate to cut our visit short," Tara explained, hugging Jovan, "but I just got a call from another client, so I have to get going."

"No problem, Tara, and thank you for coming as fast as you did."

"Call me as soon as Detective Davenport has anything, okay?" Tara asked. "And I'll look into what we discussed."

Jovan nodded. Tara turned and quickly left. Jovan stared at Timothy, and he stared right back at her. Both smiled.

"It's really good to see you again so soon," Jovan said, taking Timothy's hand and guiding him to the sofa. "Every time I see you, I have to shake my head...you're the spitting image of Cordell."

Timothy's smile vanished at the mention of Cordell. "I'm sorry," Jovan said quickly, stroking Timothy's hands. "I talk about Cordell like he's right here...and I forget that he's..."

"I know," Timothy said. "I do, too."

"Would you like something to drink? Coffee, tea, soda, anything?"

"No, I'm fine, Jo, thanks. I actually came by to see how you were doing. After I left the other day, I was worried about you and this whole crazy mess."

"I'm slowly going insane, and I may be going there while in prison."

"You can't be serious," Timothy said. "They think you had something to do with Cordell's death?"

"They found a gun today, in my office. I don't own a gun, Tim. I have no idea how it got into my house. And the other day you were here?" Timothy nodded. "Detective Davenport found evidence of an affair between Alisha Stewart and Cordell." Timothy looked away. "Tim," Jovan asked, massaging his shoulder. "Did you know?"

"I suspected," he replied. He turned to Jovan and gave a wistful smile. "I hoped it wasn't true. You didn't deserve that." Jovan couldn't respond. She wasn't ready to talk about Cordell's affair. "They have no other suspects?" Timothy questioned.

"I don't know," she answered. "But I do know they should be looking more closely at Alisha Stewart and Jameson Burke. After all, Cordell was sleeping with Alisha, and Burke just offered to buy Anderson Technologies from me. Those two reek of suspicion."

Timothy sat silent, wringing his hands. He looked distant. Jovan bumped his shoulder playfully. "Timothy," she said. "I never asked you this, but I need a truthful answer, okay?"

He faced her, his eyes probing hers deeply. "Okay," Timothy replied. "What is it?"

"I know your mother has problems with me—"

"She loves you, Jo. It's the situation that's—"

"Let me finish," Jovan interrupted, holding up her hand. "Your father has been very diplomatic, and I love him for that, but what would really hurt me right now was if you felt like your mother does. You were a close friend to me, and I would hate to lose that because of this."

Timothy broke into a smile that was so large and warm Jovan briefly thought about sinking into it.

"Jo, you never have to worry about me hating you," Timothy said.

"So you don't believe I had anything to do with Cordell's death?"

Timothy flinched, but he kept the smile on his face. "No, of course not. I could never think..."

Jovan was taken aback when Timothy broke down into sobs. She leaned to him, hugging him to her.

"I know," she cooed. "I should have known you didn't think that. I know all of this has to be just as hard on you."

"I looked up to him," Timothy whimpered. "When I went through rehab, once, twice, three times, he was there for me because he said he knew I had potential and strength. The beginning was rough..."

"Yes, it was," Jovan said, nodding.

"He blamed himself, said he should've protected me, but he always thought I could overcome the addiction."

"He believed in you, Babe, and so did I. Still do."

Timothy looked into Jovan's face, her tears shining along with his. "You were there for me too, weren't you?" he asked.

"Of course I was," Jovan answered. "I love you, Tim. Don't forget that. Even now, with this riff between me and your parents, I hope that you will continue to be there for me, and I for you."

Timothy clung to Jovan. "I will," he whispered. "I would never believe you would do anything so...so heinous, Jovan. You're not weak enough to do that."

Jovan leaned away from Timothy, a soft smile forming through the tears. "None of us are that weak, and we have to convince the police of that, and find the real killer so that we all can move on with our lives."

With a kiss to her forehead, Timothy added, "Yes, move on with our lives," before settling back into the warmth of Jovan's hug.

Pushing a shopping cart, Cheyenne zipped up and down the grocery store's aisles in search of comfort food for herself and Jovan. Even now, with the media off on another scandalous story, Cheyenne received looks and points from the other shoppers at the store. She tried to ignore the glances, the shaking of heads, all of it. She wanted to stand up on her soapbox and preach her and Jovan's innocence to the crowd, but as she strolled past the magazine rack and saw the latest local tabloid and the cover picture of her and Jovan under the headline, *Sisters in Writing and Murder?* she knew it would take more than a speech to convince the masses.

Cheyenne glanced down into the cart, viewing its contents: a gallon of orange sherbet, a couple of frozen pizzas, pretzels, popcorn, beer.

"Okay, time for checkout," she said.

"Back to college night, I see."

Cheyenne turned on her heels and stared down Ian. Immediately, her stance became erect and a steely glaze fell across her eyes. Even the half-smile on Ian's face couldn't weaken Cheyenne's stance.

"Detective Davenport," she said, turning back to her cart and moving forward. She was not only trying to get away from him, but she was standing in the frozen food section, and her silk dress wasn't keeping her warm there.

"Cheyenne," Ian called after her, quietly, not wanting to

cause a scene in the store. She continued to walk, finding a short line to step into. She placed her items on the conveyor belt and took cash from her wallet.

She noticed the cashier's eyebrow rise, but she smiled and said, "Plastic, please." Ian followed Cheyenne into the line and out into the parking lot once he paid for his things.

As Cheyenne reached her car, Ian reached out, taking her hand to stop her. "Cheyenne," he said again, this time huskily.

"What?" she asked. She raised her hands and placed her wrists together. "Are you going to arrest me?"

"Chey—"

"Don't Chey me, Detective."

"I'm sorry," Ian pleaded. "You can't possibly be mad at me."

"Why not?" she asked, looking perplexed. "You took my sister in for questioning like some goddamn criminal. Are you insane? Of course I'm mad at you, furious in fact."

"Well you tell me, Cheyenne, what was I supposed to do? We got a tip about a gun. There was a gun in your sister's office, and previously the two of you stated there were no guns in the house. Was I supposed to toss the gun, pretend I never saw it?"

When Cheyenne didn't respond, Ian added, "I have a job to do. It may not lead me down perfect roads each and every time, but I have to investigate every piece of evidence, more so with this case. The higher ups are on my ass to do this right and to do it quickly, no mistakes, so if I find a weapon at your sister's home, regardless of how I feel personally, I have to check it out." Ian took a breath to calm himself. He felt the need to explain his predicament to Cheyenne, to get her to understand where he was coming from. He liked her. He had admitted that to himself, and with that acknowledgment, he couldn't stand having her so upset at him.

After a moment, Cheyenne nodded. "I understand," she conceded. "But that doesn't make me like your position any better. Especially when your position has my sister in an interrogation room."

"Point taken." Ian watched the edge slowly ease from Cheyenne's stance until eventually she glanced his way, a small smile etching the lines of her lips.

"So," she said, rocking back and forth on her heels.

"So," Ian mocked. "Friends?"

"Technically, we were never friends, Detective Davenport." Cheyenne gave Ian one of her best smirks, and they both laughed.

"Okay." Ian chuckled. "Could we possibly be friends?"

Cheyenne turned to open her car door, dropping her groceries in the passenger seat before getting in. Closing the door behind her, Cheyenne looked out of the opened window at Ian, who had bent down to look at her.

"I dunno," she said. "I'll get back to you on that." She watched him laugh as she pulled out of her spot, headed for Jovan's place.

"I've been holding this in, but I just have to ask," Cheyenne said as she leaned against the island in Jovan's kitchen. "Why did Ian ask about you and Mark? You holding out on me?"

Jovan slid her bare foot beneath her bottom as she reached for a slice of pepperoni pizza. "There's nothing going on between us," Jovan said. "Not really."

"Girl, dish. Give details." Cheyenne moved in close and gave all her attention to Jovan.

"It's not that serious." Jovan laughed. "He saw us today coming from the park up the street, and he thought something was up."

"What is up?"

"Nothing." Jovan picked the pepperonis off and ate them before adding, "We've both lost big, suffered big, and maybe once or twice, we comforted each other."

"Comforted?"

Jovan threw a piece of crust at Cheyenne. "Get your mind out of the gutter, girl. We talked. We hugged. Maybe kissed a few times."

"Jo, do you realize this man had an affair on his wife who happens to be dead?"

Jovan stood and retrieved a beer from the fridge. After a swig, she turned and faced her sister.

"I don't know what to say, Chey." She shrugged. "We're not a couple. We're just friends. Besides, it's been a while since someone cared about me and my feelings."

Cheyenne nodded. She ran a hand through her straight hair and said, "I feel you on that. Been a while for me, too."

"But you did have a grocery store love connection."

"There was no love connection, especially on my part. I was a cold fish, I think."

"I admit, I was mad at Ian, but I understand that he's only doing his job," Jovan commented. "Can't hold a grudge against him for following the clues even when they lead to me."

"And I understand that, Jo. Now anyway. I even told him that. I can't help it if I get mad at him treating you like a criminal. But I do realize he's not doing it because he wants to, but because it's his job."

"So you two reached a middle ground?"

Cheyenne smirked, biting into a pizza slice. "More or less," she said. "If only we could catch the damn murderer already! Tonight, out on that parking lot, God forgive me, I wanted to kiss that man."

"Why wouldn't you?" Jovan asked, her beer poised toward her lips. "The man is fine."

"I think he wanted to kiss me, too," Cheyenne whispered, like a little kid.

"Changing my previous question slightly, why wouldn't he? I mean, look at *me*. *You're* beautiful!" The two fell onto each other and laughed.

"You're a mess. Who knows what will come out of that whole situation."

The doorbell rang.

"I wonder who that could be," Jovan mused.

"Every time we speak of him, he shows up."

"Could we be batting a thousand? Let's find out." Hopping from the kitchen stool, Jovan padded her way through the living room to the front door.

She opened the door and found Ian on the other side. She giggled. "I bet your ears are burning, aren't they?"

Ian tilted his head. "Why?"

"Oh, no reason. Come on in." She moved and allowed Ian to enter. The two walked into the living room just as Cheyenne sashayed in from the kitchen. Ian smiled as he eyed her dressed in a hunter green pajama set. She looked just as good in pajamas as she did in that silk dress today, he thought.

"Detective Davenport," Cheyenne said, nodding professionally before laughing.

"Ms. Parham," he answered, in mock seriousness.

"Okay, this has to be good news because we're all too giddy."

"Or too drunk?" Ian asked, looking from Cheyenne and Jovan and remembering the coolers that were in Cheyenne's shopping cart.

Cheyenne shook her hands. "We refuse to answer that question," she said. "Would just give you another reason to take us in. Anyway, what brings you by this time of night?"

"Well, we got the results back from the gun," Ian stated, receiving silence from the twins. "The gun was clean, no prints on it at all. The serial number was scratched off, so we're still trying to figure out who the gun belonged to, and even though the gun is the same caliber that killed Anderson, it's not the same gun."

Jovan raked her hands through her hair. "This doesn't clear me," she said. Cheyenne motioned toward Jovan, but she moved away.

"Someone's planting guns in my home," Jovan yelled. "I can't grieve, be angry, be anything because every little thing I do is being scrutinized. Am I the killer? That is what everyone is thinking. I couldn't possibly be grieving for Cordell, right? After all, he was cheating on me, wanting to leave me. God, I don't know how much more of this I can take."

Jovan raced out of the living room toward the sunroom. Cheyenne tried to go after her, but Ian held her back. "She needs me," Cheyenne said.

"Let her get herself together first. She's been through a lot."

He took Cheyenne into his arms when she began to cry openly. "I am so tired," she whispered into his shoulder. "Is this ever going to end?" Ian leaned back, looking into Cheyenne's tearful eyes. He wiped her tears.

"I'm going to find out who killed Cordell," he said. "Not just because I'm good at what I do, but because you two need to be able to let this rest."

"That's all we want to do. Let it rest." Ian continued wiping her tears, his fingers moving along her cheeks and softly across her lips. He felt her warm breath seep out from an audible sigh.

Cheyenne blinked twice as Ian's lips approached hers. The initial touch of their lips came simultaneously with the ringing of the phone. They jumped back as if burned.

Jovan reentered the living room, tear tracks down her face. She picked up the cordless and said, "Hello?" Cheyenne and Ian watched her face contort with fear and anger. "Who is this? What do you want from me?"

Cheyenne moved to the phone and clicked on the speakerphone.

"Did you enjoy the gift I left for you?" The muffled voice snickered. "I guess it won't be long until your sweet twin will be coming to see you during visiting hours, huh?" The line went dead, and Jovan dropped the receiver. "Who was that? What is going on?" Cheyenne took Jovan in her arms. The pair clung to each other. Ian watched the twins; he knew that he would find out who placed that call and who killed Cordell. There was more at stake now...aside from freeing Jovan from this nightmare. That *almost* kiss between him and Cheyenne ignited something in him, and he wanted the slate clean for the twins so that he could explore things with Cheyenne further.

Chapter 16

"*I* hope Mel has some good news for us this morning," Jimmy said. He sat on the corner of Burke's desk. Burke sat silent at his desk, his thick, long fingers perched together in the shape of a triangle. He was stoic; his tall, silent persona being one of the major reasons so many people feared and revered him. He was a man of few words, but the words he said spoke volumes. Jimmy turned to face Burke, who had his eyes closed. *Of course this bastard doesn't care about Mel coming*, Jimmy thought. *He's got more loot than he could ever spend.*

"It will be good," Burke commented after long moments of silence. "Why would Jovan want Anderson Technologies now? After all she has heard about her *faithful* husband, the last thing she would want is a company that would constantly remind her of Cordell."

"True," Jimmy surmised, nodding. He stroked along his pointed chin. "I just wish he would get here."

"Why?" Burke laughed, opening his eyes to reveal a round pair of black eyes, a color that matched the thick mass of wavy hair that rested upon his head. In his mid-fifties, Burke looked no older than 35 with his thick, muscular physique, healthy pink skin and full head of hair, along with an award-winning smile and charisma to woo even the Devil into his corner. "Do you have somewhere else you need to be?"

"Not really."

"Then calm down, Devane," Burke insisted. "You're about to get stinky rich. I would think you could be patient for just a few minutes longer."

"You right. You right."

Burke shook his head in disgust. He never imagined he would need the assistance of someone like Jimmy Devane to pursue such a lofty goal as getting Anderson Technologies, but Devane had sweet connections and was the cog to initiating a tremendous coup. He just hoped that getting into business with this well-known local thug wouldn't be the demise to his empire.

Unexpectedly, Jimmy began to laugh. "Man," he said, snorting like a pig. "Did you watch the news last night? It was brief, but they had little Miss Jovan talking about that gun they found in her home."

"I wonder how she got out of being detained at the precinct," Burke whispered, more to himself than to Jimmy, but Jimmy heard him.

"Hell, she's the freaking queen here, her and the twin," Jimmy retorted. "I know you've read up on them…come from a good family, two hot pieces of ass, they give money to charities, support various causes. It's like people go home from church on Sunday to read one of their books. They're one step removed from Oprah in the human goddess totem pole."

"Yes, they are a sweet pair, aren't they?" Burke asked, with a sly smile on his lips. "Despite the sweetness, the girls aren't winning any popularity contests these days."

Jimmy snorted. "I'm sure America's just waiting for Jovan to be convicted."

"You gentleman should learn to lower your voices."

Burke and Jimmy both turned their attention toward the door where Mel Stein stood.

"Your secretary wasn't at her desk, so I took the liberty of coming straight up to your office." Mel fought to keep his professional stature before the two men. He held Jovan in high regard. No matter how much of a fool her husband had been, she was always a respectable, highly moral, and giving person, and overhearing Jimmy and Burke's comments unnerved him.

Jimmy looked caught in headlights, but Burke widened a smile across his face before rising from his desk and coming around to greet Mel. They shook hands, Burke giving a welcoming pat to Mel's back.

"Glad you could come," Burke stated, gesturing toward a chair for Mel to sit in. He shot Jimmy a glance to remove his backside from his desk. Jimmy obliged.

"So," Burke began. "I'm to take it that you went to Mrs. Parham-Anderson in reference to my proposition?"

"Yes, I most certainly did," Mel answered. Although his face didn't reflect it, Mel found it odd for the tall, thin man to be in such an important meeting. *What did he have to do with this meeting*, he wondered.

"Good." Burke smiled. "So what is the good news? Has she given us an amount or would she like me to draw up a contract?"

"She doesn't want to sell."

Jimmy coughed as if choked by the Jaws of Life. Burke remained calm even though inside he was trembling fiercely.

"Doesn't want to sell?" he asked. "How can that be? Is she planning to run Anderson Technologies herself?"

Jimmy laughed with a bitter tone. "That broad knows nothing about the computer business or business period." Burke cut Jimmy a *shut it up* glance.

Mel cleared his throat. "She didn't technically say no."

Burke rolled his eyes in annoyance. "What *exactly...technically* did she say?"

"Keep in mind I just informed her about you wanting to purchase the company. Given everything she's been through, it's only reasonable that she would need time to think about what she would like to do concerning the company and other assets."

"Yes, it's only reasonable," Burke mocked, anger growing. "What the hell does she want? Is that all she told you...to give her time?"

Mel nodded. "Her husband was just murdered," he commented sarcastically, just to be sure the *gentlemen* knew of this. "She needs time to recoup."

"How much time are we talking about?" Jimmy asked, impatient. "What, a day, a month, months, years, what?"

"Devane," Burke said with authority. Jimmy put his head down to keep from viewing the glare from Burke's heated eyes.

"Jovan said she needed a few days to think this through. She also wanted me to relay to you that she would be allowing me to oversee the situation...whichever way it plays out."

Burke could no longer hold his irritation in. "Damn it," he growled, pounding his massive fist onto his desk. "Please, go to Jovan and persuade her to contact me as soon as possible about this issue," Burke continued. "This is business, not a date. I won't sit around forever with this deal on the table."

The three men turned to the knock at the door.

"Why are you so anxious to purchase Anderson Technologies?" Ian asked. "Don't you have enough money as is, Burke?"

"What the hell?" Burke commented. "Where is my secretary?"

"Wasn't at the desk," Ian answered, shrugging before stepping into the office. "I'd love to come in, thank you. How are you doing, Devane?"

"Davenport," Devane gritted between his teeth.

Mel stood, reaching for his briefcase. "I'll let Mrs. Anderson know of your wishes and get back to you shortly with her response," he said.

"You do that," Burke said, nodding. He shook Mel's hand and watched him give Ian a nod of acknowledgment before leaving the office. "Mel," Burke yelled. Mel peeked around the corner. "If you see my dimwitted secretary, let her know you received a memo from me to her...she's fired, effective immediately." Burke focused his attention on the amused face of Ian. "What can I do for you, Detective?" Burke asked, remembering the detective from the funeral.

"Actually, I'm glad and curious that you and Mr. Devane are both here," Ian said. "You do get around, don't you, Devane? Best buds with Cordell, friendly with Burke at Cordell's funeral, and now I find you here. I guess I can kill two birds with one stone."

"Detective," Burke said with a harsh, low voice. "What do you want?"

"I wanted to ask you about your whereabouts the night of Cordell Anderson's murder," Ian responded, "and the morning after."

Ian instantly caught the fidgety appearance of Jimmy Devane and noted it while Burke continued to exude his air of calm.

"Is that all?" Burke asked. "Mr. Devane and I were in Atlantic City. Actually, we took my jet to New York and from there took a limo to Atlantic City for a night of gambling."

"Why would you two even be together?" Ian asked, skeptical.

"Devane is an associate of mine," Burke responded, giving a nod toward Jimmy, who now appeared more relaxed, sure of himself.

"Devane, you went to Atlantic City with Burke? After dinner with Cordell, his wife, and her twin?"

Jimmy nodded. "I told you how the dinner didn't end on a happy note," he answered. "When I got in, I received a phone call from Burke about the trip, and I jumped at the chance. Lost my shirt that night."

"So what time did you two get back from Atlantic City?"

"About ten the next morning," Burke answered. "We left about eleven the night of the 14th and returned that following morning."

"Do you have jet logs that will corroborate your story?"

Burke laughed. "My story?" he asked. "I have the jet

logs, yes, and can get them to you as soon as possible. Is that all you needed?"

"If your story holds up," Ian stated, "yes, that's all I need."

"Well, thank you for stopping by," Burke said, raising his hand to Ian. Ian didn't take it. "I do hope you solve this horrible case and soon."

"So do I," Ian responded, eyeing Jimmy then Burke. "So do I."

Jovan sat in Deborah Gianni's office. After talking to Mel about Cordell and Anderson Technologies, Jovan felt a need to talk with her financial advisor about her money matters.

Secretly, when her mind wasn't thinking about someone breaking into her home, she was still reeling from discovering Cordell's financial indiscretions. Anderson Technologies was a viable company, but she found it hard to believe Cordell could swindle millions of dollars from his company and still have it functioning.

Shaking her head, Jovan asked, "I'm sorry, Deborah, what did you say?"

Deborah gave Jovan a small smile. She didn't want to imagine how bad this situation had been on Jovan. "I was saying that you and Cordell had three accounts; you and he each had an individual account, and then there was the joint account."

"Yes," Jovan said, "which I used to pay the house taxes, our car payments, home furnishings, other household bills."

"Correct." Deborah nodded. "Now, rest assured, your individual account is fine, great in fact. Your municipal funds, stocks and CDs are all still intact, and there has been no activity on your account since you last withdrew…" Deborah glanced down at her sheet, "...$3,000 from your account."

"You know a girl has to do a shopping spree sometimes," Jovan said, smiling softly. "And I really do hate checks and credit cards." Deborah nodded. "Okay," Jovan continued, now breathing slightly better, "I pretty much figured my account was okay. I had the statements, but wanted to be sure. With our joint account, I was a bit cloudy because a while ago, Cordell began taking care of it and making sure payments were going out in a timely fashion."

"Why was that?" Deborah asked as her fingers deftly typed in figures and uploaded documents. "You did a great job with that account."

"At the time, I didn't think it odd. I thought he was just feeling left out, so I gave him the account to handle. If I had known then what I know now..." her voice trailed off. She blinked her eyes several times. "So tell me about the joint account."

"As of today, the account has exactly what you should have in it," Deborah answered. "For the most part, the withdrawals fluctuate from $1- to $10-thousand a month depending on the purchases or bills paid."

Jovan nodded. "Yes, that's about right. When we added the sunroom last year, we took out a lot. You said *for the most part*. What do you mean?"

"Well, over the last four months, there have been several major withdrawals from the account."

"What? Not our normal withdrawals?"

"No. Cordell went to the bank and would withdraw the money from the account; however, he always replaced the funds...usually around the time you two were to pay out money for household expenses."

"Why? I just don't understand what he would need the money for. He had his own account."

"True, but his account was extremely low."

"How low?"

"Less than a thousand."

"That can't be right. He had money." Jovan stood and immediately felt nauseous. "I have to go," she whispered.

"I'm sorry, Jovan," Deborah began. "I didn't think anything of the withdrawals nor did we expect any wrongdoing."

"It's okay. I just need to go. I'll talk to you soon." Jovan turned on her heels and ran out of the office. Since all this began, she was mostly happy that Cordell was dead because she knew she would kill him if she had the chance.

"Fame! I'm gonna live forever…" Cheyenne sang while she busily typed on her computer. After spending the night at Jovan's place, Cheyenne returned home, determined to use her energy in working on the revisions of *Deadly Vows*. She tapped her feet, bopped her head, and occasionally sang a rift to songs off of her *Diva of Dance* CD while she feverishly worked. Cheyenne laughed as Riqué bounced around her, barking, as if trying to become the next Irene Cara himself. She worked hard to keep her mind light as she went through a book that bore resemblance to Cordell's death.

"This is just a book," she told herself repeatedly as she wrote. "Fiction. It's a coincidence."

Cheyenne pulled on the tank top of Jovan's she wore. She made a pot of coffee, brought it to her computer, and sat there for almost three hours, writing.

"Almost done," she whispered.

Her love of writing and the love of her sister were the only two things keeping her sane these days. Like Jovan, she contemplated when Cordell's murderer would be captured, when they would be able to rejoin civilization and live like they had done before. Revising the novel grounded her, placed her back into reality, and with it, she held onto the hope that someday soon, all this would pass, and the gray skies would clear.

Cheyenne jumped out of her seat at the sound of someone knocking on her door. She knew that Jovan would be at a meeting with her financial advisor this afternoon, and other than her, not too many other people came to visit.

"Geez, I look a fright," she muttered, realizing her normally free flowing, bone straight mane was combed atop her head in a spiky looking ponytail. When she opened the door, she inwardly smacked herself for not cleaning herself up when she first arrived home.

"Hi," Ian said, with a soft smile on his face.

"Hi back," she said, the same smile on her own face. "Come on in." *Rein it in, girl,* Cheyenne thought, lowering the wattage of her smile. "What are you doing here?"

Her eyes quickly perused Ian's dark eyes, his lips, which she was briefly introduced to, and his athletic body clad in jeans and a denim shirt.

"I thought it would be a good idea if we tapped your and Jovan's phones," he answered, giving the same perusal glance to Cheyenne. She blushed. "Maybe we can find out who called Jovan's home the other night by doing this."

"Sounds like a plan."

"I went to Jovan's home first, but no one answered. Is she okay?"

"As okay as she can be. She had a meeting today, so that's probably why you didn't catch her."

Ian nodded, removing a black nylon bag from his shoulder. "Do you mind if I do this now?" he asked. "I brought the equipment on the off chance you would say yes."

"By all means," she answered, "do it now. The sooner, the better. Maybe we can catch the bastard who's tormenting my sister."

"Great." Ian walked over to phone base that was located beside Cheyenne's computer desk. "How many phones do you own?"

"Just two…one here and one in my bedroom." The mention of the bedroom made them both blush. Cheyenne returned to her computer, before asking, "Would you like something to drink?"

"I'm cool," he said, glancing up at her from his kneeling stance at her small table where the phone sat. Riqué sidled up alongside Ian, watching him work. "Working on the novel?"

"Yep," she answered. "I tell you, not much makes me smile and feel good these days, but sitting here, plowing through these revisions has me ecstatic."

Ian smiled. Seeing Cheyenne happy made him happy. It was odd, but true. Being this close to her and seeing that smile on her face made it hard for him to think about waiting until he solved the case to pursue something with her. "Is writing the only thing that has been putting a smile on your face?" he asked, watching her intently.

Try as she might, Cheyenne couldn't keep the smile from creeping back onto her face. "Actually no," she whispered. "My sister is always a constant joy in my life."

Ian laughed. "Okay," he said. "Anything else?"

"Nope," she answered, turning back to her computer to work. Out of the corner of her eye, Cheyenne saw Ian's smile fall off, and she wanted to howl at the saddened look that replaced it. He was too easy, she thought, chuckling.

"She hurts me, and then she laughs at me." Ian sighed.

"I'm sorry. I really couldn't resist it."

His sad eyes looked at her playful ones and he asked, "So you were playing with me?"

"Yep." She gave him a wink and returned back to her computer, trying hard to pretend that Ian wasn't boring a hole into her face by his steady stare.

Ian continued staring at her while he raised his right hand to reach out for the phone receiver. He removed a small device from a case in the bag and placed it into the receiver. Neither said anything while Ian completed his task. Cheyenne's focus moved to the computer screen, and she chuckled, viewing *Ian* written on the screen several times. She quickly erased it.

"A funny scene in a mystery novel?" Ian asked.

"Kinda," she responded. Ian stood from his kneeling position and leaned against Cheyenne's desk. He caught her deleting an 'a' and an 'I'. He wondered if it was his name, but he wouldn't ask. Cheyenne closed her eyes to take in Ian's cologne and the heat that emitted from him being so close to her.

"Cheyenne?" he said, practically against her ear. She bit the inside of her cheek, trying to focus on the pain and not Ian's sweet breath near her cheek.

When the tip of Ian's index finger lightly stroked the tattooed lips on her neck, Cheyenne cringed, squeezing her legs tight and saying a prayer for strength. Instead of giving him her full attention, Cheyenne cut her eyes at him, catching Ian in her peripheral.

"Yes?" she replied.

"Okay, I'm just going to come out and say this," he said. That made Cheyenne turn to him, looking directly into his sable eyes.

"Say what?"

"You and I…we almost kissed the other night."

"I know." A hint of blush dusted along Cheyenne's cheeks. Ian knelt down in front of her, his face even with hers.

"I was really upset that we couldn't finish that kiss," he added.

Cheyenne cleared her throat and swallowed hard, watching Ian as he examined her eyes, then her lips as she responded, "I was upset, too."

"This is just so crazy," he said, standing up.

"I know," Cheyenne offered. She dropped her hands between her thighs.

"For all technical purposes, you are a suspect in a case I'm in charge of." Ian walked away, scratching the back of his neck.

"I know."

"My boss would probably kick my ass if he thought I had feelings for you."

"Having feelings, eh?" Cheyenne broke into a wide smile as Ian turned around, his golden-brown cheeks red, his eyes deepening into some emotion that made Cheyenne sit straight. Her heart raced.

"And even though you are this little spit fire, and you're tenacious and strong-minded as hell..." They both laughed. "...I can't stop thinking about you."

"I know the feeling."

Ian and Cheyenne held the other in their sight, afraid to break the connection. Cheyenne could see the debate that plagued Ian's mind. Did he want to pursue her, or did he want to keep his job?

"Then, what do we do?" Ian asked.

"Come here."

Ian's eyes widened from Cheyenne's command, but he took the steps toward her and knelt down in front of her again. She smiled, a smile that would make one think she was as sweet as pure cane sugar. Ian knew otherwise. She reached out and touched his face with her fingertips before inching up into the massive curls atop his head.

"I know I should be telling you to curb your feelings, ease off your thoughts until after the case is solved," Cheyenne said, her fingers massaging Ian's scalp through the curls. She saw his Adam's apple bob up and down as he swallowed. "But, the truth is, despite our barbed words, I'd really like to spend time with you."

Cheyenne waited anxiously for Ian to respond. She was definitely laying herself out there, and rejection right now would be painful, but at least she would have nipped it in the bud early. With the exactness of a surgeon cutting an incision, Ian's fingers sliced down the curve of Cheyenne's right cheek before tracing her smooth, full lips. Her lips parted slightly in a sigh.

"I really want to finish that kiss," Ian groaned, his eyes stuck on the fullness of Cheyenne's lips.

"Finish it," Cheyenne whispered, her eyes widening, then closing as Ian inched closer to her. They both moaned as their lips finally made contact. Ian's hands trickled along her sides, around to her back as hers rose to the curve of his neck. The kiss lasted long enough to leave them both panting.

"You know," Cheyenne said, her lips throbbing, "you could come and question me about the case. Perhaps dinner will be prepared." She watched Ian's smile spread across his face. His eyes twinkled full of mischief.

"What do you think?" she asked, almost hopping in her chair, awaiting his response. Too afraid he would say no, she leaned out and kissed him again. When he pulled away, only to have his bottom lip slide from between Cheyenne's teeth, Ian asked, "What time do you want me to come for your interrogation?"

Chapter 17

Jovan stormed into her house, her heart pumping furiously in her chest. Her hands ripped off the jacket she wore and worked feverishly to unbutton her blouse.

"You son of a bitch," she screamed at the top of her lungs. "You just couldn't be happy with cheating on me, could you? You had to take our money, doing God knows what with it." Jovan kicked off her pumps and slipped and slid across the waxed floors. "I wish I'd never met you, Cordell. I wish I'd never fallen in love with your evil ass." She stumbled and fell onto the staircase, crying out when her right knee connected with the corner of a step.

"Screw you, Cordell." Jovan took hold of the banister and limped up the stairs. She barged into the master bedroom and began ripping the sheets Cheyenne had put on the bed after the death. She pulled clothes out of his dresser and ripped clothes from hangers in the closet.

"Where did your money go, Cordell?" she yelled, breathing heavily. She blew air as she tried to get her hair from her mouth. "Did it go to these nice clothes?" She shook her head.

"Sure didn't. *My* money went to your clothes. How about your women?" When she had every hanger bare and swinging on the rod, Jovan kicked over Cordell's wicker hamper.

"Yep." She nodded. "Money went to bank accounts. To penthouses. To your bitches and your bastard child."

Jovan began throwing the clothes from the hamper on top of the growing pile of clothes in the middle of the bedroom floor.

"I'm about through giving two shits about you, Cordell," she gritted out through clenched teeth.

She sat on the empty hamper and tried to catch her breath. She stared at the clothes, mentally accumulating what would go to the Salvation Army and what would go to Goodwill.

"Damn it," Jovan muttered. "Own house is a crime scene." Jovan went into the bathroom and came out wearing a pair of clean gloves, used when she cleaned the bathroom. She began picking through the clothes and separating into two piles. "Let me at least get the dirty clothes out the pile."

She tossed a few shirts and boxer briefs back into the hamper. She came across a black pair of slacks and a black button down shirt.

She thought of that night in bed when Cordell took sex from her. That was the outfit he came home in. The outfit he wore when he left her lying in bed after he got what he needed. Jovan loved the color black on Cordell. The day she told him that, he almost exclusively wore that color. Jovan folded the shirt and placed it on the bed, remembering that Ian had planned to come by. She began folding the pants and noticed spots on the cuffs and up the legs of the pants to about the knee.

Jovan wrinkled up her nose. "You didn't even take your pants off before screwing, Cordell? You fucking pig."

As she brought the pants closer to her face, she saw that the stains were dark, maybe red. She threw the pants and crawled off the hamper.

She went to the far side of the bed and grabbed the phone. Ian answered on the second ring.

"Ian," she said, whispering.

"Is that you, Jovan?" Ian asked. "Are you okay? What's wrong?"

"Come to the house, please. I have something to show you."

Jovan sat on the staircase. She had been there since Ian left with the clothing and the shoes Cordell wore the night of Sarah's murder. The stains looked like blood to him, too. He was taking things in for testing. He would call her as soon as he learned anything.

When he left, more than two hours ago, Jovan watched him close the door as she sat on the staircase. She remained there, slowly coming to the realization that Cordell might have actually killed Sarah. Her husband could be a murderer. And to her, it made sense. Cordell could get angry. He could get furious if he didn't get what he wanted. He had told Jovan he didn't want children now. It hadn't been any different for Sarah. Maybe she wanted to keep the baby and had told Cordell.

The phone rang, and Jovan jumped. She waited for the answering machine to pick up. "Hey Jovan." It was Mark. "I saw Detective Davenport come by. You okay? Gimme a call, or come over. Bye."

"Did you kill Cordell, Mark?" Jovan asked. She didn't want to believe he could kill, but it all came together so seamlessly. Cordell was sleeping with Sarah. Mark knew. Any man who had that kind of information had to want to see the man dead. Cordell got Sarah pregnant. Cordell killed Sarah because he didn't want the child and Sarah did. Mark's first inclination was to think Cordell did it, so what did he do? Killed Cordell in retaliation.

If her writing of mysteries taught Jovan anything, it was that if the solution seemed too good to be true, it usually was. Despite that, she couldn't help but feel that everything she thought was true. She had been married to a murderer. She had begun to like a murderer. Because of these two things, she was a very stupid woman.

There was a knock at the door. Jovan threw her hands up and yelled, "Go away and leave me alone."

"Jovan. You okay? Let me in."

Jovan sighed and yelled, "Come in."

Timothy walked in and stopped after shutting the door. "Jo, what's going on?"

"Absolutely nothing," Jovan said. She laughed. "Things are just great."

"Don't do that, Jo. Don't act as if everything's okay. Talk to me."

"Do you really want to know, Timmy?" Timothy stood in front of Jovan. Nodded. "Your brother took my whole life away." Timothy's eyes almost popped out of his head from the bitterness in Jovan's voice.

"I loved him, and he never loved me," she continued. "He cheated on me. He lied to me. He used me, and now..." She stopped. She didn't want to talk any more. She didn't want to do anything anymore. She suddenly felt exhausted, and thinking and talking were not on her list of priorities. Timothy reached out to her. She stared at his hand before finally taking it. He walked her into the living room and led her to the loveseat. Jovan fell beside him and lowered her head on his shoulder.

"I'm so sorry you have to go through this, Jo," he whispered into her hair. "I didn't know Cordell was doing you wrong."

"I thought," she began, "I thought he loved me. I wouldn't care about the money if I knew he loved me. I feel so stupid." Timothy wrapped his arms around her and pulled her close.

"You're not. Come on, you're stronger than this, Jo." Timothy broke their embrace and stared at her. His hands stroked her flyaway hair. "I want you to do something for me, okay?"

Jovan wiped her eyes and nodded.

"Go upstairs, run a bath, and relax. I'll make some tea and see if you have anything to eat, and I'll bring it up to you."

"You don't have to do that, Timmy," she replied. "I can—"

Timothy rose and helped her up. "Go," he said. "Please? I want to help you for a change."

Jovan stood on tiptoe and kissed Timothy on his cheek. "Thanks."

Timothy watched Jovan make it up the stairs before he turned to the kitchen.

Jovan tossed and turned in her sleep. Her mind was full of visions, none positive. In her dreams, she replayed the day before, the tears, the possible truth about Cordell, the fact that she did not know her own husband. She was left in a tailspin, not able to talk to anyone about her pain, not even Cheyenne. That is, until Timothy appeared at the right time to help fish her out of a looming depression.

Jovan woke up with a start and found herself in the guest bedroom she stayed in. Beside her on the bed lay Timothy, fully dressed. Despite all the drama of her life these days, Jovan smiled as she remembered how attentive Timothy had been, fixing her dinner and tea, getting her into bed, and making sure she ate everything on the tray. He even offered to stay, just in case she wanted to talk.

Her hand shook as she went to touch Timothy's jaw. His skin was as smooth and chocolate as Cordell's had been. They had the same long lashes and full lips, a shade lighter than their skin. Her fingers were scant millimeters from touching his lips when her phone rang.

She jumped and looked at the clock. It read 7:15. Timothy barely moved from the sound, but he did stir when Jovan leaned over him to snatch up the phone on the nightstand. Crossing back over, his eyes opened and connected with Jovan's. She looked away.

"Hello?" she answered huskily. Her head turned toward her office when she heard the phone in there ringing. She slowly slipped out of bed and padded through the bathroom to her office.

"Girl!" It was Cheyenne.

"Hey, Sis." Jovan yawned into the phone. "Grand Central Station here this morning. Got another call on my office phone."

"That's probably Mom," Cheyenne said.

"How would you know? Don't answer that. Hold on." Jovan snatched up the cordless phone that sat perched atop her desk. "Hello?" she answered.

"Baby."

"Hey, Mom," Jovan answered. "Look, I got you on this phone, and Cheyenne is holding on the house phone, and…" The line beeped. "My God," Jovan cried out. "What the hell is going on? Hold on, Mom." Jovan picked up the other phone. "Chey, still here? It was Mom, but someone is on the other line of the phone. Hold on."

Jovan switched back to her office phone and clicked over. "Yeah?" she said in aggravation.

"Jovan, this is Elyse. Whatever channel *This Morning* comes on down there, turn to it, now."

"Why? What's going on?"

"Just do it. Please, hurry up."

"Okay, I'll get back to you in a minute. Mom is on the other line, and Cheyenne is on the house phone."

"I'll talk to you then, bye."

"What is going on?" Jovan muttered again, sighing. Sitting down behind her desk, she grabbed the remote control and turned on the TV, selecting channel 2. *This Morning* was a syndicated news show that aired every morning. Timothy stumbled into the office, and Jovan placed her finger to her mouth, signaling him to keep quiet.

183

"Okay, ladies," Jovan said, speaking loud enough for both her mother and Cheyenne to hear her, "I'm assuming you all were calling for me to check out *This Morning*, so I got it on."

"I hope you're sitting down," Cheyenne said.

"What could possibly be so interesting to me on the..." Jovan was halted by the sight of Alisha Stewart sitting on the set of *This Morning*, along with the host, Jeffrey Talisman.

"What is Alisha doing on there?" Jovan asked herself. As Timothy came to her side, she turned the volume up.

"Welcome back to *This Morning*," Jeffrey said in his most cheerful voice. "Today, I'm here with Miss Alisha Stewart, the interim president of Anderson Technologies. As we all know, the ever popular author, Jovan Parham-Anderson, suffered a tremendous loss with the murder of her husband and Anderson Technologies' founder and president, Cordell Anderson."

Jovan sat with her mouth gaped open, listening. "As of today," Jeffrey continued, "the killer is still on the loose; however, the investigation in Maryland has been focused on two people, Jovan and her twin, Cheyenne Parham."

"What the hell?" Jovan exclaimed.

"We have to kill her," Cheyenne seethed through the phone.

"Why is she making such crazy accusations?" Jovan's mother asked on the other phone.

"What accusations?" Jovan questioned.

"Alisha Stewart was kind enough to come talk to us about the situation," Jeffrey said. "As a close acquaintance of Mr. Anderson's and essentially his second in command at Anderson Technologies, Ms. Stewart felt it urgent to talk publicly about her qualms with the investigations."

"Close acquaintance, my ass," Jovan and Cheyenne growled in unison. Timothy stood behind Jovan and kneaded her shoulders and neck.

"Yes, I did," Alisha spoke, smoothing her hair behind her right ear. She was playing the role of a concerned employee and friend of Cordell's to the tee. Her attire was somber, a dark brown linen pantsuit, the opposite of what she would normally don—something short and bright in color.

"The investigation has been amateur at best," Alisha continued. "There is no proof that anyone other than Jovan or Cheyenne had anything to do with the murder of Mr. Anderson. It's been written in every newspaper in the country—no fingerprints, no weapon, no breaking and entering, no tampering with the alarm, nothing. Someone close to Mr. Anderson must have committed the crime...and well, Jovan and Cheyenne do make their living writing about murder..."

Jeffrey chuckled. "What about the rumor that you and Cordell Anderson were having an affair?" Jeffrey asked.

"Totally unfounded," Alisha said, without a flinch. "I cared for Mr. Anderson, yes; however, he and I only had a professional relationship."

"She is lying through her capped teeth," Cheyenne screamed.

"Is she stupid or something? The police have all the e-mails and letters between her and Cordell. She isn't credible."

"You know that, I know that, and you best believe Ian will tear into her ass once she gets back here," Jovan responded. Her voice was serene, a stark contrast to her sister's.

"I can't believe *This Morning* would allow her to make such a spectacle of herself," Jovan's mother said in a huff. "They have to know she's lying."

"Oh, they do," Jovan answered. "They know, and they don't care. Chey and I love to write and do well at it. That has generated a lot of publicity for us, normally good. With Cordell's murder, everyone is trying to find an angle to get a piece of the action. *This Morning* has jumped on that bandwagon and convinced Alisha to make an ass out of herself."

"What are we going to do?" Cheyenne asked.

"Like I don't have enough to deal with now." Jovan looked upward and saw Timothy looking down at her with a slight smile on his face. His fingertips pressed gently against Jovan's temples and massaged her. She mouthed, *thank you.* Jovan decided to keep to herself about the pants until she knew something definitive. Instead, she added, "Do you know that Cordell was taking money from our joint account and that his own individual account was just about cleared?"

"What?" her mother and Cheyenne replied.

"Chey, hang up. I'm gonna call you and make this a three-way." Jovan dropped the house phone and dialed Cheyenne. When she had both her mom and Cheyenne on the phone, she spoke again.

"I went to see Deborah Gianni yesterday because I wanted to know that my finances were in order."

Timothy pulled up one of the high back chairs and swiveled Jovan around to face him. He opened his hands and lowered them to Jovan's feet, silently asking her for one. She blushed, wanting to keep away from Timothy's kindness. But nonetheless, she gave him one of her pedicured feet. He massaged her feet while she talked on the phone. Jovan closed her eyes to block Timothy from her view. She bit down on the inside of her cheek to keep from moaning.

"Deborah told you that Cordell was spending the money?" Cheyenne asked.

"More or less. Fortunately, my account was not tampered with, and the money he took from our joint account he replaced every month as well."

"Girl, why didn't you call and tell me this yesterday?"

"If I called you or Mom every time something has gone wrong since Cordell's death, we'd never sleep," Jovan answered. "Besides, I didn't feel like talking yesterday. I just wanted to sleep away the problem." She and Timothy shared a smile.

"Well, Baby," their mother spoke, "you can't sleep this away. Alisha has pretty much stated that you or Cheyenne or both killed Cordell."

"Yeah, what are we going to do now?" Cheyenne asked. "I opt for sending her to Siberia somewhere. That is after we have our way with her."

"I'm going to make a visit to Anderson Technologies this afternoon," Jovan replied. "I'm sure she's jetting back here as soon as possible, and I'll have a few choice words for her when I see her."

"Ooh, can I come?" Cheyenne asked.

"No, this is something I'll have to do on my own," Jovan answered. "Besides, I don't want any witnesses."

Jovan ended the call with Cheyenne and her mother. She sat, staring off into nothing. She couldn't tell them about Cordell's pants. Not yet. The minute she learned anything concrete, she would tell everybody. Timothy included.

"Stop thinking," Timothy said as he massaged the instep on her right foot. "Alisha can't do anything to hurt you."

"I'm not thinking."

"Yes, you are. Your right eye closes slightly when you're in deep thought."

Jovan couldn't speak; however, a tear slid from her left eye, dropping down onto her pajama top. She removed her foot from Timothy's lap and attempted to get up from her seat, but Timothy took her by the shoulders and made her look at him.

"What's wrong?" he asked. "Why are you crying?"

"I feel sick," she replied, still struggling to get out of his grip. "This feels wrong. I shouldn't be enjoying this. You shouldn't be here."

"I thought we were friends." Timothy sounded hurt.

"We are, but this, the foot rub, staying over. It's too much." Timothy let her go. "You know what's messed up? You know that my right eye closes when I'm deep in thought.

Cordell probably couldn't have told me what my middle name is. It's sick. Hell, I could have been with you instead of your good for nothing brother."

Timothy tried to approach Jovan, but she backed away. When her back bumped against the wall, Timothy closed the distance between them.

"No," Jovan said weakly, her hands pressed against Timothy's chest. "I'm lonely right now, feeling sorry for myself. I don't trust you to be close to me. I don't trust myself."

Timothy took hold of Jovan's hands and kissed each before pressing against her and hugging her close. "I just want to be there for you, Jo," he said. His lips grazed Jovan's forehead. "I'm here for you, okay?"

"Okay," she said.

With reluctance, Timothy stepped away from Jovan and went back to her bed where he sat and put on his shoes. Jovan remained silent as she watched him grab his jacket and head down the stairs and to the door. The less she said, she felt, the better off she would be.

"You gonna be okay?" Timothy asked.

"As okay as I can be," Jovan replied. Timothy kissed Jovan's forehead again before opening the door. Mark stood on the other side, holding a white bag and a tray with two cups of coffee. He and Timothy stared each other down before Timothy finally walked away.

To use the word *awkward* for the situation would have been an understatement. Mark faced Jovan and neither said a word for several uncomfortable seconds.

Mark broke the silence with, "That has to be Cordell's brother. Looks just like him."

Jovan nodded. "It is."

Mark lifted the bag. "Brought some cinnamon buns and coffee." When Jovan didn't respond, he added, "Did I interrupt anything between you and..."

"Timothy."

"Timothy?"

"No."

"Okay, so, well, why the cold, silent treatment?"

Jovan closed the door behind Mark and walked into the living room. Mark followed. She walked around the living room, holding her head and trying to find the right words to say, *Um excuse me, did you kill my husband?* Or, *I'm sorry, my husband might have killed your wife.*

"Sit down please," she said.

Mark placed the coffee and the buns on the coffee table and took a seat on the sofa. He clasped his hands together and looked up to Jovan.

"What is going on?" he asked.

"Okay, look." Jovan stopped pacing and stood in front of Mark. She wrung her hands and waited for her stomach to stop doing flips before saying, "You and I are on the up and up, right?"

"Of course," he answered. "I already told you that."

"Now I need you to be 100% serious with me, Mark. No bullshitting. And I swear to God I will be truthful to you. Okay?"

Mark grabbed Jovan's hand and pulled her onto the sofa. "Jovan, damn it, just tell me."

She took a breath and said, "This is hard, okay? Jesus. It's not every day my life becomes a freaking made-for-TV movie."

After a moment, she said, "I have something to tell you, and then I have something to ask you. It's really important that you listen and that you answer honestly. My life, your life, and my feelings depend on it."

Mark's eyes widened and he nodded.

Jovan twisted around until she was face to face with Mark. She took his hands in hers and said, "I found a pair of Cordell's pants that might've had blood on them."

Mark tried to pull his hands away, but Jovan wouldn't let him. "I don't know what was on the pants. I'll probably find out tomorrow," she added. "But my gut...my gut tells me that it's Sarah's blood." Jovan watched Mark's tanned face blanch. His green eyes darkened and became moist.

"You trying to tell me that Cordell might've killed Sarah?"

She nodded.

He cleared his throat and closed his eyes. "What's your question?" he asked.

"Please look at me, Mark," Jovan said. When he did, she wiped his wet eyes with her thumbs. "I think I already have the answer to this question, but I have to ask, okay?"

"Okay."

"Did you kill Cordell?" Mark stood and marched to the door, Jovan hot on his heels. "Don't leave, Mark," she yelled. She ran to the door and blocked his exit. "I don't think you did it. I don't. I don't want to believe it. I want to make sure that we are in the clear. I want to protect us." Jovan reached out and took handfuls of Mark's t-shirt. "I have no idea what the hell we're doing, but I just need to hear you say you didn't do it, and that will be the end of that."

"I didn't do it," he said. Jovan fell against him and wept. She sighed as Mark's arms tightened around her. "Do you want me to take a polygraph?" he asked.

Jovan tilted her head to face Mark. "No, I believe you."

"I think I should. I think you should, too."

"My lawyer was looking into it. For me and Chey."

"Let's contact Detective Davenport and see what he thinks."

"Okay."

Mark kissed Jovan's forehead and then her lips, and she gave her first real, albeit small, smile of the day. She didn't feel like things were going to be okay, but she did feel quiet in her head. For now.

190

Chapter 18

Hours after Mark left, Jovan let her mind move from Mark and Cordell and Sarah and Timothy to Alisha. She funneled her anger into the visit she was going to pay the trophy home wrecker. Jovan wanted to make a statement when she walked into Anderson Technologies. She wanted everyone to know that she was confident, self-assured, and fought for what was hers. She was feeling dark and mysterious and volatile, and she wanted to make sure that when Alisha saw her, that was the image she conveyed. After selecting a black Versace, two-piece suit, one that hung nicely against her short, curvaceous stature, Jovan slipped into a pair of black Prada sling backs.

Her makeup was minimal, except for the dark red lipstick she slashed across her lips. She had pulled her hair back severely into a chignon, which gave her face an air of snobbishness. It worked for the occasion. For final clothing panache, she lazily threw a red silk scarf around her neck, bringing out the thin red pinstripes in her black suit. Once she slipped on her sunglasses and reached to pick up her small black Prada handbag, Jovan felt ready for war.

"Classy and dressed to kill," she whispered before exiting her home to pay a visit to Alisha Stewart.

Anderson Technologies was abuzz, not from busy employees, but from the fast moving mouths of the gossipers who worked for the company. When Jovan stepped off the elevator onto the main floor, you would have thought E.F. Hutton himself had spoken. Silence enveloped the entire floor, and except for Mallory, no one breathed a word.

"Hello, Mrs. Anderson," Mallory chirped. Jovan rolled her eyes.

"Hello, Mallory. Is Alisha in?"

Mallory was excited. She could barely sit in her seat.

"Yes, she just returned," Mallory answered. "From New York."

Jovan nodded, still having not removed her sunglasses. Taking a breath, she slowly stepped down the long corridor that led to Cordell's office. She felt the gaze of everyone she passed. She heard their loud whispers. If they wanted to see a fight, she thought, they just might get one today. She turned the corner, and three doors up, stopped in front of a closed door. No pomp and circumstance, no knocking or being polite.

It was beyond that now. Jovan barged into the office, slamming the door behind her, the force literally rocking the framed pictures that lined the wall. Alisha jumped from behind the desk with the phone still against her ear.

"I'll call you back," Alisha said into the phone, hanging it up.

"Who are you on the phone with?" Jovan asked, finally slipping her sunglasses off and placing them into her handbag. "Another tabloid or talk show to spread lies to?"

Alisha smirked. She was nervous, even scared of the angered presence that Jovan exuded; however, she knew that the show today would rile Jovan up, and seeing Jovan here, she knew her thoughts were right on the money.

"Oh, so I take it you saw me on *This Morning*?" Alisha asked, flinging her strawberry-colored hair over her shoulder. "They say the camera adds ten pounds, but I think I looked absolutely fabulous, don't you?"

Jovan didn't flinch; she didn't stir. She remained cool, angrily cool. "You looked great," she commented, striding further into the office, taking a seat directly in front of the desk opposite the standing Alisha. She took her time crossing her legs and smoothing her pants leg before continuing. "But looks can be deceiving, as I'm sure you are aware."

"And how were my looks deceiving?" Alisha asked, sitting down behind the desk.

"For one, anyone who has ever been around you for longer than five minutes knows that you aren't conservative. You aren't mature-looking, sophisticated. You normally would have worn something flashy, trashy, and very unclassy."

Alisha's left eye twitched. "And another thing," Jovan continued, "anyone with access to Precinct 3 or just half a brain cell would know that there is substantial proof that you and Cordell did indeed have an affair, and that this proof will come to light…and soon."

Alisha laughed. "You would let the whole world know that your husband had been playing you for a fool? That information isn't even relevant to the case at hand, so the police aren't even worrying about it."

"You really are stupid," Jovan quipped, resting her hands upon her knee. Alisha was slightly rocked by Jovan's cool veneer. She didn't know how to play her…or if she could be played.

"Did my husband fuck you into your position?" Alisha took in a sharp breath, as if slapped across the face. "Sure, you're pretty, beautiful in fact, but not very smart. Do you think I care what the public thinks of me?"

"Without the public, who will continue to make you the darling of the literary world?" Alisha shot back.

"Alisha, the books that Cheyenne and I write will continue to sell because we're excellent writers," Jovan stated simply. "And, unfortunately, bad press is good press. This whole, shitty situation really has nothing to do with me. I didn't kill Cordell. Neither did Cheyenne. Anything that Cordell's done, he did, not me.

"Every day, I learn new things about my husband, nothing positive. I'm not going to let his shady dealings affect my life. Point blank."

"So you're completely untouched, unfeeling about all of this?"

"Of course not, but you know what? I have a clear conscience, and I definitely don't feel the need to go on national television and slander innocent people for sheer pleasure."

A panic came over Alisha, and silent tears fell from her eyes.

"Oh, don't cry yet," Jovan said, "because I'm not done with you." Alisha rose, her eyes questioning. "Do you think I came here just to slap your wrist for embarrassing me and my family on television?"

"Why did you come here?" Alisha asked, steeling herself and trying unsuccessfully to control the quiver that took home in her bottom lip.

"There are so many reasons." Jovan smiled, drumming her fingers along her knee. "I don't know where to begin, so let me just jump in. One, you will be hearing from my lawyer about your little stunt today on TV. Did you think you could call me a killer and not suffer any ramifications?" Jovan asked, her nostrils flaring, the only sign of anger coming from her icy appearance. "Two, as of this moment, you are fired."

"What?" Alisha cried. "You can't do that."

"Oh, but I can," Jovan responded, nodding. "You see, Anderson Technologies, as well as the few dollars the two of you managed to keep within the company now belong to me. "I was a fool to let you stay after Mel Stein came to me about the discrepancies. Today, however, I see more clearly. I'm more focused, and there's simply no need to have you here any longer."

"You can't do this to me." Alisha came around the desk, looking down at Jovan. "This company will fail without me."

"Well, there may not even be a company when I'm through. Whatever the fate of Anderson, it doesn't matter.

You'll be out of a job."

"You bitch," Alisha screamed, trying to grab at Jovan and wrench her from the chair. Jovan was quick, moving to the side before bouncing out of her seat. "You're just doing this because Cordell loved me…me! I won't let you get away with this."

"He loved you. He screwed Sarah. She carried his baby. Hell, he might have even killed her because of it. It's so funny because you're just this small dot on the spectrum of insanity." Jovan leaned into Alisha, causing Alisha to lean back onto the desk.

"Don't get mad now because you tried playing with the big boys and in return, they kicked your ass. You screw my husband. You help in taking money from my husband's company. You go on TV and slander my sister and me, and then you have the nerve to threaten me now? You should consider yourself damn lucky I don't beat you right here and now."

"You wouldn't dare," Alisha yelled. With Alisha's words, Jovan stood straight, raised her left hand, and hauled it across Alisha's alabaster face with a hard, quick slap.

Alisha grunted.

"Don't you ever, as long as your frail white ass exists, ever try to dare me," Jovan screamed. She looked down at the tearful Alisha, who had blood trickling from her mouth and nose. The sight extinguished some anger from Jovan, but not quite enough. She still felt like a volcano not yet flowing with hot molten lava. She did, however, step back from a shaken Alisha and took hold of her handbag that lay on the seat she was sitting in.

"Once upon a time," Jovan began, her eyes serious, "there was a young woman, naïve and talented, who loved with her heart on her sleeve. She fell in love with a man whom she believed was her happily ever after."

Jovan reached into her purse and retrieved her sunglasses, flipping them on. "The young woman's prince charming was murdered," Jovan continued, "and she found out he was truly a frog with a toad as a mistress. The young woman locked up her heart, tossed away her naiveté, and from then on ruled her life like those around her."

Alisha looked at Jovan with eyes of wonderment, wanting to know the significance of this tale. "The moral?" Jovan asked, watching as Alisha wiped at her nose and mouth with a tissue from the box on the desk. "The moral is simple. Don't fuck with me. I'm living like the big boys now. I'm a quick learner and have mastered a lot thus far.

"The old Jovan would have gone to her tower, crying, hoping for the best. The new me, however," she added, with a wry, almost wistful look, "is coming out fighting. Be warned."

Cheyenne paced her apartment, her cell phone pressed tight against her ear.

"Jo, are you there," she said into Jovan's voicemail. "Did you go see Alisha? Call me. I'm doing something big tonight, and I need to tell you about it. You know how you can always calm me down when I'm feeling frazzled. Are you there? Okay, call me when you get in. Love ya."

Cheyenne needed Jovan to convince her that she wasn't a desperate, single woman trying to grab onto the first man who showed interest. She needed someone to tell her that before Ian arrived. All day long, her mind filled with negative thoughts about asking Ian to come to her place. Was it a good idea? Was she desperate for asking him to come the very next day? While her mind played tricks on her, her heart remembered the glow and smile on Ian's face, and it confirmed and reaffirmed for her that she wasn't the only one feeling euphoric about the upcoming date.

"Any minute now," she whispered to herself, feeling the flutter in her stomach. Her apartment was spotless, her orange chicken and lo-mein was in a warming dish waiting to be devoured, and Cheyenne was busy styling her hair into a smooth, sleek bob. After changing into a wardrobe of outfits, Cheyenne finally decided to go with a casual look and chose a soft, navy, crewneck top and a pair of her favorite, fitted blue jeans. She added her navy-colored mules for the final touch.

She was in her kitchen, taking out two wine glasses and a bottle of white wine when the soft knock at her front door caused her to almost drop the wine.

"Come on, girl," she whispered, rubbing the willies from her stomach. "You can do this." Try as she might, she couldn't contain the smile that lit her face when she opened the door.

"Good evening, Miss Parham," Ian said, smirking, despite the professional tone of his voice. "I was hoping I could ask you a few questions."

Cheyenne swallowed to keep from laughing before responding, "I guess. Just for a little while." As Ian entered, Cheyenne whispered, "I have a date tonight."

Inside, the two walked into the living room, laughing uncontrollably. "Now, was there really a reason for the Dick Tracy moment?" Cheyenne asked, before sitting on the sofa. "Have a seat."

Ian sat beside her and replied, "Well, you never know. Somebody could be hiding in your stairwell, hoping to catch you in the act."

"Whatever." Cheyenne chuckled as her eyes scoured her apartment. From the living room where they sat, one could see every room in the apartment, minus the bedroom and bathrooms, which were hidden behind doors. Cheyenne fell in love with the apartment at first sight, citing its lack of walls as a major selling point. To her, the big area was a canvas on which she could section off and draw her own rooms. With her creativity, she had done just that.

When her eyes came back around and landed on Ian, she didn't speak until she began to feel antsy under his scrutiny. "What?" She laughed. "Something wrong?"

"No, everything is just fine." He smiled back. "You look so beautiful." Cheyenne shushed him with the waving of her hands.

"Get outta here," she spoke. "A shirt and jeans hardly make someone beautiful. And you need to stop being all forward. It's so not like you."

It was Ian's turn to laugh. "Maybe it's the fact that I'm here and we're not discussing the case," he began, continuing to stare at Cheyenne, "but I feel free to say what's on my mind. Is that a problem?"

"Of course not. I would be insulted if you didn't tell me what was on your mind."

Ian reached out with his left hand and caressed Cheyenne's cheek. Her eyes fluttered closed. Just as her eyes began to open,

Ian's lips came into view as they descended onto her lips for a brief kiss. Cheyenne moaned, immediately trying to squelch the burning heat that surfaced from her. "Kissing you was on my mind," he whispered, winking at her.

"You are so bold," she said, smacking at him. "Come sit at the dining room table. Dinner is ready, and you need something else to do with your mouth."

Ian moved across the room to Cheyenne's Nydala dining set while she retreated to the kitchen. Though Cheyenne entered the kitchen through a swing door, the island that connected the open space with the kitchen allowed Ian to still see her, busily moving around. Sitting on one of the black and oak veneered chairs, Ian surveyed the apartment.

"You really do have eclectic taste," he said. He viewed the dining area in one corner, her living area on the other side of the room and her computer area next to the door that led to her bedroom. "I would like to thank IKEA for my beautiful place," she said, exiting the kitchen with a steaming tray. The dining table was already set with black and brown cutlery and plates. "I always said that when I got a place of my own, I would IKEA it to death."

Ian chuckled, taking a deep sniff of the tray Cheyenne sat at the table. "Wow, smells delicious," he said. "Orange chicken, right?"

"Yep, hope you like."

"Love is the operative word."

Cheyenne smiled. "Well, lemme get the wine and glasses, and we can chow down."

As Cheyenne turned on her heels to get the wine and glasses, Ian watched the soft sway of her backside and sighed. "Behave," he said to himself under his breath.

After dinner, Cheyenne found herself sitting on the sofa with Ian as they shared wine. Maybe it was the loosening of the lips from the alcohol or perhaps it was how comfortable the pair seemed with each other, but conversation flowed seamlessly. They talked as if they had always known each other and about things most people shared after being together as a couple.

"I'm sorry," Cheyenne whispered as she rested her hand on Ian's raised knee.

"It's okay," Ian said, a brief sadness swishing past his eyes. "At the time, I felt like my world was over. My parents were very important to me. Like yours are to you and Jovan."

"But to lose them both." Cheyenne frowned. "Who was there for you?"

"No one. I was an only child, and I didn't have uncles or aunts. I was 25, out of college, and in the police academy. When my parents died in the car crash, I had to comfort myself."

Cheyenne felt tears sting her eyes as she took a breath.

"Now don't get weepy on me," he said, smiling. "I've gotten over the pain. It was hard, but now I focus on the joy they brought to my life, while at the same time, continuing to make them proud by living a good life."

"You definitely are an inspiration," Cheyenne whispered, her voice still tight. "Losing your parents, your divorce. I'm surprised you're even looking at women after everything she did to you."

"Oh, I haven't been," Ian insisted, laughing. He placed his glass on the coffee table. Cheyenne followed suit. "Since the divorce two years ago, I never glance at the opposite sex unless it is to question them in a case. I guess I was still in the *licking my wounds* phase."

"So," Cheyenne said. "What made you look at me?"

Ian smiled, shyly, causing Cheyenne to laugh. "Wow." She chuckled. "You can kiss me on a whim, but blush when I ask an innocent question."

"Do you really want to know?" he asked.

"'Fess up, Detective."

"Truth is, on the most horrific day of your and Jovan's lives, I was like wow. I saw all that fire and attitude and have not been able to stop thinking about you since."

"Whoo," Cheyenne said in a low whistle. She felt her heart triple beating under her skin and her entire body flushed. "All that, huh?" she asked.

"Mmm hmm." He nodded. "I had questioned your innocence that day and was still attracted to you."

"Gee, thanks." Ian inched closer to Cheyenne, resting his left hand to the right of her, his face directly in front of hers.

"I know you're innocent now," he whispered, his warm, sweet breath brushing along her face. "I also know I shouldn't be here, but I want to stay away unless you want me to go."

Ian kissed Cheyenne. Her hands stroked along his face, around to his neck, deepening their kiss.

"No," she whispered into his lips. "I don't want you to go."

As Ian lowered himself onto a reclining Cheyenne, tucked away in the back of his mind was the hope of quickly solving the case, so he and Cheyenne wouldn't have to hide their feelings. Cheyenne had the same thought.

Chapter 19

Sweat poured from Jovan and Cheyenne's faces. In the small white box of a room, the girls took turns slamming a blue ball into the wall.

"Got it," Jovan yelled, propelling her body to her left, connecting racquet to ball before landing hard on the shiny, hardwood floor. In an instant, she was back up, though hobbling a bit, and when the ball came back to her, she angled it into a corner, a move that had the ball whizzing by Cheyenne. "I win," Jovan said, raising her tank top in an unladylike manner to wipe her face.

"Dang." Cheyenne puffed. "You spanked me—15-3. You eat your Wheaties this morning or something?"

"Girl, I feel like a million bucks. Wanna go another match?"

Cheyenne shook her racquet at Jovan. "Hell no." She laughed. "I think beating me 15-6 and 15-3 tells me that I won't be beating you today. Let's head to the cafeteria for breakfast."

Picking up their towels, balls, and racquet cases, they turned off the light in the racquetball court and stepped out into the hallway. A few stragglers were lingering, watching games, waiting to use a court. Several people stood out front of Jovan and Cheyenne's court. Jovan could read the onlookers' minds, but instead of getting angry, she waved her racquet at the small crowd, as did Cheyenne, and spoke. "Good morning."

Turning on their heels, they continued down the hallway, watching the other early birds who were up sweating it out on the court.

"Sis, you were a little lethargic out there today," Jovan quipped, playfully jabbing Cheyenne in the side with her racquet.

"Oh, just because I'm not superwoman doesn't mean I wasn't giving it my all." Jovan raised her brow at Cheyenne, who chuckled. "Okay, so I was a tad bit tired, but I still didn't want you to win both games."

They entered the cafeteria, and Jovan grabbed a tray and utensils and asked the cook for a plate of scrambled eggs, sausage, and pancakes.

"After whipping your butt this morning, I'm starving," Jovan joked, ducking a swing from Cheyenne. As soon as the two were seated, they made eyes at one another.

"There's obviously a reason for your glow," the sisters said simultaneously. "Don't you think the twin thing is getting a bit old?" Jovan asked.

"Hey, as long as you and I exist, we'll never get out the other's head," Cheyenne answered. "So anyway, what's up with you? After yesterday and Alisha on *This Morning*...what happened?"

Jovan took a swallow from her orange juice. The cafeteria was cool and quickly dried her sweat, but left her with a chill that edged up her spine. Shaking it out, she replied, "You wouldn't believe me if I told you."

"Ooh, did you smack her? Please tell me you smacked her."

"Now, now, Chey, didn't Mom teach us that violence never paid? Look at you, wanting World War III and whatnot."

"Girl, shut up, just tell me you hit her, and I'll be happy for the rest of the day."

Jovan shook her head. Raising her right hand to the nape of her neck, she rubbed there. "Okay, I smacked her," she replied smoothly.

Cheyenne dropped her fork and stared at Jovan, gaped mouth.

"What?" Jovan laughed. "You said you wanted to know. There, I told you." She moved both hands to the back of her head and tightened her ponytail. "I went to Anderson

Technologies cool as ice, Sis," she explained. "My clothes, my walk, my voice, everything was just too smooth. Alisha didn't know what hit her—"

"Until you hit her." Cheyenne roared.

"Exactly, but she deserved it, Chey. She was so unbelievably smug and dared me not to. I told her to clear her things and get the hell out of my company, and before I left, she got a taste of my anger."

"I can't believe you did it," Cheyenne whispered. "I mean I'm glad you did. She deserved it, but it's so against your nature to smack or attack."

"I know, and some of my excitement left when I saw the blood come from her nose and mouth—"

"Dang, how hard did you hit her?"

"Hard enough for her to know that I'm not playing with her anymore."

"Damn," Cheyenne said, biting into a bagel. "I'm sorry I missed that, for real."

"Well, do you wanna come with me today?" Jovan asked. "I decided to go have a preliminary meeting with Jameson Burke. I want to feel him out in regards to selling Anderson to him."

"You *have* changed," Cheyenne said, eyeing her twin, what felt like for the first time. She could see a calmness radiate through Jovan's body, and she prayed that the dark cloud she and Jovan had been living under recently was on its way out. "Once upon a time, you might have let these things collect dust, praying for them to go away, but now, you're right there, handling Alisha, handling Anderson Technologies…I'm really proud of you, Jo."

Jovan winked at Cheyenne. "Thanks."

The two ate in silence for a few moments, Cheyenne looking up eventually to add, "Unfortunately, I can't go with you today. I was going to finish up our edits to *Deadly Vows* yesterday, but got sidetracked. I'm going to do that today, and then air mail it to Elyse, so we can keep everyone happy."

"Sounds like a plan." Jovan smiled, forking in eggs. "So, uh, what kept you detained yesterday?" she added with a knowing smirk.

It was Cheyenne's time to light up as her cheeks flushed and her lips curled into a smile. "With all the commotion yesterday, I forgot to tell you that I had a meeting last night that I had to prepare for."

"Meeting my ass, you had a date with Ian, so 'fess up and tell me all the details."

"Jo, it was pretty amazing," she gushed. "I was never so nervous in all my life…and so was he. After all, you and I aren't exactly cleared in the investigation yet—"

"But we will be," Jovan reassured her.

Cheyenne nodded. "I know, and Ian knows it, too. He finally believes us when we say we had nothing to do with Cordell's murder."

"Thank God for small favors." Jovan sighed.

"Because of the case and all, we had dinner at my place. Orange chicken and lo mein, with wine. We laughed and talked."

"Sounds like you two had a great evening." Jovan smiled wistfully, faintly remembering a time when she and Cordell were so enraptured in each other and clearly remembering her moments with Mark. She struggled to keep her thoughts on Mark to herself. She wasn't ready to share them, not even with Cheyenne.

"It was wonderful, Jo. It's going to be hard, keeping this a secret until the case is over and done with, but we're both excited about investigating the goings on between the two of us, so we'll figure out a way to make it work."

Jovan reached across the table for her sister's hands, holding them in hers. "I just want you to be happy, Chey," she whispered, her voice tightening.

DEATH AT THE DOUBLE INKWELL

"I want you to be happy, too, Jo. Someday, we're both going to receive everything we've ever wanted. Just you watch."

Tap tap tap. Taptaptaptap. Incessantly, for ten minutes straight, Jovan drummed her fingers along her steering wheel, attempting to calm her nerves. She had parted from Cheyenne with a cloudy mood. She was lucky she hadn't gotten into a car accident on her way to Burke International even though she did have her fair share of horns being blown at her. Moments of past-times flashed before her eyes, times that felt like moments from someone else's life now. She could see, so clearly, flashes of happier times with Cordell, times that made her heart ache.

For the last day, Jovan had felt so in control of her life, had felt as if she was going to be all right, that someday all this pain and deception would be a thing of the past, and she would get a chance at being happy, but as she turned off the ignition and went to unfasten her seatbelt, an odor attacked her nose, an odor so potent, she looked frantically around the car for the source.

She smelt death...blood. She saw the stained comforter, Cordell lying lifeless on the bed. In that instant, all the hatred and bitterness had evaporated. Her husband, the love of her life, had been killed, in her home, right under her nose, and to her, life had seemed to stop existing.

"Oh my God," she wailed as a monsoon of tears fell from her eyes. "I loved you so much, Cordell...why, why did this happen? Why did someone kill you? Why did you cheat on me?" Jovan beat the steering wheel as she streamed off a string of expletives. "I've never loved...and hated someone, so much in all my life. I should say fuck this company, sell it to Burke for a buck and move on with my life."

A rapping sound at her driver side window startled her. With tears in her eyes, she turned her head and came face to face with Jameson Burke.

"Are you sure you're okay, Mrs. Anderson?" Burke asked again as he and Jovan entered his office. He took his coat and Jovan's and placed them on the coat rack that stood to the right of his office door.

"Yes, I'm fine, Mr. Burke," she reassured him, rubbing her hands together for warmth, as if the heat from her body had been zapped. "You know, it's been a very stressful time for me, and sometimes one needs to release the stress."

Burke pulled out a chair for Jovan before moving behind his desk and sitting. "Please, call me Jameson," Burke spoke, softly. Jovan nodded. "I do offer you my condolences in what has to be a very hard time for you."

"Thank you, Mr. B...I mean, Jameson."

"Have there been any leads in the case?"

Jovan shook her head. "But there are some pending leads."

"You must be frightened," he responded. He lifted a small piece of lint from his charcoal gray suit.

"Me? Why would I be frightened?"

"I wouldn't want to put fear in you, Mrs. Anderson. That's not my agenda," Burke began. "But they haven't caught Cordell's killer yet. Aren't you afraid they could come back for you?"

"I'm not worried about that," she answered. "If they wanted me, they would have certainly made that known by now." Jovan squirmed a bit in her chair before continuing, "I'm sure you're not interested much in the case, except for how it pertains to the selling of Anderson Technologies, which is why I'm here, correct?"

Burke let out a small laugh full of deep timbre. "Yes, you're correct, Mrs. Anderson. I did contact you in the hopes that we could talk about you possibly selling Anderson to me. I was hoping my—" Burke's words were cut off as Jimmy barged through the door, slicking his hair with one hand and smoothing his suit jacket down with the other. Jovan's hands gripped her chair as an uneasiness settled in her.

"Jimmy Devane?" Jovan whispered, looking from Burke to Jimmy.

Jimmy threw on a smile and stepped toward Jovan. He took her hand in his and shook it. "Hello, Mrs. Anderson," he said with reverence. "I'm sorry I'm late, Burke, I had—"

"Okay, I'm confused," Jovan said, shaking her head. "You two know each other?"

Burke gave Jimmy a quick, disgruntled glance before sliding his manners back into place. "Mrs. Anderson," he began. "Jimmy is a business acquaintance of mine—"

"Yeah." Jovan groaned, rolling her eyes. "He was one of Cordell's, too." Jovan knew Jimmy wasn't the type of business acquaintance that was usually signified by that term. She knew Jimmy dealt in gambling and whatever else he could get his ratty little hands on. She just didn't know why two very successful businessmen would include him among their peers. Always having an eye for detail, Jovan noticed how the air in the room changed from one of good nature to one of tension as Jimmy entered. Was he even supposed to be here, she pondered, but didn't have enough time to think out the situation before Burke spoke.

"Mrs. Anderson," he stated, hoping to sway her attention back to the matter at hand. "I took the liberty of having my attorney draw up a proposal that describes in detail what Burke International is willing to pay for Anderson Technologies and what we'd like to have in return. Would you like to look at it now?"

Jovan stole one more glance at Jimmy, who sat to her left before responding, "Please."

Reaching across Burke's expansive desk, Jovan took hold of the proposal, quickly skimming through the 15-page document.

Burke wanted the company lock, stock, and barrel. He was offering $75 million, plus offering Jovan personally a lump sum for her stock in the company. The document stipulated that Burke planned to make Anderson Technologies a subsidiary of sorts of his own company, and within a year, incorporate the company fully into his own. He made plans to keep the majority of Anderson employees.

Jovan's mind whirled back to when Mel informed her of all the shady dealings of Cordell, and she wondered if the company was even worth $75 million. She knew that by selling the company to Burke, this chapter of her life would be closed forever; she would no longer have any thoughts lingering about Cordell or Anderson Technologies because neither would be in her life any more. A definite plus.

I did say I would sell it to him for a dollar, she thought, remembering her earlier tirade in the car. This was too big a deal to seal it now and with her uneasiness of having Jimmy in the room, Jovan thought it best to take a breather, to let Mel read through the proposal first before jumping the gun.

"I will say this," Jovan began, clearing her throat, "this proposal is very well thought out, offers nice money, and would basically clear me of ever having to think of Anderson again."

"A win all the way around, I think," Burke responded, folding his thick hands on his desk.

"However, I would like for my attorney, Mel Stein, to have a look at this."

"I would have it no other way, Mrs. Anderson. Believe me, we want this to be an extremely fair and profitable venture for the both of us."

Jovan slipped the proposal into her attaché case before

rising from the chair. Burke rose also. "I will contact Mel as soon as possible, so he and I can discuss the matter," Jovan said. "Hopefully we—you, Mel, and I—will be able to get together soon, and make this official."

Jovan cut her eyes at a sitting Jimmy who smiled at her. She shivered.

"Excellent," Burke replied, raising his hand to Jovan. She took it, feeling its hard warmth enclose hers. "I will be looking forward to talking to you again, Mrs. Anderson." With a nod and a withering glance toward Jimmy, Jovan turned and walked briskly out of Burke's office.

"Didn't I tell you not to come here?" Burke exclaimed as soon as his door was closed.

Jimmy shrugged, still sitting. "This is major, Burke," Devane said. "I wanted to be a part of this, see if Jovan would sell today…or make us wait."

"For a man who's afraid of being wrongly accused, you sure don't take precautions, do you, Devane?"

"What's that mean?" Jimmy asked.

"For God's sake, Devane, use your head. Jovan spends her life writing mysteries. You think she didn't find it suspicious, you being here? You were at her house the night Cordell was killed. It wouldn't take a genius to conclude that maybe, just maybe, you might be the killer."

"But I ain't the killer," Devane cried out, jumping from the chair. "I got an alibi. I was with you."

"You know you're not the killer, and I know that— making the police believe that would be a whole other matter."

"That detective Davenport don' already checked us out. Our alibi is tight," Devane said, his tone lowering, the panic slowly leaving him. They did have the alibi. "Jovan can think all she wants, but with that alibi, I'm in the clear."

Ian was on a mission. A mission that was sealed with the kisses he and Cheyenne shared the night before. With those kisses, he promised Cheyenne and himself that he would find the killer of Cordell Anderson, and he would do it soon. Jovan deserved to have her life back, and he deserved to bring what could be a budding relationship with Cheyenne out into the open.

He arrived at the precinct just after the sun woke up from its nightly slumber. As he did every day since the murder, he poured over every piece of evidence, of information the investigation came up with, and once again, he found himself back at point zero. There was no evidence, nothing that pointed to anyone anyway. In his attempt to place the folders of the investigation into some pile of order, his black notebook fell to the ground. As he bent to pick the opened notebook up, his eyes read *Devane and Burke?*

"If ever there was an odd couple," he whispered, sitting back in his chair. Though he had made a call to Burke's private hangar and had the log faxed to him, Ian felt the urge to get some air and to travel to Aberdeen, Maryland and check out the place in person.

Adjacent to Burke's hangar was a small building, probably offices, Ian had thought. Finding the doors unlocked at the entrance of the building, Ian walked in and found himself standing in front of a desk. There was a nameplate on the desk. Tremaine Stokes, the person he talked to on the phone.

Seconds later, a slight man walked into the office from a side door and stopped in his tracks when he saw Ian.

"Uh, may I help you?" the man asked as he walked behind the desk. Ian opened his jacket, revealing his badge.

"I'm Detective Ian Davenport, Mr. Stokes. We talked on the phone."

The man smiled and shook his head. "I'm not Mr. Stokes, Detective. My name is Lyle Cage. I'm his assistant. What can I do you for?"

"Is Mr. Stokes in?"

"Nope. Day off."

Ian leaned against the desk before saying, "Mr. Stokes was to make copies of a flight log for me."

Lyle rummaged through papers on the desk. "Well, I don't see any copies. Give me the dates, and I'll make them for you now."

This was easier than Ian thought it would be. When he talked to Tremaine on the phone, he practically had to give his first son up to get the log.

"April 14 and 15, please," he said.

Within five minutes, Ian had a warm copy of the flight log in his hands. He quickly scanned the log, sighing.

"They were right," he muttered, groaning. "Shit." Ian stood, making eye contact with Lyle. "Thank you for doing this." He shook Lyle's hand.

"No problem," Lyle replied. "From the look on your face, you didn't get what you hoped."

"You win some, you lose some." Ian nodded in Lyle's direction and turned to leave. As his hand touched the doorknob, he felt as if a massive lightning bolt had struck him.

He jumped back and turned around. "Hey, tell me something," Ian began, feeling jittery, hoping that this new instant brainstorm would come up with positive results.

"I'll try," Lyle said.

"The night of Jameson Burke's flight to New York, were you here?"

"Yep." Lyle chuckled. "I'm here so often, I joke that I should just live here.

"So, you saw Burke and Devane get onto the jet?"

"Of course. They both signed the log sheet…you saw that."

But I didn't see them, Ian thought.

"Okay," Ian said, trying to curb the excitement in his belly, "Do you remember what Devane looks like? The last time I saw him, he looked like he needed a meal or two."

"You can barely miss him, literally." Lyle smacked the desk and laughed at his own joke. "He must have gotten three or four meals since the last time you saw him. The man has to weigh every bit of 300 pounds."

Bingo, Ian thought. He shook his head, laughing. "He must have found himself a woman," he said. "You know when you settle down, you tend to settle *out*, too."

"I guess that would explain why I'm so thin. No woman yet to fatten me up."

"Thank you for your help, Mr. Cage," Ian said. "I've taken up enough of your time."

"I'm sorry I couldn't be of more help."

Leaving the office, Ian whispered, "You were the best help I've had in this case." He raced to his car, adrenaline coursing all through him. He was on a mission to find Devane and ask him a few questions. His phone rang just as he sped off.

"Davenport," he answered. After a few seconds, Ian drove his car to a curb and parked. "Are you a hundred percent sure?" He banged his hand against the steering wheel. "Okay, I'll tell her."

Hanging up, Ian drove off again, this time slower, not looking forward to making his destination.

Chapter 20

Jovan and Cheyenne tapped their crystal champagne flutes together.

"How many times can I say I love you?" Jovan asked, sipping from her glass.

"As many times as you want," Cheyenne replied. "Feed my ego."

Jovan grabbed the bottle of Veuve Clicquot La Grande Dame and led Cheyenne out to the deck in the backyard. She refilled their glasses before the two sat in lounge chairs and enjoyed the smell of freshly cut grass, honeysuckles on vines, and roses from Jovan's garden.

"I guess we have made everyone happy today, huh?" Jovan asked. Cheyenne slipped an arm behind her head while she drank from her flute.

"Well, I told El that I mailed the book overnight," Cheyenne said, "and she was very surprised and ecstatic." "I'm just glad it's out of our hair now." Jovan sat up, swinging her legs around to the side. She faced Cheyenne, her eyes wet.

"Thank you for reining up the strength to finish the edits, Chey. My heart wasn't ready to do it."

Cheyenne reached out and patted Jovan's knee. "We're a team, Jo. There's no need to thank me. I had some moments of jitters as I wrote, but I knew that it would be one more thing off our shoulders."

"That it is." Jovan tilted her flute skyward and drained her glass.

"Damn, Jo, slow down." Cheyenne laughed. "You know you're not a real drinker."

Jovan filled her flute again and wrapped her hands around the cool glass. "I know," she said. She hunched her shoulders up and down and rolled them, trying to release tension that began to build between her shoulders. "Guess I just feel like I need something to numb me a bit. I'm so tired of drama. I'm surprised I still have hair. Or that it hasn't turned gray. How do we do it?"

"We just do." Cheyenne shrugged. "I know that isn't much of an answer, but it's all I have right now. I feel in my heart that everything will end soon and will be okay. You've been through so much. I don't think God would put you through too much more, so soon."

"From your lips to God's ears," Jovan said. "Sis?"

"Yeah?"

"Will you help me clean the house?" Flashes of the pile of clothes she left in the master bedroom illuminated her mind. "You know, of Cordell's belongings?"

"Of course, I will. You don't even have to ask."

Jovan rubbed her forehead and inched her fingers through her curly mess of hair. "I need him out of this house."

Cheyenne sat beside Jovan and threw an arm around her shoulder. "I'll do whatever I can to help you."

When the phone rang, Jovan stepped into the sunroom to answer it.

Timothy's voice quickly sobered her up.

"Hi," she said, turning away from the deck.

"How are you?" Timothy asked. "Been thinking about you."

"I'm fine."

"You didn't miss me?"

"I'm kinda busy right now. Chey's here."

"Oh, okay." Jovan heard the disappointment in his voice.

"Call me later?"

Jovan promised and hung up. The last thing she wanted was for Timothy to become romantically interested in her. Despite her love for him, she would never do something like that after all that had happened.

"Who was that?"

Jovan spun around to find Cheyenne leaning in the doorway leading to the deck.

"Grab the Veuve," she answered. "We can start on our late lunch." Jovan left out of the sunroom, but Cheyenne grabbed the champagne and checked the phone's Caller ID before entering the kitchen.

"Timothy called, huh?" Cheyenne said, sitting the bottle down. She picked out a strawberry in the bowl on the counter and bit into it before washing it down with champagne.

"He's lonely these days."

"And so are you." Cheyenne stood behind Jovan and massaged her shoulders. "You two being lonely together?"

"No." Jovan shirked herself out of Cheyenne's grip and pulled packages of shrimp and scallops from the fridge. "That's...it's just...no. He's my brother-in-law. Not cool."

"I know the circumstances are not the best, but—"

"No buts. Every time I see Timothy, I see Cordell, and I remember all the pain and hurt. I remember seeing him in our bed lifeless. I see all this negativity and know that nothing positive can come from it."

"Okay." Cheyenne retrieved the rice from the pantry. "Jo." Cheyenne hiccupped, her voice squeaking. "What about Mark? I mean, you like him, I think."

Jovan turned to face Cheyenne. She absentmindedly flipped a loose strand of Cheyenne's burgundy hair out of her face.

"I kind of like him, yeah," Jovan said. "It's way too soon to even give a full blown like. I can't even begin to know what I really want until all of this is over."

Cheyenne hugged Jovan. "It'll be over soon, Jo. I promise you that."

"Have you talked to Ian? You know something I don't?"

"Nope," Cheyenne answered, shaking her head. She gave Jovan a serious look before adding, "Haven't gotten that after date call."

"Don't make me laugh." Jovan smirked. "As much as I would love to hear about the Ian and Chey drama, I wanted to know if he talked to you about the case."

Cheyenne hid her huge smile behind her hand before saying, "Nope on that, too…no news is good news though."

"I guess." After several silent moments, Jovan added, "I went to see Burke today…felt like an episode of *The Twilight Zone*."

"How so?"

Jovan walked into the living room, Cheyenne in tow, and fell into the thick-cushioned chair.

"Okay, get this," she began, "Jimmy Devane was there."

"That little weasel looking guy?"

"One and the same."

"What the hell was he doing there?"

"Well, it seems that Mr. Devane is an acquaintance of all the major players here in Maryland and Lord knows where else. He didn't say too much at the meeting, but I could see this hunger in his eyes, like my signing away Anderson Technologies would be a windfall for him."

"How much did Burke offer for the business?"

"Seventy-five million, plus a lump sum for my stock in the company."

"Wow." Cheyenne low-whistled. "Sounds like a done deal to me. Hell, after all the behind-the-scene maneuvers Cordell and Alisha pulled off with AT, you'd get a nice chunk of money for a company you don't want anyway."

"I know, and believe me, I was *this* close to signing away the company, but something told me to wait, to talk this through with Mel, so I need to hook up with him and get this over and done with."

"It'll work out," Cheyenne said. She finished off her glass of champagne and smiled. "Maybe my giddy mood is affecting my senses, but I think Ian will find Cordell's killer, and things will turn around soon."

"Ever the optimist," Jovan said, trying to keep a smile on her face.

"No," Cheyenne responded. "But I'm trying to keep the faith."

There was a rap on the door, and Jovan went to answer it.

"Well hello, Ian," she said, smiling. "Come on in."

Almost immediately, Cheyenne was at the door, grinning at Ian. Almost as fast, her grin fell. "What's wrong?" she asked.

"I have the results on the blood test," he replied.

"What blood test?" Cheyenne asked.

Jovan stood, motionless. She knew the result.

"Jo, what's going on? What test? Are you okay?"

"You didn't tell her?" Ian asked.

Jovan shook her head no. "I found a pair of Cordell's pants," she said. "They're from the night Sarah was killed."

"She wasn't sure what was on the pants, so she called me," Ian continued, noticing that Jovan was about five seconds away from losing it. "She wanted to know what the stains were before she told anyone about them."

"So what are the stains?" Cheyenne asked.

"Sarah Brockman's blood," Ian answered.

"God," Cheyenne said. "That mean...no, that's not true." She looked at Jovan. "Jovan, Cordell didn't—"

"Yeah, he did," Jovan said. "That bastard killed Sarah."

"We don't have a weapon," Ian said. "But there is enough blood on his pants that suggest he was there, in the room when she died."

"He did it." Jovan laughed. "And I know why. He didn't want kids. He did want to live happily ever after with

218

Alisha and for some reason, he screwed Sarah, and she and that baby threatened all his goals. He couldn't let that happen. He was selfish. I have to give the bastard credit though. Even when he's dead, he manages to screw all of us around."

"God is good. God is good. God is good." Ian repeated his new mantra during his ride from Jovan's home to downtown Baltimore. He needed some good news today. He needed to begin putting two plus two together and getting this murder solved for everyone's sake. As he pulled his car in front of Jimmy Devane's brownstone on Park Avenue, Ian said, "What the hell is Devane doing living in one of these 'stones?'"

He knocked on the door and rocked back and forth on his heels, counting to ten before knocking again. On his third rap, the door swung open, and Jimmy appeared, draped in a black silk robe, with matching boxer shorts and nothing else.

"Detective Davenport," Jimmy spoke, spreading out each syllable like peanut butter on bread. "To what do I owe this honor?"

Ian kept his optimistic glow in check as he gave Jimmy his stern detective stare. "I had a couple of questions to ask you—"

"Lemme guess, about the Anderson case, no doubt," Jimmy said. "Didn't Burke and I already clear this up with you?"

"Well, it appears, Jimmy, that there has been a minor discrepancy with your alibi, and if you would let me in, we could clear this up."

Jimmy and Ian stared each other down, neither backing down until Ian added, "We can talk out here. After all, I'm sure your neighbors in this nice neighborhood would be happy to hear about what I've come to tell you." Ian's left brow cocked upward, and Jimmy rubbed his hand nervously over his hair.

"Come on," Jimmy said gruffly, louder than needed as he opened his door wider. Ian let out a whistle as he stepped into Jimmy's contemporary digs.

"For an *associate*," Ian began, "you keep a great looking home."

"I do what I can." Ian's eyes devoured every crevice of the living and dining areas, before moving his attention back to Jimmy, noticing his sweaty brow and roving eyes.

"Something wrong, Jimmy?" Ian asked, feeling the tension in the room increase with ferocity.

"Naw," Jimmy said, shaking his head. "You just disturbed me from—"

"From?"

Jimmy paused a beat before adding, "So what did you come here for, Davenport? You say you got news. How about you tell me now?"

With slow movements, Ian opened his jacket, taking out his pad. He pretended to be engrossed in the words on the page even though the page was blank.

"The last time I talked to you," he began, "you told me that the night of the 14th, morning of the 15th, you and Jameson Burke took his jet to New York, and then his limousine to Atlantic City, where the two of you spent the night gambling."

"Yeah," Jimmy answered, looking indifferent. "And I told you I lost my shirt that night."

"You may have lost your shirt, but you appear to have gained a whole lot of weight."

Jimmy froze. "I have no idea what you're talking about," Jimmy stuttered. The two were jolted from their conversation when a soft, yet audible thump sounded down the hall. Ian turned his attention to it.

"I guess I did disturb something," Ian responded, his eyes connecting with Jimmy. "Who you got back there?"

"That's none of your damn business, Davenport," Jimmy said, taking the defensive. "This whole conversation is meaningless…I was on the jet. I went to Atlantic City. Burke has the jet logs to prove all this, so whatever you think you've found is—"

"What I found," Ian interrupted, "was a person who didn't know he was supposed to lie about what he saw the night of the 14th when you and Burke boarded the jet."

Before a stunned Jimmy could respond, a noise came from down the hall, followed by a soft, seductive voice asking, "What's taking you so long, Baby?" Ian and Jimmy motioned toward the hallway at the same time. Alisha waltzed out into the living area, wearing only a black negligee and fire red pumps. Her hair was slightly teased and fanned out from her slender face. When her eyes finally zoned in on Davenport's figure, she stopped moving, and her already pale complexion became practically translucent.

"Well, well, well," Ian said, unable to hide the rising smirk that christened his lips. "How quickly you move on, Miss Stewart."

"You don't understand," Alisha began, rushing to Ian's side to plead her case. "Jimmy and Cordell were—"

"Shuddup, Alisha," Jimmy snarled, taking her roughly by the arm and pulling her to his side. Ian watched the interplay between the two, wondering if he would have to ask for his answers or would they volunteer them in their state of confusion.

"I was just gonna say," Alisha began, trying to unlatch Jimmy's hand from her arm. She was unsuccessful. "You two were friends. Jimmy loved Cordell like a brother. Cordell's death was hard on us all."

"So, the two of you came together in your grief to console each other?" Ian asked, wanting to laugh, but opting to remain stoic.

"Exactly," Alisha went on. "That's exactly right." Alisha looked into Jimmy's eyes as if to tell him that she would handle this. Turning her attention back to Ian, she continued, "You…

know that Cordell and I were lovers, and we loved each other deeply. We were going to be together forever—"

"Even though he was married to Jovan Parham-Anderson?"

Ian asked, crossing his arms over his chest.

"Sometimes, the things we do are the wrong things for us. Cordell realized late in his marriage that Jovan was the wrong woman for him, but he didn't want to hurt her. He had hoped that the two would split amicably."

"In this day and age?" Ian laughed. "I know he wasn't dumb enough to think that. So how do you explain Sarah Brockman?"

Ian watched Alisha's cheek burn red.

"I don't know about that," she said. "I know that Cordell loved me and just me, and while he and I were making our plans to be together, Jimmy and Cordell were friends. I didn't know Jimmy at the time...we sorta came together after Cordell's passing. We needed someone to lean on, to grieve with."

Ian looked at a silent Jimmy, who managed to contort his face into something that bore a resemblance to sorrow. Ian was ready for the show to end. "You know," he said, "this all sounds quaint and innocent enough, but your lover, the grieving Jimmy Devane? Well, it appears that he didn't go to Atlantic City the night of Cordell's murder, so he's without an alibi."

Jimmy opened his mouth to speak, but Ian once again interrupted him by adding, "Don't give me any bull, Devane. A little birdie told me that an obese man passing himself off as you got onto that jet the night of the 14th. You lied to me, and that ain't good." Ian sat on the armrest of the black sofa before adding, "I'm not leaving this place until I get some answers... we can do it here or downtown...which will it be?"

Chapter 21

*J*ovan's Sunday mornings usually entailed the same thing. Wake up at eight, shower, dress, have a little breakfast and pick up Cheyenne before eleven o'clock church service. This morning as she stepped out her shower, she had altered the plans a bit. Right after service, she would go see Mark, tell him about Cordell, and then take him and Cheyenne to the precinct and see about polygraph tests.

After toweling herself dry, Jovan dropped the towel and went pillaging through her closet for something comfortable to wear.

She heard the doorbell followed by a knock on the door.

"Lord," she muttered. She grabbed a robe, tied it tight and ran down the steps. Timothy stood on the other side, smiling as he held a bag and coffee. Instantly, Jovan thought of Mark and smiled.

"This was so sweet, Tim," Jovan said. "Come on in."

Timothy followed her up the stairs and into her office.

"Let's see what ya got," she said. She pulled out a chocolate chip muffin and snagged a coffee. "Thank you, Timmy." She kissed his cheek. She looked at him and concern rocked her. "Are you okay?"

"Yeah," he replied, nodding. Though there was some vibrancy in his big, brown eyes, there was also something vacant, something that needed to be filled. She had seen that look on him before.

"You wouldn't lie to me, would you?" she asked.

Timothy looked around the room before settling back on Jovan.

"Never," he said.

Jovan sat at the window seat, but she still watched Timothy, hoping he wasn't falling back into what he once

223

called "His Darkness."

"You never called me back yesterday," he said.

Jovan paused from eating her muffin and watched Timothy's smile diminish. "Um, I'm sorry," she said. "A lot of stuff happened yesterday. It's kind of why I'm in a bit of a rush this morning." Jovan reached up, touched her slightly damp mane, and laughed. "I must look a fright right now," she said.

"No. You don't."

Jovan noted the sultry undertone of Timothy's voice. She began to feel naked sitting there with only a robe on. She pulled the collar of her robe together and tried to act nonchalant as she smoothed the robe down over her taut thighs.

"So what's going on, Timmy?" she asked, trying to switch subjects. "How are you and your parents?"

"Detective Davenport called Mom and Dad yesterday," Timothy replied. A frown marred his handsome face. Jovan couldn't look at him. She knew what Ian had to tell. "So you know about what Cordell did?" he asked.

Jovan nodded. "Found out last night."

"I can't believe he would do that. That's not the brother I remembered. Mom's ready to hire every lawyer in America to prove his innocence."

"Of course she would. She's the mother. All I can say is that Cordell masqueraded to everybody."

Timothy rubbed his face and stared at Jovan.

"I should be getting dressed," she said, looking down at the floor. She couldn't look up. The look in Timothy's eyes scared her. Between lust and anger. Two things she never saw in Timothy before. When she attempted to stand, he took her by the hand and guided her back to the window seat.

"Can we talk for a minute?" he asked.

She nodded and whispered, "Okay." Jovan noted how he gently massaged her hands; she took in the concerned look in his eyes, but she also took in a sadness that began to build a bubble around him.

"Are you okay?" she asked. "What's wrong?"

"You know I care for you, right?" he asked. Jovan swallowed and nodded. "I've always cared for you... but there was a time when—"

"When what?" Jovan's heart began to race. She pulled Timothy onto the window seat and looked directly into his eyes. "What?"

"Cordell told me things," he said. "He made me think you were doing bad things to him."

"Bad things?" Jovan's mind sped with questions. "Like what? Did he say I was crazy? Did he say I didn't care for you? For him?"

"Just believe me when I say that they weren't good things. He was relentless about it, and for a time, I believed him. I don't know why I could ever believe you to be evil." He closed his eyes and looked away from Jovan. "You're the kindest woman I've ever met, and I believed Cordell. I feel so bad about that."

"Timothy." Jovan touched his cheek and turned his face toward hers. "Cordell made a few people believe I wasn't right in the head."

"But I shouldn't have believed that, Jo. You helped me so many times, even times when my own brother was too ashamed to be there for me. I shouldn't have believed him."

Timothy stiffened and sniffed, trying to hide the pain that threatened to show its face.

"Don't act tough with me, Timmy," she said. "Show your emotions. We've never hid them before." A stray tear escaped from Timothy's right eye. Jovan wiped it away. "Tell me. Do you believe what he said now? Do you think I'm crazy or whatever he said?"

Timothy's fingers traced along her bare neck. "No," he said. "And I'm so sorry that I did, and that all this has happened to you. You didn't deserve this."

Jovan felt her own tears run hot down her face.

"None of us deserved it," she whispered.

Timothy's soft fingers stroked the nape of Jovan's neck before sliding into her damp hair. "I would never hurt you," he said. "I'm so sorry."

Jovan froze. "Timothy," she said, but before she could finish, he kissed her and pried her lips open with his tongue.

"Jo," he whispered in her ear before kissing her there. "I'm sorry."

She wanted to yell no, to tell him to stop. She didn't want this to happen. Not between them. But the feel of Timothy parting her robe and sliding his warm hands to her breasts made Jovan's voice catch in the back of her throat.

She had forgotten how it felt to have a man touch her. She purred when Timothy batted her aroused nipples with his thumbs.

She tried not to think of Timothy as her dead husband's brother. She tried not to think that Cordell had only been dead for almost a month and a half.

"Jo," Timothy kissed into her neck. "You're so soft."

Jovan pushed Timothy away. "I can't." She panted and pulled her robe around her. Mark had told her she was soft. A dead husband wouldn't stop her. The dead husband's brother wouldn't stop her. Mark did. "I'm sorry," she said.

Timothy sat on the floor, his breathing labored.

"No matter how good this would feel," Jovan added, "it's wrong on so many levels."

Timothy crawled to her. "What levels?" he asked. His eyes were wide and wild. He looked at Jovan's mouth before taking in her eyes again.

"You're Cordell's brother. We are both in pain. We both need comfort because of the pain. Your mother would kill me."

"I don't care what my mother thinks."

Jovan reached a hand out and stroked Timothy's cheek.

"I just can't do that, Timmy. I love you, and I don't want to do something I will regret."

Timothy nodded, then leaned in and kissed Jovan fully on the mouth. "Okay," he said. "I'll respect your wishes." The kiss was good. Damn good, and Jovan mentally patted herself on the back for not backing down and deciding to get her needs fixed.

"Jovan…Cheyenne, I want you to know that the entire congregation is praying for you right now." Reverend Peters held on to the hands of the twins as they stood outside of the Mt. Airy Methodist Church. Hundreds of people filed out of the church, nodding and making nice with the Reverend's wife as he talked to the twins.

"Thank you so much," Jovan said, hugging Reverend Peters. "It's been a very trying time for us, and this was the first time since the funeral that we've been able to come to church…you know, with the press and all."

"I understand, Sister," Reverend Peters commented. "As long as you keep God in your heart, and know that He and His Son are looking out for you, all will be well, believe in that."

"We'll try," Cheyenne offered, smiling. With final hugs and goodbyes to the Reverend and his wife, Jovan and Cheyenne made their way to the parking lot, getting into Jovan's car. "Okay, what's up?" Cheyenne asked as soon as they were inside the car.

"Nothing," Jovan replied, her mind still stuck on her being on her office floor with Timothy.

"You didn't even get into the songs today. Normally you the loudest one there."

Jovan chuckled. "Well, I decided to let someone else be the star."

"Okay, fine, don't tell me." Cheyenne slipped out of her black pumps and squished her toes into the car's thick carpet. "So, are we heading to Mark's place?"

"Yeah, but first we can have a little lunch. I made some chicken salad before church."

"You go 'head, Miss Thang," Cheyenne said. "I'm starving, so put your foot on that pedal with some force."

"Aren't those Cordell's parents in front of the house?" Jovan maneuvered the car up the oval driveway, staring up at the house. Cordell's parents stood on the front steps. "I will bet any money that it's the whole Sarah and Cordell thing," Jovan said. "Timothy told me Ian called them yesterday."

Jovan wheeled the car into the garage, and instead of going through the house from the entrance in the garage, she and Cheyenne walked along the driveway to the front steps. Cheyenne took her hand, whispering, "It's going to be okay... if they're here to battle, we can battle right back."

Jovan felt awkward. Normally, when she came into contact with her in-laws, she greeted them with huge hugs and warm smiles, but so much had changed. Instead, she walked to them leaving ample personal space between them and her.

"Hello, Margaret, Dean," she spoke quietly.

"Jovan," Dean responded, taking his wife's hand into his.

"Um, I don't mean to sound rude," she said, "and excuse me if I do, but I'm really surprised to see you two here."

Margaret took a step toward Jovan, her eyes as dark and penetrating as her sons. "Why," Margaret began, her voice low and menacing, "are you spreading rumors about Cordell?"

"I am not spreading anything, Mrs. Anderson," she said. "There was blood on Cordell's pants. They tested it. It was Sarah Brockman's blood. Sarah is dead. The police put two

228

and two together. Not me."

"Why did you give them the pants, Jovan? How do we know that you didn't put the blood on the pants?"

"Now wait one minute," Cheyenne said.

"Chey, no," Jovan interrupted.

Cheyenne stepped in the space between Jovan and Margaret. "I know you are in pain," Cheyenne said. "But let's stay realistic, shall we?"

Dean opened his mouth to speak, but Cheyenne plowed through. "Now I don't mean to be rude, but I am really tired of you downing my sister. She did not kill your son. She loved your son. She loved him more than he probably deserved to be loved by any one person."

"Cheyenne," Jovan whispered.

"No, Jovan. Mr. and Mrs. Anderson, I'm sorry for your loss. It must be excruciating to lose a child, and I do pray that God helps you through this, but I don't ever want you coming here and harassing Jovan again. Your son got himself tangled into a lot of mess. Before you start blaming Jovan, you might want to learn a little bit about your son, about who he really was.

"Ask Detective Davenport about Cordell. And *listen* to what he says. No one is out to get Cordell or tarnish his memory. We're out to find the truth. Period."

Margaret glared at Cheyenne, but she said nothing.

"Now," Cheyenne said, clapping her hands, "Jovan prepared lunch," she said. "Would you like to join us?"

"Thank you, but no," Dean answered. "Margaret cooked before we left for church this morning."

"I had another reason for coming," Dean said after several awkward minutes of silence.

"Yes," Jovan said.

"Would it be possible if we retrieved some things of Cordell's?" Dean's right cheek twitched. "We just want something of his, that he touched."

"Definitely. Come on in," Jovan said.

Cheyenne opened the door and led everyone in. "I'll get lunch together, sis," she said.

"Thanks."

Jovan hugged her sister. There was a part of her that wanted to throttle Cheyenne, but overall, she was proud of Cheyenne for standing up for her.

Jovan led Dean and Margaret upstairs.

The walk down the hallway appeared to last forever. Except for the clothes tirade, Jovan hadn't been on that end of the house since Cordell's death.

When they reached the master bedroom, Jovan took hold of the knob. Margaret's hand clamped down on hers. She bit down on a yelp from the pain. She was stunned that Margaret would even touch her; she could still sense the hostility that Margaret carried toward her. With a shaky hand, Jovan creaked open the door. Long gone was the smell of death she was hit with the night of Cordell's murder. Clothes were still sprawled over the bed and the floor.

She still couldn't stare at the bed for too long. That would be the first thing to leave the house. As if afraid to awaken the dead, Margaret took small, baby steps around the room, her eyes resting on a framed portrait of Jovan and Cordell taken during one of their earlier, happier times. Her fingertips trailed along the gold frame, her eyes settling on the euphoria that appeared to resonate from the picture.

Jovan stood back and watched Margaret walk around the bed and stare at the spot where Cordell's body lay that night. Dean stood behind her, his hands resting on her shoulders.

"God, why?" Margaret wailed. "Why did you take my baby?" She knelt beside the bed.

"Mama Anderson," Jovan said as she came to her. She knelt alongside her, hugging her. Margaret shook Jovan's arms from around her. Jovan stared into her eyes, eyes that were mixed with love and hate.

She doesn't trust me, Jovan thought.

"I can't imagine," Margaret sobbed, "why someone would kill my baby. Please tell me why."

Jovan wiped at her own tears. "I don't know, Mama Anderson," she responded, choking back tears. "But we will find out who did this, and they will pay...I promise you that."

Margaret stared long and hard at Jovan. When Jovan lowered her hands along with Dean to help Margaret up, she took them. Dean and Jovan both aided in guiding Margaret outside the bedroom.

"We can do this later," Jovan said. "When you're feeling stronger. There's no rush." Margaret simply nodded, too distraught to verbally respond.

Together, Dean and Jovan helped Margaret back down the stairs and into the living room, sitting her down upon the sofa. Cheyenne waltzed into the room from the kitchen and viewed the desolate expressions on the faces of all three.

"Is everything okay?" she asked.

Jovan shook her head no before answering, "It will be."

"I made a pot of tea, and I have a tray prepared, so let me go and get it." Within a few seconds, Cheyenne returned with a silver tray containing a teapot, teacups, a small canister of milk, and a bowl of sugar. After pouring each a cup of tea, Cheyenne sat on the loveseat, alongside Jovan.

The room sat in complete quiet as the four sipped from their cups.

"Like I mentioned upstairs," Jovan said, "you can come pick out things some other time. Chey and I will be going through Cor...Cordell's things soon. I'll let you know when."

"Thank you, Jovan," Dean replied.

"So how are you two doing?" Jovan asked, then thought of how stupid that question was. "I'm sorry. That was insensitive of me." Margaret leaned her head onto her husband's shoulder and cried.

"I know this may sound weird to ask," Dean said, "but have you talked to Timothy lately?"

Jovan's hand began to shake and she quickly placed her cup back on the tray. She felt caught under the glaring light of an interrogation room. She already had herself on trial and all she had done was kiss him.

"We've been talking," she answered as she held her hands tightly. "Why?"

"We haven't heard from him the last couple of days."

Jovan sat up, alert. "Really? That's weird. We…we had breakfast together this morning," she stuttered out. She felt the right side of her face burn as Cheyenne cut her a glare.

"Where?" Margaret asked. Jovan could hear the desperation in her voice.

"Here."

"How did he seem?" Dean asked.

Jovan answered, "He seemed okay."

"Did he…" Margaret looked over at Dean who nodded, "look high?"

Jovan's head snapped to attention. She never wanted to think of Timothy falling back into drugs. She debated whether to tell them about the look in his eyes. Maybe she was being too nervous.

"Oh no, Margaret, Dean," she reassured them. "He definitely wasn't under the influence, and I don't think he has been either. He's upset, obviously, and he's been talking to me about his feelings."

"He shouldn't be talking to you," Margaret said. "He should be talking to his family." The sting of Margaret's words caught Jovan right across the face, but she forced herself to stay calm. She felt Cheyenne's hands on hers and her breaths began to come slow and steady.

"I'm his family, too," Jovan said. "I love you all, and that definitely includes Timothy."

Though faint, she heard Margaret mumble, "She won't hurt my only son," into Dean's suit jacket. Jovan cringed, embarrassed and hurt.

"Have you gone to his apartment?" Cheyenne asked, trying to stop the situation from escalating.

"We have called and gone by, but he wasn't home," Dean replied. "We even checked with the police and the area hospitals, too, but no luck."

"He's okay," Jovan said though she couldn't help but wonder why he came to her if he had been M.I.A. for the last few days. "I know this is a hard time for him, for all of us, but he's so strong now. He won't backslide."

"He has before—more times than I can count," Margaret said. Jovan avoided looking directly into her eyes.

"But that's not now," Jovan pleaded. "Timothy has changed. He has. I saw him today, and he was fine. He just needs time. Give him time."

Margaret fell into her husband's arms as Jovan turned to her sister, who hugged her.

"It's going to be okay," Cheyenne whispered in her ear. "And you will tell me about this...breakfast."

Timothy sat at the desk in his dimly lit apartment. He stood out on the fire escape, his back pressed against the wall each time his parents got the super to let them in. He didn't want to see them. Or anyone. Just Jovan so he could apologize. His tears made the words he had written in his journal smear. When he noticed the blurriness of the text, he ripped the page out and started over again. The more he wrote, the faster he wrote, and the faster he wrote, the more he needed to run, run in the fresh air and collect himself. He felt fidgety and instantly, his mind thought crack, heroin, weed, anything that would put him in a slightly comatose state.

But those remedies were things of the past for him. Yes, he had the taste, just like a person on a diet, or someone trying to cut back on booze, or the woman trying to stop smoking, but he was determined to stop for good this time, and for almost a year, he had done just that. But this was different. This was life or death. Hell, to him, this was death. He looked at his answering machine and noted the flashing light. His parents called, asking if he was okay. And he was. And he wasn't, both at the same time. The only person he wanted to be around was Jovan, and the only thing he wanted to remember was this morning when he kissed her, and she forgave him.

He remembered the crush he had on Jovan throughout her marriage and how he never entertained the thought of being able to dwell in her smile as more than just a brother-in-law. He felt that the only thing he could do, or even wanted to do was to make sure Jovan always smiled and was always happy because none of this should have happened.

He flipped his journal closed and circled his small apartment, picking up stray items of clothing and straightening up. Afterward, he laid spread eagle across his bed and looked up at the white ceiling.

"God," he said into the darkness of his bedroom. "You always do what's right. Please help make this situation right. Help my family to get through the pain and suffering, and especially help Jo to get her life back. She never deserved any of this—" Tears fell from his eyes and leaked into his ears. "She didn't, and as long as you let me, I'll make it up to her, I promise."

He ignored the knocking at his door. If it wasn't Jovan, he didn't want to be bothered. She was the victim in all this, and she deserved to have someone love her and make her top priority, and he hoped that person could eventually be him.

"Tim, open up." Fear compressed Timothy's heart into a small dime-shaped circle as he heard the familiar deep voice.

He didn't want to see him and be reminded of all that had happened. Two loud bangs on the door followed the command, and Timothy finally rolled off the bed and stepped to the door.

"D," Timothy said when he opened the door. "What's up?"

"We need to talk, Tim. We're finally gonna make everything right." Timothy didn't believe him. In his mind, nothing would ever be right again.

"Okay, okay, I'm coming!" Cheyenne jogged her way down the hall, opening the front door. "What can I do..." she halted, finally looking up to see who was at the door. Ian. The two stood, momentarily dumbstruck at the pleasure of seeing each other. "Oh, Detective Davenport," Cheyenne said. "You remember that me, Jovan, and Mark passed our polygraphs, right?"

Ian laughed. "Yes, I do."

"And you remember that it is rude for a man not to give an after-date phone call, right?"

Ian leaned against the door jamb. He smiled in Cheyenne's direction, but got nothing back but attitude and hands on hips.

"I already said I was sorry down at the precinct," he said.

"Oh, but I'm riding this for a minute, Dear. Be forewarned."

"What if the man had some information?"

Cheyenne's brow rose, as did her interest. "Then the man might be forgiven."

Ian laughed. "Can we start this back over? I don't want attitude."

"Okay, fine." Cheyenne shut the door in his face and chuckled, awaiting his knock. When he did, she opened the door. The look on his face was priceless.

"You are such a smart a—"

"Watch your mouth," Cheyenne said as she covered her mouth and laughed. "And keep it down. Sis is out in the sunroom meditating."

"Does the meditation help?"

"No, but I guess it counts that you at least try. Why are we standing at the door? Come in." Ian stepped toward Cheyenne, giving her a small kiss on the cheek before entering.

"You know, actually I'm glad that you're here because I have some news on the case, and I came by to fill Jovan in."

Cheyenne took Ian by the hand, leading him through the hallway and to the sunroom's entrance.

"Oh my goodness," she said. "I hope it's a lead because we really need something positive."

Cheyenne nodded toward the sunroom door before rapping on it and entering. "Sis, guess who's here."

Jovan was sitting Indian style on a large cushion, eyes closed tight and hands resting outward, palms out. She smiled when her eyes made contact with Ian's liqueur colored ones.

"Detective Davenport," she said, rising from the floor. "What brings you by? Good news, I hope."

"You could say that," he responded.

"Well you better sit down right here and tell us all about it," Jovan said, sitting on a wicker chair.

"As you two know," Ian began, "I talked to Jameson Burke and Jimmy Devane about their whereabouts the night of Cordell's murder, and they had an alibi, one I thought was airtight."

"But it's not, is it?" Cheyenne asked, excitement evident in her voice.

"Nope. I actually found this out last night, but with the polygraphs and all, I didn't have—"

"We don't care about when you found out," Cheyenne said. "What did you find out?"

"Okay, Miss Feisty. Anyway, I went to Burke's hangar to talk to the hangar's manager about that night. The flight log shows that Burke and Devane took Burke's jet to New York; however, Devane was not on that jet...not the real one anyway."

"Wait a minute," Jovan said. "Are you telling us that Devane lied? He has no alibi?"

"Not a good one. After finding out this news, I went to see Devane last night, to confront him and get the truth out of him."

"And did you?" the twins asked in unison.

"I found more than I would have liked." The girls bent forward, anxiously awaiting his tale. "Devane wasn't alone. Alisha Stewart was there, and let's just say she wasn't selling Girl Scout cookies."

"They were there...together?" Jovan asked. Ian nodded in the affirmative. "Well, tramps need a warm body, too, I suppose." She sucked her teeth in disgust.

"Alisha came up with some story about how she didn't know Devane until after Cordell was murdered, and that they sought comfort and solace with each other in their grieving of Cordell."

Cheyenne laughed. "Surely you don't buy that," she said. Ian gave her a dirty look.

"Anyway," Ian continued, ignoring Cheyenne. "Needless to say, Alisha and Devane have no valid alibis for the night of the murder, but unfortunately, we still haven't found a weapon, haven't uncovered one fingerprint in this entire house, except those of you two and Cordell."

"So we're back at square one," Jovan said, sighing.

"No, not square one," Ian answered. "Devane and Alisha know something. I can feel it, and I plan to bring them in for additional questioning. I'm considering giving them both polygraphs just for my own state of mind."

"Knowing them two," Cheyenne said, "they would find a way to trick the test."

"Probably," Ian said. "I can't wrangle them too much, especially Alisha. She would have her lawyers on us immediately if we hauled her in or locked her up."

Closing her eyes, Jovan skimmed her fingertips along her hair, letting out a long, desperate moan. "I say, if your intuition is strong, forget about Alisha's attack dogs and bring her ass in. Devane's too, while you're at it."

"I just want you two to know," Ian stated, glancing at both twins, "that this case is very important to me. I pride myself in immersing my all into a case and solving it quickly."

Cheyenne softly patted Ian's shoulder as Jovan gave a small smile.

"I know you are a great detective, and I know you will follow through as best as you can with this case," Jovan said. "I just wished this would unravel like our novels normally do."

"Isn't this about the time we would throw in a surprise element?" Cheyenne asked. "Like revealing that the wife had a secret agenda...or the housekeeper had a love child by the murder victim...I mean something."

"Any minute now, my lover is going to call, and the gig will be up," Jovan offered, with a hollow laugh. Cheyenne and Ian jumped when the phone rang, each eyeing the phone, and then turning attention toward Jovan.

"Hey, I was kidding," she said. Jovan rose from the chair and picked up the cordless. "Anderson residence," she answered. She smiled. "Um, hey. I'm busy right now, but I will call you back, okay? Bye." Jovan hung up.

"Who was that?" Ian and Cheyenne asked. The phone rang again, and Jovan thanked the caller. It got her out of explaining the first call. Technically, Mark wasn't her lover, but that was just semantics. "Hello," she answered. "Yes, I know Timothy Anderson. He's my brother-in-law." Ian and

Cheyenne quickly directed their focus to an ashen Jovan as she gripped the phone with both hands. "Yes, yes, I'll call his parents and we'll be there as soon as we can." Jovan hung up and haphazardly tossed the phone onto the table.

"Timothy is in the hospital," she said, her voice dry, her body shaking. "We have to go now." She turned to run out of the sunroom and quickly stopped. "I gotta call Margaret and Dean." Cheyenne raced to a tearful Jovan's side, hugging her.

"Take a breath, Jo," she whispered.

"I'll drive behind you two," Ian said, kissing Cheyenne's forehead. "I want to make sure you two are okay." Jovan snatched the phone up and dialed.

After three rings, the Anderson's answering service clicked on, and she rattled off the message, "Margaret, Dean...this is Jovan. I wish to God I didn't have to leave this on your service, but I just received a call from St. Agnes Hospital...Timothy is there. They didn't give me much information, but please, get there as soon as you can."

Hanging up the phone, Jovan scanned the room for her shoes. Having changed into jeans and a tee once Margaret and Dean left, she reached for her mules and slipped them on while Cheyenne stepped into her black pumps.

"What did the doctor tell you?" Cheyenne asked, grabbing their purses.

"Drug overdose." Jovan wept, eyeing her sister and Ian. All Jovan could do on the ride over was pray that Timothy would be okay and that this was all a nightmare.

"Oh God, Jimmy," Alisha crooned into his ear as he rocked the two of them into an orgasmic explosion. Jimmy looked down into Alisha's sweat-drenched face, her passion screaming from every pore. He smiled.

"Yeah," he grunted, thrusting himself deeper, feeling her small breaths on his shoulder. "You feel so good, 'Lish. We're almost there."

"Jimmy, I'm there with you." She panted, matching him stroke for stroke. As they climbed the mountain of their erotic peak, the phone rang. They were totally oblivious to it, pumping and grinding and moaning until they each tumbled down the mountain in climax. After three rings, the ringing ceased, and then began again for two more rings before stopping. When the phone rang again, Jimmy jumped to answer it.

"Yeah," he said. On the other end of the phone call, a muffled voice spoke, "One down, one to go." Jimmy looked over at a spent Alisha and responded, "Gotcha," before hanging up.

Chapter 22

*J*ovan, Cheyenne, and Ian sprinted through the hospital hallway to the nurses' station. When they reached the station's counter, the portly nurse behind it eyed the three with interest.

"Excuse me," Jovan said, out of breath. "We're trying to find someone who can tell us about Timothy Anderson." The nurse glanced at Jovan and Cheyenne before looking through the submission log.

"Are you family?" she asked.

"Yes, I'm his sister-in-law. The hospital contacted me to come down."

"The doctor is with Mr. Anderson right now; however, his parents just arrived and are down the hall, to your left."

"Thank you," Jovan called out, before retreating down the hall with the others.

"Mrs. Anderson," the nurse yelled out. The trio halted, turning around. "You and Cheyenne's novels are so wonderful. I've read all of them and can't wait until your latest is released."

"I cannot believe..." Cheyenne groaned out in aggravation. Jovan took her by the hand and turned back toward the hallway. They spotted Margaret and Dean in the far corner of the waiting room, rocking on their heels, clinging to each other.

"I can't lose both my babies," Margaret cried into her husband's shoulder.

"Margaret...Dean," Jovan said as she neared them. She was surprised to have Margaret reach out and embrace her. "Have you heard anything?"

"No, we just got here about ten minutes ago," Dean answered. "And the doctor hasn't come to speak to us yet." At that moment, a tall, thin doctor burst through double doors and headed toward the group, the blue of his eyes determined and focused.

"Mr. And Mrs. Anderson," he said. "I'm Dr. Richards, and I've been attending to your son."

"How is he?" Margaret asked. "Can we see him?"

"First let me tell you what happened," Dr. Richards said. "Your son, Timothy, overdosed on a combination of cocaine and heroin."

"Oh my God." Margaret clutched her husband as he sat her into a chair.

"There was a 911 call placed by someone at Timothy's apartment. We think it might have been Timothy, calling before he fell unconscious. By the time the paramedics arrived, he was unresponsive and not breathing."

"Please," Jovan said, "please don't tell us that he's..."

"We managed to get his heart beating again, but I have to tell you that it's touch and go for the next 24 hours. He has gone into cardiac arrest two times since we brought him in, and there are a lot of drugs in his system. We're attempting to detoxify his system, but the next 24 hours will determine if his heart is strong enough to fight."

Dr. Richards patted Dean's shoulder before giving it a comforting squeeze. "Your son desperately needs your prayers tonight."

"Can we see him?" Dean asked.

"We're transferring him to a room soon. I'll be back to let you know when you can see him."

"Thank you, Dr. Richards," Dean responded, reaching out to shake his hand. The group stood in silence, unable to find words in which to speak. Leaning against a wall, Jovan watched as Dean consoled Margaret, and Ian hugged Cheyenne. A shot of loneliness stole her breath away, and she doubled over for a minute to catch her breath. When she wrapped her arms tightly around herself, she imagined them to be Mark's.

Jovan moved to a corner away from the family and unclipped her cell phone. She dialed and waited.

242

"Hello."

"Hey, Mark." She sniffed.

"What's wrong?"

"Timothy. He, um, overdosed. It's serious."

"I'm so sorry, Jovan. Are you at the hospital now?"

"St. Agnes."

"Would you like me to come? I know you're worried what others might think, but..."

"Please come."

"I'll be right there."

Jovan rested her forehead on the wall and let the tears fall.

"You okay, Jo?" Cheyenne asked. Jovan looked up and saw the quartet staring at her. She took a deep breath, wiped her eyes, and coughed.

She nodded before saying, "We're going to be here all night. I know we may not have the appetite, but we need to keep our energy up, so how about I jet down to the cafeteria and get coffee and sandwiches for everybody, my treat?"

"I can do that, Jovan," Ian replied.

Jovan shook her head. "I don't mind," she answered. "I could use a moment to myself," she added in a whisper. "Can you call in and see what they've found at Timmy's apartment?"

"Can do that," he replied.

Making rounds to give everyone a hug, Jovan ended with Margaret, holding her the longest and hardest. "It's going to be okay," she whispered. "We're going to help Timothy get better." Margaret looked into Jovan's eyes and nodded.

With that, Jovan left the waiting room, running down the hall and past the nurses' station to the elevator. Once alone inside the elevator, she fell to her knees in a crying heap. "God, please don't take him away from us."

Four floors down, Jovan prayed to God as she wailed, begging, praying for Timothy's recovery, and as the elevator doors slid open on the first floor, Jovan was standing, tears wiped clean and an icy expression on her face, as if she was afraid for the public to see her in complete shambles.

"Damn it," Jovan growled as she marched along the semi-dark parking garage of the hospital. "You need money to buy things."

Reaching the car, Jovan rested her forehead on the car's cool steel. She took a few breaths and stretched before pulling out her keys and sliding one into the lock. She could see her purse lying on the floor of the driver's side.

From a distance, she heard the faint sound of footsteps. She stopped, listening. Nothing. She opened the car door and retrieved her purse.

"Now back to the cafeteria," she thought aloud, locking the door. As she was about to turn away from the car, Jovan again heard footsteps, this time running toward her, then stopping. "Hello," she called out, only to have the word echoed back to her. "Somebody there?" Jovan's hand shook as she tried to slide her key back into the lock.

"Shit," she whispered, her chest tightening with fear. She dropped the keys and bent to pick them up. Standing, she managed to get the key in the lock and as she turned the key, a heavy force pummeled into her from the back. Her forehead connected with the side of the car.

She yelled in pain from the impact, already feeling lightheaded from the blow. Her legs went wobbly but before she could crumple to the ground, someone grabbed her by the neck and dragged her away from the car.

"Help," she croaked as she frantically clawed at the gloved hands around her neck. She opened her mouth to scream, but only air squeaked through her pipes. Jovan's eyes fluttered closed, and she felt her brain cells shut down one by one as the hands clamped around her throat tighter.

Jovan tried desperately to pry the fingers off her neck. She began to choke, but quieted when she heard a clicking sound coming their way.

Heels, she thought. Her heart beat wildly, almost ripping from her chest. She tried to keep her eyes open, but she felt tired and weak. She sucked in air when the hands loosened around her throat, but quickly, an arm came around her neck and she was briefly lifted off the ground. She kicked her legs and managed to connect with her assailant but not enough to be let go. With the slits of her eyes, she saw the faint light above her.

Inwardly, she begged to hear the heels again and when she did, she thanked God. They approached her in a quick pace, but her joy turned into more pain as she felt a knee lodge itself in her midsection. Before she could react, she was flung to the pavement, her neck snapping back as her face bounced hard against the paved ground. She groaned, feeling the weight of her attacker on her back. Opening her mouth to scream, her cries for help were thwarted by a blow to the head from the attacker's weapon.

Seconds away from complete darkness, she moaned and groaned from the flurry of kicks and punches that her body took. Even in her near unconsciousness, she knew there were two attackers. She closed her eyes, tasting blood in her mouth. She feigned unconscious in the hope of halting the attack and succeeded. The attackers slowly began to let up, as one snatched her purse.

Her face felt like it was on fire, and her ears were ringing, but she detected sounds around her, coming to the conclusion that the attackers were talking. Amidst the clanging of the bells in her ears, she heard the word *bitch* come from one of the attackers before the two fled. With her last drop of energy, she opened her eyes, straining to look toward the sound of the fleeting feet. Drifting into darkness, her closing eyes saw red.

Cheyenne doubled over in her chair, her hands clutching her stomach. "Oh God," she moaned, rocking in her chair. Ian stroked his hand through Cheyenne's hair.

"You okay, Chey?" he asked, kneeling down before her. "What's wrong?"

"Just feel," Cheyenne replied, sucking in air, "feel like I've been kicked in the gut." Ian's hands stroked her cheeks, noticing the wide, crazy look in her eyes.

"Want me to call a doctor over?" Ian asked. "A nurse?"

Cheyenne shook her head vigorously. Before Ian could respond, Cheyenne went limp for a split second, her head dipping onto Ian's shoulder.

Slowly, Cheyenne lifted her head and looked from Ian to Margaret and Dean across the waiting room, holding hands and asleep. She grabbed Ian's left wrist and checked his watch.

"We need to go look for Jo," she said. "Is she making the coffee and sandwiches herself? It's been 30 minutes. I'm worried."

"Wonder twin powers, huh?" Ian asked, a slight smile on his face.

Cheyenne frowned. She stood and faced Ian. "Whatever, I'm going to see if Jo needs help. See where she is." Cheyenne tried to walk past Ian, but he took her hand.

"I'll go with you," he said. As they passed the nurses' station, he added, "We can go down to the first floor and help her bring the food up." Cheyenne gave him a smile, not big enough to say he's forgiven for the wonder twins comment, but enough to say he was out of the doghouse. Ian took her hand, jumping onto a closing elevator. The doors of the elevator slid open on the first floor.

"Clear the way! Clear the way!"

Ian and Cheyenne jumped back against the closing elevator doors as a gurney was being rushed down the hallway. The sheet that covered the patient was stained with blood, and she heard one of the nurses yell, "I can't believe she's still alive."

Cheyenne turned her face towards Ian's chest, cringing.

"God," she moaned, "I'm definitely not a lover of blood."

"Yet you write murder mysteries?"

"Hush, and come on." They continued on their way, making a right in the direction of the cafeteria.

"Cheyenne!"

Ian and Cheyenne turned and found Mark rushing to them.

"What are you doing here?" Cheyenne asked.

"Jovan's been hurt."

"What? Where?"

"They just rushed her into the emergency room a few seconds ago...right down this hall."

Cheyenne shook her head, and instantly felt faint.

"No," she screamed. "The gurney that just went by? That was my sister?"

Cheyenne went limp, and Ian was there to catch her. Both Ian and Mark helped Cheyenne into the nurses' station in the emergency room.

Ian showed his badge to the nurse behind the counter. "Where is Mrs. Jovan Anderson?" he asked.

A doctor who was behind the counter faced them.

"Are you Mrs. Anderson's sister?" he asked.

"Yes," Cheyenne answered. "Where's my sister?"

"I'm Dr. Jarvis, please come with me."

Dr. Jarvis led Cheyenne, Mark, and Ian over to an empty corner of the lobby.

"Miss Parham," Dr. Jarvis began. "Your sister suffered an apparent robbery attack out in the parking garage."

"Parking garage," Cheyenne yelled. "What was she doing out there?"

"We don't know. About fifteen minutes ago, this gentleman," Dr. Jarvis said, pointing to Mark, "came in and told us that Jovan was badly beaten out in the garage, and we immediately went out to get her."

"Is she okay?" Cheyenne asked. "Can I see her?"

"I'm still examining your sister, Ms. Parham," Dr. Jarvis replied. "I don't want to alarm you, but your sister sustained a lot of injuries. I want to assure you that we will do everything we can to help her."

"I need to see her now, Dr. Jarvis."

"I would prefer that you wait until I finish examining her. We'll be moving her to a room after we attend to her injuries."

"How long will that be?"

"I can't say for certain, Ms. Parham, but I will have a nurse come and direct you to your sister's room when I'm done. If we need you, we'll come find you."

"I'll be right here," Cheyenne said flatly as she leaned against Ian. Dr. Jarvis offered her a slight smile before disappearing through a pair of doors.

"Chey," Ian whispered. "Are you okay?"

"No," she yelled. "I'm not. My sister is hurt, and I need to see her, touch her, make sure she's okay." Ian sat Cheyenne down into a chair a few feet away in a small waiting area. Cheyenne broke down in Ian's arms, weeping.

She looked at Mark and asked, "What happened? What did you see?"

Tears stained Mark's face. "Jovan called me," he began. "Told me about Timothy and asked me to come be here for her. I parked my car and was walking through the garage when I saw someone on the ground. Never thought it would be Jovan."

Mark walked away, headed down the hall.

"She's going to be okay," Ian offered, stroking Cheyenne's back and kissing her forehead. "Jovan is tough. She's made it through everything that has been thrown her way. She'll make it through this, too."

"I felt something was wrong," Cheyenne whispered. "I knew. I felt something was wrong. She was gone for too long. I'm her twin. I felt her pain. I should have—"

"Stop it, Chey," Ian said, gently taking hold of her shoulders, bracing her. "It's not your fault. You have to be strong right now for your sister. She's been through a lot, and right now, she's feeling violated and scared."

"I just wish I could have been there for her."

Ian stroked the tears from Cheyenne's face and kissed her forehead.

"You're her sister. Believe me, you are always there with and for her, and she knows that." Cheyenne nodded, but remained silent.

"Thank you for being here, Ian," she whispered.

"There's no other place I would be," he replied.

Chapter 23

$\mathcal{D}$an felt someone tapping on his shoulder, and he jerked awake. He saw a nurse quickly take a step back.

"I'm sorry, Detective," she said. "I didn't mean to scare you." Ian looked at a sleeping Cheyenne curled up in her chair. Mark jumped and walked toward the nurse.

"Is there any news about Jovan?" Ian asked.

"She's being moved up to the fifth floor, room 512," the nurse answered. "Dr. Jarvis wanted me to inform you that you can go see her now."

"Thank you." Ian shook Cheyenne awake.

"What's wrong?" she asked. "Something wrong? How's Jo?"

"Calm down. They moved Jovan to her room." Cheyenne instantly woke up and grabbed Ian's hand. Ian stood and took Cheyenne into his arms, holding her tight. "It'll be okay," he reassured her. She nodded.

"I'm ready," she insisted. "Let's go."

The nurse continued to stand there looking at the trio. "I wanted to prepare you," she said. "Your sister has been badly hurt."

"How hurt?" Cheyenne asked. The nurse hesitated. "Give it to me straight, please."

"Well, she has broken ribs, a broken ankle, facial abrasions, her jaw was fractured, she suffered a concussion, and she has several other cuts and abrasions on her body from the beating."

"Oh my God," Cheyenne said, her hands covering her mouth. The nurse reached out and touched Cheyenne's hand.

"Don't be too frightened. She suffered a lot of swelling, and yes, she's going to be in pain, but in time, she will heal."

"Thank you." Cheyenne watched the nurse walk away. She reached out to Mark and hugged him. She took Ian's hand in hers and said, "Let's go. My sister needs me."

The lights were out in Jovan's hospital room except for a small lamp on the stand beside her bed. The door creaked as Cheyenne opened it. She reached her hand out to turn the light on.

"Mmm mmm," came a rough, muffled voice from the bed across the room. Cheyenne quickly flipped the lights back off.

Looking back at Ian and Mark, Cheyenne walked into the room, marching up to her sister's bed. "Oh," Cheyenne groaned, swallowing a scream. Before her laid Jovan, her usually smooth, cinnamon complexion marred by swelling, deep purple bruises, cracked lips that were swollen and red, and a white bandage wrapped around her head. Her jaw and chin were twice their normal sizes.

Cheyenne took in the two puffy slits that used to be Jovan's eyes. Jovan squinted, only seeing fuzziness.

"Chey," she whispered without moving her thick lips.

"Jo," Cheyenne said. Gingerly, she took one of Jovan's hands, kissing it several times. "Don't try to talk, Sis. I know it must be painful as hell."

"Hurt," Jovan squeaked out. In her foggy sight, Jovan spotted the avalanche of tears drift down Cheyenne's face. "No cry," she whispered, wincing at her own tears trying to fall.

"Honey," Cheyenne said. "Ian and Mark are here."

"No Mark," she whispered. "Ugly."

Mark walked across the room and stood beside Cheyenne. Not once did he flinch as he looked down at Jovan.

"You're not ugly, Jovan," he said.

Jovan began coughing as the tears that tried to fall turned into sobs. Mark gently lifted Jovan and rubbed her back until she stopped coughing.

"Stop crying, Jovan," he said. "I'm not leaving. You're not ugly. We're here to help you, okay?" He grabbed a tissue from the stand and softly dabbed at the tears on her face.

"Mmm hmm," Jovan said.

"Jovan," Ian said, his hands gripping the foot of her bed. Jovan tried to open her eyes, but moaned from the pain. "Don't strain yourself. Just lay back, keep your eyes closed, and relax."

"Chey," Jovan whispered. "Vite."

"What, Baby?" Cheyenne asked.

Jovan's eyes moved from Ian to Cheyenne and then over to the table where a pitcher of water and pad and pen sat. She scratched Cheyenne's arm again.

"I think she wants to write something," Mark said, looking at Jovan. She grunted. Ian retrieved the pad and pen and placed the pad on the bed before slipping the pen into her hand.

"What do you have to write, Jo?" Cheyenne asked. Through winces and grunts, Jovan scribbled on the pad. She looked at Cheyenne to pick it up. On the sheet was written:

$ in car
people beat me
took purse

"People?" Ian asked. "It was more than one person?" Jovan groaned. "How many?"

"Two," Jovan pushed between her lips.

"Two men?" Mark asked.

"Mmm mmm."

"One of each? Two women?" Cheyenne asked.

"Each."

"What did they look like?" Ian asked. Jovan blinked and moaned. Her face scrunched up from a rush of pain that

252

attacked her. She shrugged and cringed. "She didn't see them," Cheyenne said. "Do you remember anything else?"

Jovan closed her eyes. After several minutes, she whispered, "Red."

"What do you mean, red, Jovan?" Ian asked.

Jovan scribbled on the pad again.

kick choke beat me

thud, click

see red

"Thud, click," Ian said. "What's that?"

"I don't know," Cheyenne answered.

"Walking?" Mark asked.

Jovan took a breath and whispered, "Yes." After another breath, she added, "Click heels." "The lady wore heels?" Cheyenne asked in a high voice. Jovan groaned. "Red heels?"

Jovan nodded and tried to smile. She sighed, crumpling onto the bed, trying to regain her strength. Mark maneuvered himself to the other side of Jovan's bed where he held her hand and watched her.

"Good girl," Ian said before rubbing Jovan's free hand. He whisked Cheyenne over to the door.

"What's wrong?" Cheyenne asked, frightened by the expression on Ian's face.

"I need you to check on Timothy Anderson and make sure he's okay," Ian stated, "and then, I want you to stay with Jovan at all times."

"You know who did this, don't you?"

"This, and maybe more," he whispered, kissing her. "Check on Timothy, and come right back to this room. I'll be back as soon as I can."

"Okay." With a gentle stroke of Cheyenne's cheek, Ian fled from the room, whipping his cell phone out of his jacket and dialing the precinct. He might need backup for this.

"What a rush," Alisha squealed as she and Jimmy lay on the sofa naked, except for Alisha's red heels.

Jimmy ran his hands over the small curves of Alisha's body.

"Nothing like kicking ass that adds to the sex, huh, 'Lish?"

Jimmy asked.

Alisha moaned. "Nothing," she whispered.

"Released some pent up frustrations, didn't ya?" Jimmy asked, guffawing.

"Hell yes. I think I have some of that bitch's blood on my shoes I was kicking her so hard."

"Damn, 'Lish, you don't sound like the debutante sweetheart I fell for."

"Yeah, well I'm in another element now," she said. She sat up and straddled Jimmy. "That woman always rubbed me the wrong way, and I got the chance to return the favor."

"We got her good, all right," Jimmy said, still laughing. "I like to meet the person that could survive that."

"I just wish you would have left the purse," Alisha whined. "I don't like us having it."

"I had to make it look like a robbery, 'Lish." Jimmy smacked Alisha's ass and slid from under her. "Now no one is the wiser. They'll assume it was a robbery gone wrong, and now, the broad is gone, Timothy's gone, and we don't have to worry about the cops bothering us over their asses."

"God, we need to celebrate," Alisha hollered. "Did you chill a bottle of bubbly?"

"Screw chilled bubbly in the house. Jameson will be here any minute, and the three of us are going out on the town tonight… dinner and champagne 'til we see double." Alisha pulled Jimmy atop her and kissed him deeply. "Maybe even a little nose candy. We deserve it."

"Well let's go wash off a hard day's work and paint the town red." Alisha leapt from the sofa and began trotting down the hallway when the sound of someone knocking on the door halted her moves. She grabbed the trench coat she wore earlier and put it on.

"J.B. already?" She laughed, walking toward the door. "He's just as excited as we are."

"If he's here already," Jimmy said, giving Alisha a sly glance, "then you and I will have to share a shower."

"Ooh, deal." Alisha unlocked the door and opened it, exclaiming, "J.B., you're here—" Ian's broad smile stopped her in her tracks. His eyes took in the red heels she wore, and his smile broadened even further.

"Spoil your little party, did I?" he asked.

"If you're here to bother me about the Anderson case again," Jimmy complained, rushing up behind Alisha, "I'll have to call my attorney and file harassment charges."

"Okay, well you do that," Ian said. His hand moved around his waist, pulling out a pair of handcuffs from a latch. "And while you're getting that one phone call downtown, let him know you've been arrested, too."

"What?" Alisha yelled, frozen to the spot. "Why are you arresting Jimmy?"

"Don't worry, Miss Stewart. You're going, too."

Jimmy began to back up from Alisha and Ian, his eyes wandering the room. "Don't move another muscle, Devane," Ian called out. "You and your pretty little assistant are under arrest for the assault and attempted murder of Jovan Parham-Anderson. You have the right to remain silent, and anything you say can be—"

"Attempted?" Alisha screeched. Her eyes moved between Jimmy and Ian. "Attempted murder? She's not dead?"

"Shut the fuck up, 'Lish," Jimmy screamed. Ian kept an eye on Alisha while trying to hold Jimmy in his view.

Alisha began crying, and Ian turned his attention to her. Jimmy stumbled back onto the sofa, turning quickly to dig under its cushions. Taking Alisha by the arm, Ian whipped his gun from its holster, pointing it at Jimmy.

"Devane, don't make me put a hole in your ass," Ian yelled.

Jimmy jumped to his feet, pointing a 9-millimeter at Ian and a trembling Alisha. "Don't be stupid. Drop the gun before I have to use mine." Ian noticed the shaking in Jimmy's hands and hoped to use it to his advantage.

"You drop the gun, and I'll put mine away," he coaxed. "This doesn't have to end with you dying."

"Put the gun down," Alisha yelled. "You might hit me, Jimmy," she added, her tears choking her voice.

"Hell," Jimmy sneered, taking a small step back. "I could take out Columbo there, and then you, and be outta here before another cop showed up."

"You bastard." Alisha ran toward Jimmy and Ian grabbed her around the waist with one hand while keeping his aim steady on Jimmy. "I thought we were in this together."

"If I gotta die or go to prison for this, forget that shit." Jimmy stared down Ian, the two with guns poised to fire. Jimmy took a few steps back toward the swinging door of the kitchen. "Detective, it was nice talking to you," Jimmy added.

"Devane," Ian said. "Don't do it. It's not worth it."

"I got nothing to lose. Now." Jimmy turned and ran through the kitchen door. A shot rang out from Ian's gun, nipping the corner of the door as chips of wood and dust flew. A barrage of officers came rushing into the apartment as Ian tightened his hold on a hysterical Alisha.

"Drop the gun or lose your life," a cop yelled upon entry.

"It's me guys," Ian said, throwing his hands up. He nodded toward Alisha and added, "Detain her for the assault and attempted murder of Jovan Parham Anderson, and send some guys over to St. Agnes."

Ian rushed out the door, hoping he could make it to the hospital in time to stop Devane.

Chapter 24

"Mmm," Jovan moaned as she awakened from her drug-induced sleep. Despite the beating her body took, she was feeling light, almost drunk—she was feeling no pain.

"Good stuff," she mumbled, referring to the Demerol she was given. With squinted eyes, she viewed Cheyenne sleeping in a chair to her right. With slow, silent movements, Jovan bit down on a scream as she tried to turn her body. Something kept her from moving any further. Trying to see in the dark, she realized that she was hooked up to monitors and had an IV drip stuck in her right arm.

"What are you trying to do?" Cheyenne asked as she rose from the chair and came to the bed. "Girl, lay back down before I have to push you back in that bed." Jovan lay back down.

"Do you know that you have two broken ribs and one cracked rib? Minus a whole slew of other complications?" Cheyenne continued. "Why the hell are you trying to get up?"

Jovan closed her eyes and remained silent.

After a few minutes, Cheyenne said, "I'm sorry, Sis. You just scared me, trying to climb out of bed. I thought you might be sleepwalking or something."

"Timmy," Jovan pushed through her lips.

"What about him?"

"He 'kay?"

"Last I checked, he was still unconscious."

"See him."

"You want to see him?" Jovan nodded. "Jo, there is no possible way that can happen. You are hooked up to machines." Jovan licked at her lips. "Want some water?"

Jovan nodded.

Cheyenne poured her a glass and held it while she sipped through the straw.

After a few sips, Jovan said, "You go."

"Go where?"

"Timmy."

"I was given instructions not to leave you alone."

"Mark?"

"He's down the hall talking to your doctor."

"He be back. Go." Jovan coughed. "Worried."

Jovan's chest rose high and fell. A coughing spell attacked her, and she howled from the pain of trying to calm it down. Cheyenne jumped up and gently rubbed Jovan's chest. When the coughing subsided, Jovan closed her eyes.

"Okay, I'll go," Cheyenne said. "Just for a minute, and I'll be right back." Jovan offered her sister a weak smile as thank you. Cheyenne looked back one last time before opening the door and heading out into the hallway. The floor was practically deserted, except for a nurse at the station who appeared to be napping. Up on the wall was a sign that stated rooms 520 and above were to the left, so Cheyenne quickly made a left toward Timothy's room. When she reached room 550, Cheyenne noticed Timothy's headboard light on, and his parents lying on an empty hospital bed, sidled up close to each other. She bypassed them, finally reaching Timothy. His skin was gray and ashy, and his lips, dry and cracked. Though his eyes were closed, she could see the hollowness to them. She stifled a few tears that threatened to fall.

"Damn, Timothy," she whispered, reaching out a shaky hand to touch his cool brow. "Jo said you were doing so well. Why now?" Cheyenne allowed her tears to fall. "She and Cordell were so proud of you. You love my sis, so you know I have nothing but love for you, Timmy. We're going to make it through this."

Her eyes looked up at the heart monitor, which tracked a very slow and unsteady heartbeat. Her own heart plummeted. "Come on, Timmy," she said. "Don't die." Cheyenne took in a silent breath when she saw Timothy's eyelids twitch before

259

opening. She could tell he was confused by the expression on his face.

"Where am I?" he asked in a wheezy voice. "Jo, how did I end up in the hospital?" Timothy closed his eyes, as if trying to concentrate on his thoughts.

"Jo? No, Timmy, I'm—"

"I'm so sorry," Timothy said, interrupting. Tears spilled from his eyes. Cheyenne saw the rattling of his chest as he breathed, and the effort it took for him to speak, and her heart broke. "I never meant for any of this to happen."

Cheyenne let Timothy continue to believe she was Jovan. She didn't want to upset him any further. She stroked his cheek. "We're just glad you're awake, Hon," she said. "It's going to be okay."

"Jo, please forgive me," Timothy whispered.

"What are you talking about, Timmy?" Cheyenne asked. "Forgive you for what?"

"Cordell's dead, and I let the police think it was you. It's all my fault...I...I tried to hurt you. I can't believe I did that."

"Timmy, what are you talking about?" Cheyenne asked, this time, her voice a little higher. She trembled. "I'm okay, see? And you didn't kill Cordell. You didn't. Once the drugs are out of your system, you'll be okay, and everything will be back to nor—"

"Nothing will ever be the same," Timothy said. Cheyenne turned back for a second, looking at Timothy's parents sleeping so soundly, as if the world was okay, when she had an eerie feeling that no one's life would be the same again. "I made horrible mistakes, and I didn't know," Timothy continued. "I didn't know it was all a lie, and I hurt you...betrayed your love for me."

"Timmy," Cheyenne cooed, stroking his forehead, hoping that touching something solid might stop the fluid feeling that was taking over her body. "Rest yourself. You're getting excited, and you're not thinking clearly."

For one moment, Timothy's eyes bore into Cheyenne's, neither able to look away. With a flat, lifeless tone, Timothy said, "I killed my brother."

"That's not true," Cheyenne said, her eyes growing wide, refusing to look away from Timothy. "You loved Cordell. He was your brother. You would never—"

"I didn't know," he interrupted. "They told me you'd be there instead, but I killed him...I killed him..."

"I'd be there?" Cheyenne asked. She shook her head. *Jovan*, she thought. "Where? Who are they?"

Cheyenne ran off a string of questions, none of which were answered because Timothy was stuck on the phrase, "I killed him." The heart machine began to make a sound that reflected a thousand raindrops hitting one directly behind the other.

Margaret and Dean knocked Cheyenne out of the way. Margaret held her son's hands as she cried, and Dean pushed the emergency button above the bed.

"The bed," Timothy croaked. "You were...to be in the bed. Not Cordell."

"Calm down, Timmy," Cheyenne pleaded. Her tears fell fast down her cheeks.

"Baby," Margaret said. "Don't talk. Just relax. It's okay."

Timothy's eyes rolled upward. "Please, forgive me, Jovan," he whispered.

"No," Cheyenne said, stepping backwards, her hands clasped around her abdomen. She felt the urge to vomit. "It's not true," she cried out. Nurses rushed in, along with doctors. Cheyenne stumbled into the doorway and once out into the hallway, she slid down the wall and dropped her head onto her raised knees.

"Jovan," she said, "Not Cordell." No one paid attention to Cheyenne as she wept over Timothy's revelation. They were too busy trying to keep Timothy alive and keeping his parents from having heart attacks through their own pain.

"You just couldn't die, could you?" Jimmy looked down at Jovan, sneering at her sleeping figure. "This could have been so perfect."

With the butt of his 9-millimeter, Jimmy scratched his forehead before looking back at the door, making sure no one was behind him.

"I should have listened to 'Lish and kicked your ass some more," he continued. Jimmy turned the gun in Jovan's direction and lowered it to her face. He tapped her forehead with three swift, rough taps. Jovan's eyes popped open as far as they could, and she cried out in agony. When she took in Jimmy, she moaned loudly in an attempt to scream.

Jimmy laughed. "Can't scream, can ya?" He chuckled. Jovan pulled every available drop of her energy together to keep from moving. Her eyes slowly followed the gun as the end of it trailed over her left cheek, down to her bottom lip.

"It's nothing against ya," Jimmy said as he bent down a bit, his face less than a foot from Jovan's. "I don't even really know you, but you're in the way of me getting what's mine."

"Please," Jovan whispered. "Don't."

"This is already in motion," he replied. "It's been in motion for a while, but that all ends tonight, right here."

Jovan couldn't take her bruised eyes off the gun as she tried to use her battered mind to keep Jimmy talking, to give her one more second of life.

"Motion?" she gritted out. "What?"

"Your demise, of course." Jovan stopped breathing for a second as she saw Devane's face turn sinister. "It's been in the cards since...well since Cordell bit it."

Jovan flinched. She shook her head no, but stopped when Jimmy brought the end of the gun back to her lips.

"Cordell, Timothy," Jimmy spat. "Nobody could do this job right. I always say, if you want something done right, do it yourself." He cocked the gun and slithered the end between Jovan's full lips. Jovan didn't blink, didn't breathe, didn't move.

All her thoughts were on the gun, Jimmy, and God in hopes He could pull her out of this one alive.

Jovan blinked several times. She could have sworn the door opened, but her vision was still blurry and she couldn't see well out of the corners of her eyes. In the time it took her to blink again, Mark rammed into the back of Jimmy, knocking the gun from Jovan's mouth.

She cried out as Jimmy fell on her legs. He quickly stood and landed a punch in Mark's stomach.

Jimmy snatched the gun from the bed. "Now isn't this sweet," he said. "Two people get together after the girl's husband kills the boy's wife. Couldn't make that up."

"You leave her alone," Mark said, lunging for Jimmy. Before Jimmy could get a shot off, Mark had them both on the floor. The gun went off and for a moment, all was quiet except for the machines. Jovan couldn't see the ground, but she could hear someone moaning in pain. Jimmy stood and Jovan cried out, "No. Mark."

"Now," Jimmy said. "I won't finish him off first. You've been through far too much already." He slipped the gun back between Jovan's lips. "I'll do you first, then your boy. Say hi to Cordell and his baby mama for me."

Ian leapt out of the elevator with a crew of armed officers. It was still late into the night, and no one wandered the fifth floor but a few nurses that Ian managed to whisper away from the scene. His body plastered to the wall, Ian walked swiftly toward Jovan's room. Five rooms before hers, he came face to face with Cheyenne, as she turned the corner down the hall on her way back to Jovan. She froze when she saw him with a gun in hand. Ian noticed the tear streaks down her face.

"Is Jovan…" he began.

"She's fine," Cheyenne said.

Ian placed his index finger to his lips, signaling Cheyenne to keep quiet.

"Stay here."

As he and his men moved forward, he whispered for one of the officers to keep Cheyenne at bay. Ian approached Jovan's door and peeped inside the small, square window. His heart caught in his throat as he took in Jimmy holding a gun on Jovan. He saw that the gun was cocked and placed close, if not in, Jovan's mouth. Mark was on the floor, shot.

"Shit," he mouthed, making sure not to make a sound. He turned to his men, pointed at two, and through mime, positioned them on the other side of the door. Cheyenne crept down the hall a few steps before Ian pleaded with his eyes for her to stay. She did.

When Ian looked into the window again, he caught a glance from Jovan who caught his gaze and let it go as if it never happened. He saw Jovan's fingers twitch and then Jimmy moved the gun a fraction from her face. Her mouth moved, slow, deliberate, and as Jimmy moved the gun closer to his side and appeared to pay attention to what Jovan had to say, Ian lunged into the room, men in tow, yelling, "Freeze or die, Devane."

Jimmy spun around and raised his gun, but Ian was quicker, peeling off two clean shots to Jimmy's chest before lowering his gun. Jimmy examined the holes in his chest as if amazed by the blood oozing from the wounds.

Jovan found the force to scream. Her voice pierced through Cheyenne's heart, and she came running down the hallway in neck breaking speed. With a burst of energy, Jimmy pointed his gun toward Jovan, aiming to shoot, but he was hit again, this time with a bullet from an officer to Ian's right. The hit ripped through Jimmy's throat, and he gagged before looking down at Jovan with eyes void of emotion and falling to the floor in a lifeless heap.

The officers immediately raced in to tend to Jimmy while Cheyenne ran to Jovan's bedside and Ian checked on Mark.

"Mark," Jovan whispered. "Mark dead."

"No," Ian said. "His pulse is weak, but he's breathing. Was shot in the stomach."

Jovan watched nurses bring in a gurney and place Mark on it. She watched until they wheeled him out.

Cheyenne took tissues and wiped specks of blood from Jovan's cheeks. Cheyenne tried to speak, but no other words would come out.

"Are you okay, Jovan?" Ian asked. Jovan blinked and slowly nodded her head yes. Her face was tight and drawn as if she was afraid to reflect on how she might be feeling. "What did you tell Devane to make him pull the gun away?"

"Offered money," Jovan whispered.

Cheyenne continued to coddle Jovan as Ian stepped back, his mind full of the corruption, deceit, greed, and lies that would culminate in such deadly situations.

Chapter 25

Jovan's attention was drawn to her one sock-covered foot and one cast-covered foot as they swung forward and back, inches away from touching the floor.

"Ow," she groaned, attempting to stand again. For the last five minutes, she had told herself that she would be up and dressed before Cheyenne arrived to pick her up. Cheyenne sauntered into the room, and Jovan was still in her hospital gown.

"I don't want to be pushed in some freaking wheelchair like an invalid," she said, pouting.

"Hospital rules, Sis. Consider it your limo ride out to the car."

"Yeah, yeah, yeah." Jovan rolled her eyes. "I signed my release papers, so now it's just time for me to get dressed and head to the precinct…see what Detective Davenport has to tell me about everything."

"Are you sure you want to do that today?" Cheyenne asked, reaching into a small closet to retrieve Jovan's outfit. "I think I told you enough to occupy you for a couple of days. Maybe I should just take you home so you can rest."

"I've been in this hospital for over a week and was high most of that time," Jovan argued. "I barely remember what you told me. Now that I can move and can talk better, I want to go. I want to get this out of the way."

Cheyenne raised her hands in surrender before laying the clothes onto the bed. "Whatever you say," Cheyenne replied. "I think I liked you better when you couldn't speak at all."

Jovan struggled for the umpteenth time to get up from the bed. "Sis, can you hand me the crutches?"

"You sure you want to try them now?"

"I have to go to the bathroom," she said in a defeated voice.

Jovan slipped the crutches under her arms and with slow determination she made it to the bathroom. "Nurse Jane helped me shower this morning," Jovan said. "I'm still sore, and it hurts to use the crutches."

"It's okay to need help, Sis," Cheyenne said. "You're still healing."

The toilet flushed, and then Jovan said, "Chey?"

"Yes, Hon."

"Come help me, please."

Cheyenne shook her head and laughed. She guided Jovan back to the bed where she helped Jovan dress.

"You see Mark?" Jovan asked.

"You know I have. He went home yesterday. I took him, sat with him, got him situated. Went to see him this morning before coming to get you. He told me to do this." Cheyenne kissed Jovan's forehead. Jovan couldn't help but to blush and smile.

"I'm glad he's okay." Jovan broke into tears as Cheyenne put the Reebok on Jovan's good foot.

"What's wrong, Sis?"

"I did all this. If it wasn't for me, Mark wouldn't have gotten hurt."

"You didn't do this. Cordell did this. Alisha and Jimmy did this. Burke did this. Timothy did this."

Jovan sniffed and wiped her face with tissue from the stand.

"His funeral is tomorrow," Cheyenne said.

Not a muscle in Jovan's face flinched as the words entered her ears.

"Mmm," Jovan moaned. "Lace too tight on my foot." Retying the shoe, Cheyenne rested herself beside Jovan. She draped her arm over Jovan's shoulder.

"Aww, Honey," Cheyenne said. "It's okay to show emotion. You loved Timothy."

"I just can't believe Timmy killed Cordell."

"We don't know everything," Cheyenne responded as she rubbed Jovan's back.

"Did Ian tell you anything yet? I know I've been out of it, so if you told me anything, I really don't remember it."

Cheyenne shook her head. "I didn't want to hear anything until you and I both could hear it." Jovan took her sister's hands into hers and held them tightly.

With a tear-choked voice, Jovan said, "At the very least... it's over."

"Thank God, and we're both alive to tell the tale."

"In this whole thing," Jovan said, "you have been the only person I can trust. It's always been you and me, through the good and bad times." "Now we have Ian and Mark. And we also have Mom and Dad who are at the house, waiting for me to bring you home, so are you sure you don't want to go there first?"

"I need this behind me, once and for all. We see Ian, and we can finally close the cover of that horror novel and move on with our lives, or at least try to."

Cheyenne scanned the room, picking up stray items of Jovan's and placing them in an empty bag she brought in with her. On cue, Nurse Jane appeared, wheelchair in hands.

"Come on, my dear," Nurse Jane chimed. "Let's get you to the car."

Jovan wiped her face with her hands and tried to offer the grandmotherly sweet nurse a smile. Cheyenne helped Jovan into the wheelchair, and as they departed the room, Cheyenne bent down toward Jovan's ear and whispered, "Jo, I'll always have your back. We're blood, and I love you." Jovan offered Cheyenne a teary-eyed smile as Nurse Jane wheeled her out of the hospital.

Jovan sat in Ian's office; baffled was the only word to describe how she felt. "So you're telling me that there was a host of people in on trying to kill me?" she asked.

Cheyenne sat in a chair beside Jovan, holding her hand while Ian sat behind his desk, a thick folder opened before him. His face looked tired, his sable colored eyes dark, almost black.

"Let me backtrack a bit," Ian began, leaning back into his chair. "The night you were attacked, you mentioned the color red, and you also mentioned hearing two people there."

"Right."

"The night before, I went to see Devane, and Alisha was there wearing red pumps. I put two and two together and figured they were in on it. I got to Devane's place, and he and Alisha were celebrating. Hell, your blood was still on Alisha's heels. Devane took off, and he went to the hospital."

"And was killed," Jovan added in a soft voice. Ian nodded. "What I don't understand is why Alisha hated me so much. She and Jimmy. Why would those two try to kill me?"

"Once Alisha found out about Devane's death, she fell apart," Ian replied. "She confessed to the attack though it didn't matter. We had the evidence. She made the claim that Timothy was the trigger man behind Cordell's murder."

"But Timothy told me that he didn't mean to kill Cordell," Cheyenne said. "He thought it was Jovan."

Jovan shuddered in her chair, dipping her eyes toward the ground.

"It was hard for me to believe that Timothy wanted to kill his own brother," Ian said. "And with him dead, I couldn't ask him, so I got a search warrant and went to his apartment."

Jovan sat forward in her seat, finding the strength to look Ian directly in his eyes. "So what did you find out?" she asked.

Ian looked away, his eyes swaying toward Cheyenne.

"Please, just tell it to me straight, Ian." Ian opened the drawer of his desk and pulled out a thick, oak colored journal. Jovan took it, a perplexed expression on her face.

"What's this?" she asked, looking at Ian.

"Timothy's journal. We found it in his apartment. I asked his parents if you could read it, and they said yes." Jovan's hands shook as she tightened her grip on it.

"But why do I have to read this?" she asked, coughing, as her throat tightened.

"Ian," Cheyenne pleaded.

"It appears that this is a journal that Timothy began keeping the last time he went into therapy," Ian began. "Cordell's death, your attack, it's all connected to a deception that is so tangled, the only way I think you can fully understand it is to read the journal."

"Give us the *Reader's Digest* version," Cheyenne said, wringing her hands and cracking her knuckles. "How tangled is tangled?"

"Okay," Ian said. "Cordell Anderson initiated the beginning, middle, and end of this whole thing."

"That's crazy," Jovan said. She struggled to stand, but a low burning fire erupted in her knees, causing her to grimace. She settled back into her seat, shirking off Cheyenne's attempts to comfort her. "So what you're saying is my husband wanted me dead?" A sick smile grew on Jovan's lips. She wouldn't wrap her mind around that thought. It was too insane.

"We compared Alisha Stewart's confession, Burke's conversations with us once we picked him up at his hangar trying to get the hell up outta dodge, and then we tied those in with Timothy's journal." Ian wanted nothing more but to tell Jovan that her husband loved her and that this was all a lie, but he could only offer her the sadness in his eyes. "From what we know, yes, Cordell wanted you dead, Jovan." He lowered his voice before adding, "I'm sorry."

The tension in Jovan's face slacked, and she was left with a gray, ashy look to her normally sweet, brown complexion.

"Cordell told Timothy that he feared for his life, that you had become unstable," he said. "According to Timothy's journal, Cordell had been prodding him for almost a year with stories about you. He had convinced Timothy that you needed to be killed so that he could live."

"How could Timothy believe that?" Jovan asked. "He knew me, he loved me, he would know that I would not want to do someone harm."

"But Cordell was his brother, Sis," Cheyenne reasoned. "If I came to you and for a whole year, told you that someone was trying to hurt me and I was afraid, you would have been my protector."

Jovan's silence egged Ian on. "Alisha knew that Cordell was plotting to get Timothy to kill you, and Alisha told Jimmy Devane."

"Why would she do that?" Cheyenne asked. "I mean she was Cordell's mistress. How did she know Devane?"

Ian let out a loud sigh, shaking his head. "It appears Alisha and Devane were an item before she even got with Cordell, and of course you know that Devane was an associate of both Cordell and Burke. After a year of convincing, Cordell broke Timothy down, and Timothy agreed to... kill you."

Jovan reached for a few tissues out of Ian's box and wiped at her eyes before blowing her nose. She took a clean one and began to shred it.

"Go ahead," she whispered as she breathed deeply.

"Cordell thought of everything. He gave Timothy the access to the security system, a key, even staged an argument between you two, knowing that you would be sleeping in the guest room."

"That bastard." Cheyenne sneered. She leapt from her chair, trying to find an outlet to her anger. When none became available, she fell back into her chair, a scowl on her face. "That night with him and Devane, and he was acting like such a bitch. He staged it all."

"If Cordell told Timothy I would be in the guest room, then why did he go to the master bedroom?" Jovan asked.

"Because of Alisha," Ian answered. "With help from her friends, Devane and Burke. Alisha knew about Timothy's drug addiction, and how he was in the beginning stages of recovery, and she used that to her advantage.

"She already had a Manhattan penthouse and money in an account from Cordell, and she felt that with Cordell dead, she would become president of Anderson Technologies, Burke would buy the company, and Devane would be given some highly paid job in the company. A win-win-win for everyone."

"Okay, so the deceit comes in where?" Cheyenne asked.

"Open the journal to the first page," Ian instructed. Jovan opened the journal, finding a piece of paper folded in half. On the paper, in Cordell's handwriting was the note, *Jovan will be in the master bedroom…NOT the guest room. Cordell.*

"Why would Cordell write this?" Jovan asked. "That would be like suicide."

"Cordell didn't write it," Ian answered.

"Yes, he did. That's his handwriting."

"No, that's the handwriting of a person who has spent years around Cordell, who knows his every habit, every movement. Alisha."

"Alisha wrote this?" Jovan asked. Ian nodded.

"She wrote it, Timothy got it, and went to your house, went into the master bedroom, and killed his own brother. He didn't find out until the next morning that he had mistakenly killed Cordell."

"I can't believe they would go through such a detailed scheme to kill Cordell," Jovan said. "For money…for power. It's insane."

"Screw that," Cheyenne yelled. "Cordell wanted *you*

dead. This whole damn situation would have never taken place if he didn't begin the vicious cycle. How sick was he to think, oh, I can kill Jovan so I can have my life with Alisha, a tramp who was screwing him over from jump."

"But did he really want Alisha?" Jovan asked. "I mean where does Sarah come in to this?"

"I think that was purely a Cordell thing," Ian replied. "No one else seemed to have known about it. From what I can gather, Cordell used Sarah simply for sex. Once she became pregnant, he used her as evidence for your death."

"Meaning?" Cheyenne asked.

"There had been robberies in the neighborhood. Sarah was killed. Jovan, you were mugged. If you were killed, we could have easily seen a pattern and might not have looked at Cordell."

"Cordell mugged me," Jovan whispered.

"Well, we don't know for certain, but..."

"He did." Jovan laughed. "It makes sick sense."

Jovan picked up the journal and pressed the worn leather book to her lips, breathing in its woodsy scent and vicious secrets. Tears fell from her cheeks and moistened the pages.

"I'm not the only victim in this," she said. "They tricked Timothy. He OD'd because of his guilt."

"He didn't overdose," Ian stated.

"But..."

"We found a syringe and various narcotics at his apartment. None of them had his fingerprints on them; however, we did find Devane's fingerprints on the syringe. Alisha has been close-mouthed about it, but we suspect Devane and the gang drugged Timothy to make it appear like a suicide."

"And with Timothy dead, they figured they would bump off Jovan, too," Cheyenne added. "That way, their tracks would be burnt, and they could go on with their happily ever after."

"Exactly," Ian concurred.

Jovan sat in silence. Her brain was pulsating against the skin surrounding her skull. Cheyenne and Ian glanced at each other before directing their attention to Jovan.

"You okay?" Cheyenne asked, but Jovan didn't respond. "Sis?" Jovan placed the journal beside her in the wheelchair and began to back up.

"Thank you for everything, Ian," she whispered, reaching his doorway in a slow stroll. "I appreciate all you've done to get this case solved."

Cheyenne quickly rose and placed a soft kiss on Ian's cheek before rushing to Jovan's side.

"I'll talk to you later," she said. He nodded and watched as Cheyenne pushed Jovan out of the precinct. "Jo," Cheyenne said once they reached the car. "Talk to me. What's going through your head?"

Jovan looked straight ahead, her eyes opened, wide and alert. "I need to go see him," she stated.

"Who?"

"Cordell."

"Are you sure you want to do this?" Cheyenne asked, the car still running. Jovan looked out her car window, down a small hill that led to Cordell's resting place.

"I need to do this," Jovan answered. "Could you just help me down the hill?"

"Jovan..."

"Please, Sis. I can sit on the bench beside the grave."

Cheyenne sighed, getting out of the car, and making her way to Jovan. She opened the door and gave Jovan the crutches. Cheyenne stood beside Jovan, her hand resting gently on Jovan's arm.

After many slow, tiny steps, they finally reached Cordell's grave. Out of breath, Jovan rested herself on the bench and wiped her brow with the back of her hand. "Gimme a second, please," Jovan said. Cheyenne patted Jovan's shoulder before turning to walk back up toward the car.

Jovan took a deep breath before speaking. "Dear Lord, please forgive me, for I may sin," she whispered, making the sign of the cross.

"I didn't even know you," Jovan began, looking down at Cordell's headstone, which read *Beloved Husband and Friend.* "Did you ever love me? My God, for a year you planned my death. You used your own brother to do it. What? Were you too much of a fucking coward to kill me yourself?"

Jovan rubbed her hands together as if freezing in the warm, soon-to-be summer weather. "You thought you could screw my friend and then kill her. You thought you could kill me and be with your trophy girlfriend, but you didn't even know that she was cheating on you with Devane."

Jovan took in the azure sky with gauzy, white clouds coasting by. "I can't even cry for you any more, Cordell. I can't even begin to analyze and understand what had to be going through your mind. It's too sick and twisted. I'm going to leave you here, and I'm going to go and live my life."

Jovan performed the sign of the cross and prayed fervently. She felt a warm hand touch her shoulder and kiss the top of her head.

"Sis, you're going to make it through this," Cheyenne said. "You're a good person, beautiful inside and out. This was not your fault. I swear to you, I will be there, right beside you to make sure you come through this."

"I know I will be all right," Jovan stated. "You can't go through all this and not be all right."

"You ready to go?"

Without assistance, Jovan stood and slipped the crutches under her arms.

"Got my back?" she asked, looking into her sister's eyes.

Cheyenne walked behind her, her hands loosely at Jovan's sides.

"Like I told you in the hospital," Cheyenne began, "I got you. You can't get rid of me." She monitored as Jovan took baby steps up the hill, all by herself.

"You go, Girl," Cheyenne yelled, hugging Jovan gingerly. "I didn't have to hold you one time."

"Those were the first steps of my body's recovery," Jovan replied, her eyes wandering down the hill. "That was my first step at recovering my mind." "You're going to be okay, Jo." "In time, you're probably right," Jovan said.

Epilogue

*B*arnes and Noble was crowded. Customers packed the main entrance, attempting to make their way through the line to see the authors in attendance for a book signing. Along the line, men and women, young and old stood, with books—purchased and brought in with them—discussing their enjoyment of the mystery genre, as well as how beautiful the authors were in person…as opposed to the photo on the back cover of their novels.

The line began at Borders' front door but ended at a long table with three posters—two dotting the ends of the table and one behind the table. The posters were of authors, Jovan and Cheyenne Parham, and their latest bestseller, *Deadly Vows*.

"Say cheese!" Jovan and Cheyenne hugged a female customer as their publicist took a photo of the trio.

"Thank you for coming out to support us and *Deadly Vows*," Cheyenne commented, offering the woman a parting hug. "I swear it's a rush to be around the people who actually love your work."

"I know," Jovan replied, shaking hands with the next customer. "Whom should I make this out to?" she asked the teenage girl.

"Tisha," the girl said, shyly smiling as she patted her short 'fro. "I love the way you two write. I'm actually trying my hand at a novel now because I felt inspired after reading your books."

"Thanks, Tisha," Cheyenne said. "And you know, Jo and I are in the beginning stages of creating a writer mentoring program, so please, take a press kit and consider applying." Cheyenne signed the book as Tisha leaned across the table to pick up a folder.

"I don't think we've ever had a turn out so huge," Marcia, the bookstore manager exclaimed as she made her way over to the twins.

"Marcia's right," Cagney, the twin's publicist, stated. "This book can't stay on the shelves."

"Drama sells," Jovan replied, rolling her eyes. "Months later and we're still news. What's that saying, there's no such thing as bad publicity?"

"All that past crap," Cheyenne replied, "is exactly that, past crap. These people are here because we've written a damn good book."

"I won't deny that." Jovan laughed. "I wrote half of it, and I at least know *my* part of the book is good." Cheyenne playfully punched Jovan in the arm, emitting laughs from the customers.

"Lord," Cagney sighed, glancing toward the bookstore's entrance. "Speak of the devil and she shall appear." Jovan and Cheyenne glanced up toward the entrance and watched Linda Hayes walk into the bookstore, pad and pen in hand, and a cameraman in tow. Linda bypassed the customers, leaning her weight onto one of her long, slender legs. With a flip of her brunette hair, Linda smiled and spoke, "Jovan, Cheyenne, it's so good to see you two again."

"Every time we see you, it's never good," Cheyenne responded. "Here to write another scandalous story for the tabloids? Perhaps showcase it on your show, *Trash Chick*?"

"That's *Trés Chic*," Linda corrected, amidst the giggles of the twins and everyone within hearing distance. "Actually, news has it that Jovan is in the beginning stages of writing her first solo project. We wanted to know if a riff between the twin love façade was emerging."

Jovan shook her head before sucking in a deep breath. "Sorry to burst your bubble, Linda," she replied, before offering a smile and a signed novel to a customer. "My solo project is a one shot deal. Chey and I will most definitely continue writing our mysteries together."

"So tell us about your new book," Linda coaxed. "Will it be a tell-all novel about your horrific ordeal from last year? Are you hoping to battle with Alisha Stewart, who is planning to write her own book about the situation from prison?"

"Well, when she turns 60," Cheyenne said, "maybe Alisha can reap the benefits of her book. That is, if she gets parole."

"Hey, Cameraman," Jovan called to Linda's sidekick. "Be sure to get my good side. I'm only going to say this once." The cameraman maneuvered himself and the camera in front of the table, gently pushing customers back. "My solo project is titled *Picking up the Pieces*. It's not a tell-all. It's not about sensationalism or lies, like Ms. Linda Hayes promotes on her show and in her articles.

"It's a book about weathering storms, about learning to pick one's self up, move through the pain, and come out better and more loving of self. There's no publication date set; however, Chey and I are currently writing our seventh novel, and plan to have it out in stores in a little over a year."

"Now," Cheyenne said, blocking the cameraman's view of Jovan. "If you don't mind, we have people we would love to meet. Have a nice day." Linda sucked her teeth before flipping her hair.

"Thank you two for your time," she said as she plastered on her fake, for the camera, smile.

As she walked away, Linda said, "Tomorrow, some rag is going to have you two on the cover, with the headline, *Mystery Writer vs. Murderous Mistress…head to head in tell-all book war.*"

"Well, whatever," Jovan said. "I have long since placed drama out of my life. Miss Trash herself doesn't even register a blip on my radar."

"You go 'head, Girl," a militant sister in line said as she stood before them. "It takes a strong woman to have gone through what you have and still make your life so open like this. I really do admire you and can't wait to read *Deadly Vows*."

"Thank you," Jovan replied. "You know, it's people like you that keep me going." Jovan looked out at the line and spotted Mark walking into the bookstore. She smiled.

"Linda just missed Mark," Cheyenne said.

"I'm sure she caught him outside," Jovan responded.

As he walked up, Cheyenne asked, "So have you promoted Mark to real boyfriend yet? I've been really good at not nagging you every week about it." Jovan laughed. "And I thank you for it. We are good friends, if you must know."

"Good friends, my ass," Cheyenne whispered.

Mark came around the table and gave both girls a hug. When he hugged Jovan, Mark whispered, "Hey you."

"You hey," Jovan responded.

"Can I kiss you later?"

"Perhaps." Jovan covered her mouth and giggled. It was new to her to feel so giddy and giggly. She was apprehensive to put a name on what she and Mark had. For now, they were friends with *monogamous* benefits.

"Beep beep. Beep beep. Can I cut in line?" Ian rushed up to the table, hands laden with their books. "I'd like to get each of these signed, with the inscription, *To the sexiest detective around... we're hopelessly dedicated to—*"

"Next," Cheyenne yelled, laughing, leaning over the table to push Ian out of line. "You are such a nut."

"I try," Ian replied, smiling as he sidled up to Cheyenne and hugged her before dropping a kiss to her lips.

"Whoo," the people in the line whistled.

"You better be glad Linda and her trusty sidekick are gone," Jovan said. "Mess around, and you'll be joining me on the front page tomorrow."

"I already told our roving reporter that the next time she confronts me, I'll slap the cuffs on her myself," Ian responded.

"I'm sure that's just the way she likes it," Cheyenne added. Jovan snuck her hand around the back of Mark and pinched his butt. He jumped. She laughed.

"Couldn't resist," she whispered.

"Hi there," Cheyenne said, welcoming the next customer to the table. "I see you just purchased *Deadly Vows.*"

"Yes," the blonde-haired lady answered. "I have the others and thought this would be a great time to pick up the book and see you two. I absolutely love all your novels."

"Thank you," Jovan said. "We try to better our writing with each book."

"You know," the lady said after reciting the inscription she wanted in the book, "my book club had a discussion the other week about you and Cheyenne."

"Oh really?" Jovan asked, signing her name before sliding the book to Cheyenne.

"Yes. We wondered if you and Cheyenne ever thought about going into the law enforcement field."

Ian quickly jumped in between the twins, answering, "I think these two have found their calling...writing."

"Afraid of a little competition, are you?" Cheyenne asked.

"Afraid you might *write* a better ending to a case than actually solve it," Ian joked. "That's about it."

"I think it would be a great idea," the lady offered. "You two, helping out the police, offering advice."

"Actually," Mark said, "I think these ladies get into enough trouble just writing books."

"Amen to that, brother," Ian added.

Jovan looked up into Ian's begging eyes, chuckling. "I don't think the police need our help...or even want it," she said.

"I think we'll stick with what we're good at," Cheyenne added. She looked at Ian and smirked. "Maybe."

About the Author

Shonell Bacon is an author, doctoral candidate, editor, educator–everywoman. She has published both creatively and academically–novels, short stories, textbooks. She has had an essay of hers developed as part of a live theatre documentary production, and currently, while she works on penning more stories for her readers, Shonell is pursuing her Ph.D. in Technical Communication and Rhetoric at Texas Tech University. You can learn more about Shonell and her work at her website: http://shonellbacon.com.

www.ingramcontent.com/pod-product-compliance
Lightning Source LLC
Chambersburg PA
CBHW071308170626
46809CB00001B/368